ZELESTINA URZA IN OUTER SPACE

Basque Originals

Zelestina Urza in Outer Space

A Novel

David Romtvedt

Center for Basque Studies
University of Nevada, Reno

This book was published with the generous financial support of the Basque government.

The Center for Basque Studies
University of Nevada, Reno
www.basque.unr.edu

Text and cover design: Daniel Montero
Cover photo courtesy of Kristin Pegan

Library of Congress Control Number: 2015936630

For Simon and Dollie Iberlin—happy days

Contents

Part One

1

A Funeral

When Zelestina Urza died this winter, it was for the second time so people took a wait and see attitude. Resurrection is as plausible as the moon landing and we may as well get something from Christianity besides a guilt ridden sex life.

It was Zelestina who convinced the Wolf Basques to accept me. Without her, I would have been out in the cold for good—no pun intended. And I don't mean to criticize—Basques have been under attack for over two thousand years—first from the Celts, then from the legions of the Roman Empire, then from the Muslim armies that conquered the Iberian Peninsula, and finally from the French and Spanish who drove the Muslims out to impose their own version of what people nowadays call nation building.

For many of those more than two thousand years the Christian missionaries were there, too. In the missionaries' view, the most memorable thing about the Basques was that their language approximated the squawking of crows. Me, I like crows.

All this colorful history culminated in the rise of the fascist caudillo, dictator, and generalissimo Francisco Franco about whom I will say nothing more for the moment. Google Gernika and you'll understand why Basques might be cautious about welcoming newcomers.

At Zelestina's funeral, the new priest, an American who knows nothing about the Basque people, and who has asked to be called Father Bill, lifted the brass crucifix from the coffin and handed it to Jone Zabaleta. Unable to close her hands fully because of her heavy winter gloves, Jone nearly dropped the cross and Father Bill lurched forward as if he were lunging into the other world.

They say that in the last moments before dying our entire life passes before our eyes. I can't say how many nights I've lain in bed trying to observe the moment when I go from waking to sleeping. And the next thing I know it's morning and I'm opening my eyes. I know this is not death.

I could hear Zelestina, trapped in her satin bed, pounding on the inside of the coffin lid and shouting, "What kind of a name is that for a priest? Father Bill—it sounds like an Episcopalian outreach ministry in a shopping mall."

Jone and Father Bill nodded to each other and looked down. Then the cemetery board secretary started the electric motor that turns a set of pulleys allowing the coffin to drop slowly into the ground. A green velvet skirt attached to a set of aluminum poles blocked the view. The diesel generator running the electric motor roared from behind a row of poplars that had been planted as a windbreak.

In Arnegi where Zelestina was born, the men would have pulled off their jackets and lined up around the grave, each man with a rope in his hands, the rope slung under the coffin. They would have carefully let the rope out, the coffin banging the sides of the grave and a little dirt crumbling along the walls. Even in the rain they would have been sweating, the weight slowly settling into the water-laden earth.

But nobody did anything. The men, uncomfortable in ill-fitting suits and topcoats, rubbed their gloved hands together and shifted their weight from one foot to the other trying to stay warm. We all breathed while the motor whirred. It was like the hum of light coming from distant stars.

These men were too old for hard physical work anyway. They had bad backs from sixty years of bending over to shear sheep and bad knees from spending the same years climbing up and down hills. What if one of them stumbled on the rumpled indoor-outdoor carpeting that had been laid down on the snow around the edge of the grave? He might have broken a hip and with old people a broken hip often means the end. Or tumbled over the aluminum poles and fallen into the hole.

"Watch it there," Zelestina would say, and reach her hand out to push the man back into the land of the living.

I used to ask if she thought of getting a boyfriend. "Doesn't matter if you're old," I suggested in my young person way. "There are lots of other single old people in Wolf."

"I know that," she'd answer then turn her head, look into some remembered room I'd never seen, and say, "A good man is hard to find." She knew I imagined myself a writer and she'd read a lot so I wondered if she was messing with me. Did Flannery O'Connor have a boyfriend? I'd have to look that up. And even being dead, I wonder if Zelestina is still messing with me. In the O'Connor story, the man's not very good.

It took a long time for the coffin to drop. Nobody fell into the open grave. When the first frozen clod of dirt was thrown down, it hit the lid like a meteor hitting the earth. Maybe the closest thing humans get to eternity is a funeral. Jone wondered if the crucifix shouldn't have been given to Zelestina's friend Yellow Bird Daughter who'd come down from Lame Deer for the funeral. Somebody else said to give it to me. But neither Yellow Bird Daughter nor I was family. Jone wasn't either but she was Basque so Father Bill gave it to her. As she took it, she looked at the crucifix with the expression of someone who'd just shoplifted something she didn't want and had been caught by the security guard while trying to put the damn thing back.

It was hard to see in the glare of winter light bouncing off both the snow and the polished top of the coffin—walnut or some other hardwood that doesn't grow in Wyoming. And brass fittings—at least they looked like brass, but nowadays it's hard to tell—big fat fake world. Maybe the crucifix was fake, too. Whoever chose that coffin looked to have done it mainly to offend the abiding sense of frugality that marks every Basque rancher I ever met. Cheap sonsabitches but they can work and I admit that if you're in trouble they'll help you. One day I was up on a windmill tower with one of those ranchers—back then I was doing any job I could find, windmill maintenance included. We'd forgotten a part so we had to climb down and drive back to town. When we got there, my rancher boss got out of the pickup leaving the key in the ignition. Me being raised in a city, that seemed pretty odd so I asked him, "Don't you want to take the keys with you?"

"What'd I do that for?"

"I don't know. What if somebody saw those keys hanging there? Anybody could just drive your pickup away."

"Well, that's possible, but it might be that somebody needed that truck, maybe they had an accident and had to get to the doctor. They could take the truck. You can't ever tell. All kinds of emergencies. What if a person died not being able to get to the doctor fast enough?"

The sun kept bouncing off the snow onto the coffin, and Father Bill kept turning his head and squinting. Jone took a pair of oversized red sunglasses with amber lenses out of her purse and handed them to the priest. When he put them on he looked like a mafia hit man pretending to be an FBI agent disguised as an insurance salesman on vacation at a hurricane ravaged Caribbean resort on the verge of bankruptcy. Only it was winter. Between that and the unwanted shoplifted artificial crucifix, I felt a little better.

The coffin finally disappeared but you could still hear the whir of the motor and the hum of light from the stars and the rasp of the old men breathing. I pulled out a two-row diatonic *trikitixa* accordion and played two songs for Zelestina, feeling my fingers slowly stiffen in the cold. Then the cemetery board secretary cut the power and the funeral was over. When everyone left, a county road and gravel crew man came and, using a miniature Bobcat loader, moved a pile of frozen earth and filled the grave in three hurried strokes, leaving a wash of dirty snow where we'd stood.

Stomping our feet in the snow and slapping our sides with our arms, we walked from the cemetery back to the church— Our Lady of the Mountain—*gure mendiko andereren eliza*. My Basque is pretty cracked so I'm not sure that's exactly right. In any case, we went to the church and lined up in the hall to eat American food served on paper plates.

It wasn't until I got home that it really hit me that Zelestina was dead. She was like one of those basketball sized deep space probes sending radio signals back to earth. Only the probe is getting farther and farther away and the signal is getting weaker and weaker and one day it'll be gone.

2

Yellow, Police Seat Doan

Sixty-seven years before the first American set foot on the moon, Zelestina Urza, of the village of Arnegi in the Basque province of Nafarroa Beherea, stepped down from the train in Clearmont, Wyoming. It was February and cold, though not exceptionally so for northern Wyoming. She was sixteen.

Zelestina was the first baby born in Arnegi in 1886—New Year's Day a little before dawn. People being the hopeful souls they are, a lot of the villagers thought the birth was a sign of better times to come. Neighbor women were smiling and singing. The men were sharpening knives and testing ropes and getting drunk. It's true that the Basque Country now is pretty rich but in those days it was dirt poor. And poorer in Iparralde—the north—where Zelestina's family lived.

I always wondered about the name Urza, an uncommon Basque name. She shook her head sadly and said, "The truth is we're not really Basque."

"What do you mean 'we're not really Basque'?"

"Well, we're not, my family came to Euskal Herria from Alsace Lorraine."

"Alsace Lorraine? But it's not—how do you say it? —an Alsatian or Lorrainian name either."

"No, but that's where we came from—along the French-German border."

"I know where it is. So you're not Basque but when did your family move to the Basque Country?"

"Oh, I'm not sure, I think about seven hundred years ago."

"Seven hundred years."

She didn't even smile.

Arnegi sits on the border—Spain on one side, France on the other, the Basque Country crushed in between. In between what? In between a line is just about nowhere.

The sun was barely up when neighbors began to arrive at the new parents' house bringing cheeses and chickens, fresh vegetables, and homespun wool cloth. They might have been poor but they ate well and dressed warmly. Someone put a chair next to the laying-in bed, and the new mother, her baby nestled against her, sat serenely while the midwife wrapped her in blankets. Four men picked her up, chair and all, and carried her to the *enparantza*—the town square. They put another blanket over both mother and child after which the old women, shawls tight around their shoulders, came forward to comment on the baby's beauty. Across the square, boys played handball with their fathers. The thwack of the ball at the *pilotaleku* splintered the air.

The new father roared around the *enparantza* waving a *xahako*—a goatskin winebag—over his head. "Behave yourself, Potxo," people shouted. Potxo—Chubby. He was a fat baby, a fat child, and a fat young man. Now he was a fat father. Nobody in Arnegi knew his given name. His parents claimed they couldn't remember it and the priest, when pressed, shook his head to apologize then explained that the church registry had disappeared in a fire. At any given moment in Spain, someone is building a church and someone else is burning one down. In this case the Basque Country shares something with the Spanish state. Of course Arnegi is on the border so it's neither Spanish nor French.

The black and white colors of the goatskin swirled as Potxo reeled from side to side. At irregular intervals, he would uncap the *xahako*, hold it above his face at arm's length, and squirt wine hopefully toward his mouth. Mostly he missed and his brilliant white shirt, soft from hundreds of washings, was stained and sour.

"Oihane," the new mother's friends called, "*Senarra dela esaten duen mozkorti hau non aurkitu zenuen?*" But Potxo was a kind, gentle, and hardworking man and his neighbors liked him very much. I don't know if you can ask much more than that from life, no matter who you are. My father could work harder than about anybody but no one would call him gentle or kind and he wasn't so well liked. Another story.

One of the crones who fancied herself an herbalist and fortuneteller sidled up to Potxo and leaned forward, pressing her lips to his ear. When she whispered her prediction, he could feel a little spittle frothing at the edge of her mouth and falling onto his shoulder. "She's an important baby and she'll be an important woman."

Potxo grabbed her by the shoulders, pulled her face up close to his and, lifting his arms, said, "God knows, an important baby. Thank you, *andere ona*."

"I'm not joking."

"*Ba, ba*, of course you're not joking. *Bera garrantzitsua da*—important. *Zurekin ados nago baina bera gure alaba da*—she's my daughter—so who knows." He leaned even closer to the fortuneteller and said, "*Astakeria*. You know what this village needs? A labor contractor not a baby. Maybe a shipyard on the coast and a whaling fleet, a sawmill and a railroad. *Noski garrantzitsua dela*. Who do you think I am?"

I added the Basque to give you a feel for it. I don't know how important it is to translate it but the neighbor women joked: where did Oihane find this drunk who claimed to be her husband, and *astakeria* means nonsense.

By the time Zelestina was a young woman, two out of three young men in Arnegi had left the steep hills and the muddy roads of Iparralde for Amerika—for Argentina and Venezuela and California and other rich nations where they were going to make great fortunes and come home rich. The few who did this were called *Indianoak*—Indians. They went to Amerika, made money, and came back to build mansions and lord it over the stay-at-homes, live a life of ease, drinking their *ebakiak* or *kafesneak* every morning at 11:00. You can still see the great houses of those *Indianoak*, a lot of them now serving as small-town museums.

Most of the young men who left never came home. They went to Amerika and disappeared. And a good chunk of the young women did the same. Mostly, the women were sent as brides for the lost men. But some of them—like Zelestina— went on their own.

Potxo dropped the *xahako* and fell to his knees, staring up at the sky. A few stars still shimmered in the pale blue. Ursa Major, the Great Bear, turned toward the earth. Potxo Urza, the fat bear, drunk from fear at the birth of his daughter. He laughed and fell face first into the damp earth. The wet cold filled his nose. When he looked up, the sun was brighter, the stars were no longer visible, and the bear had disappeared over the Pyrenees.

During Zelestina's childhood, Potxo and Oihane often spoke about leaving Arnegi. Zelestina would lie awake and listen to her parents while her younger brothers grunted and snored in the beds next to hers. "It's not only Zelestina," Potxo said, "but Iñaki and Andoni and maybe, God being the provider he is, there will be more. Only one can take the farm. Are the rest to become priests and nuns? Or go to Marseilles or Poitiers and work in shops and factories only to become Frenchmen. Even in Baiona they would become Frenchmen."

Potxo spat and shook his head. "And Spain is worse—it's full of Spaniards."

There's a song called "Maiteak galde egin zautan"—My sweetheart asked me.

Maiteak galde egin zautan lana banuenez,
maiteak galde egin zautan lana banuenez.
Lana, lana banuela baina, gogorik ez, gogorik ez.

Maiteak galde egin zautan poltsa banuenez,
maiteak galde egin zautan poltsa banuenez.
Poltsa, poltsa banuela baina dirurik ez, dirurik ez.

Gaixoa hil behar dugu guk biok gosez,
gaixoa hil behar dugu guk biok gosez.
Gosez, gosez hil behar baina elkar maitez, elkar maitez.

That's part of the song—no sense in overwhelming anyone with a little known language. Here are all the lyrics in English:

My sweetheart asked me if I was pretty.
I said yes but I'm pretty brainless.

My sweetheart asked me if I was the firstborn.
I said yes, but my family has no house for me to inherit.

My sweetheart asked me if I had a job.
I said yes but I wished I didn't.

My sweetheart asked me if I had a pocketbook.
I said yes but there's no money in it.

My sweetheart asked me if I felt embarrassed.
I said yes but never with you.

My sweetheart asked me if I had any marijuana.
I said yes but no papers to roll it in.

That last couplet with the marijuana joke is new. The others though were sung in Zelestina's day. Past or present, eventually the joking ends. Then comes the turn. The singer says, "Maybe the two of us will die of hunger." It's even stronger—"we need to die of hunger." What does that mean? Finally, hunger or not, "We'll die together with love." That's how it was. Maybe another plan would be better.

Just after Zelestina's sixteenth birthday, Potxo took her in the cart pulled by a single horse down the bank of the Errobi Ibaia—the river the French call La Nive—from Arnegi to Donibane Garazi—the town the French call Saint-Jean-Pied-de-Port. She'd told her parents she wanted to go to Amerika, she could take care of herself, and they wouldn't have to worry. Youth and ignorance gave her confidence—even a child could see how much easier life would be if there were fewer mouths to feed—but at the same time she was a little bit scared out of her wits.

In Donibane, Potxo negotiated passage for his daughter with a hay merchant. For a moment it seemed that the man looked slyly at the sixteen-year-old girl. "You are ugly," Potxo reassured Zelestina, "and so, in this world, safe."

"*Mila esker eta beharrik, Aita.*" Thanks and thank goodness. She took her father's hand and smiled at him. When he smiled back, his eyes nearly disappeared into the flesh on his face.

Aita eta ama—father and mother. *Nebak*—brothers. *Etxe*—home. Euskara *eta* Euskal Herria—the Basque language and the Basque Nation—both so small they barely exist. She began to cry and Potxo held her, stroked her hair, and cried, too. This is the only way it could have happened.

At Baiona, Zelestina took a boat to New York, and from New York a train to Chicago. In Chicago, she found her way toward another train, riding dizzily across the continent. The Union Pacific line became the Burlington line and the towns grew smaller, more distant from one another—Broken Knife, Spotted Horse, Arvada, Clearmont.

Her hair was dirty and her dress wrinkled and stained. It had been impossible to wash and she stank. She stepped onto the platform between two cars and leaned out, hoping the cold wind might wash some of the smell away. Hills rose away from the tracks on either side of the train. They were old hills, rounded and, under snow, smooth. They reminded her of her body—her narrow hips and long thighs, her breasts so recently and, it seemed to her, so fully arrived from the distant land of womanhood. She turned away and went back into the car.

At Clearmont, Zelestina stepped down from the train, slipped on a patch of ice, and pitched forward. The wind lifted her and she thought of the baby princess in the fairy tale her mother had told her. In the story, the princess has no gravity and so her parents, the king and queen, must tie weights to her legs to keep her from floating away. Zelestina had plenty of gravity and when she landed she fell backward and hit her head on the step down from the car.

The stationmaster, who also served as the light keeper, water tank master, and switchman, ran toward the fallen woman. When he reached her, he stopped and stared down. Zelestina's dress had flown up and her legs, encased in tight full-length undergarments whose style the stationmaster had never seen before, were, to some extent, exposed. Enough to see, anyway, that it was obvious she had great legs.

"My God," he said, uncertain if he should lift her or call for help. Then he imagined her legs locked around his waist, strong and comforting. He blushed and as his eyes moved upward along her body he was confronted by her breasts. By the time he saw the large square face that Potxo had called ugly, it was too late. Anyway, she was not so ugly.

It was eighteen below zero. But as we say in Wyoming—it felt colder. It's like today—April 8, eleven degrees and six inches of new snow. Winter just won't give up. When Zelestina regained consciousness, she was lying on a cot in a low ceilinged room across the frozen road from the railroad tracks. A green wool blanket covered her and a fire burned in an iron stove. Her two bags had been set against the wall. The air was warm but so dry that the inside of her nose felt raw. Her lips had cracked and, as she wiped her tongue across them, she tasted blood. Somebody must have picked her up and carried her in here. Someone's hands holding her. In the heated room, her smell was even stronger than it had seemed on the train.

The wool blanket scratched her neck and cheek. She pulled it off and sat up then stood to straighten her skirt and blouse. She stepped across the room away from the stove that glowed red from the heat of the wood burning within. Still, only a few feet away the air was cold. Her coat had been folded neatly and laid across a chair next to her bags.

Iñaki and Andoni had told her it would be cold in Wyoming. "Colder than you can imagine," they said as she packed. How they'd learned about Wyoming's cold, Zelestina didn't know. Still, her younger brothers' words had made her nervous and she'd sewn an extra layer of wool into her good winter coat.

Maybe it was the cold, or the rough wool blanket, or her doubts rising in her throat that made her shiver. She pulled up a sleeve and saw that her skin, normally smooth and olive toned—her best feature, her mother said—now appeared splotchy, a bluish gray. She rubbed her arm then hugged herself. Her nipples, hard in the cold, hurt.

She turned back to the stove then went to the window, which was frosted over and impossible to see through. She scraped a little ice off with her fingernails. The sound of the scraping made her shiver again. When she leaned forward and put one eye close to the frozen glass, she saw that the train was gone. The wind had dropped, the temperature had risen, and it had begun to snow. The light was pearly and there were no shadows.

Zelestina laughed when she told me about that first snow. "*Amarru handia*," she told me. "A big trick—about the only time in fifty years that the snow fell with no wind."

Fell straight down out of the sky like in a storybook winter. Of course, it never really snows that much here. They say that it snows a foot or two in October then it blows around for eight months until it wears out at the end of May. Zelestina loved that joke.

She scraped a little more ice off the window expecting to see God out there disguised as a priest or a cowboy. She knew what the priest would look like but she could only imagine the cowboy with his six-shooters and big hat. He'd smile and wave, then lift his shoulders and shrug.

Zelestina went to the door, opened it, and poked her head out—no cowboy, no priest, no God. Just the hills disappearing behind the curtain of thickening snow. The cold sucked the breath out of her and when she tried to inhale her lungs burned.

"Here there," a man's voice called, "we can't have you falling twice in one day."

For the rest of her life, when something seemed particularly perplexing, Zelestina would say, "here there" and shake her head. "What does that mean? Here there."

He came from the tracks across the street, touched her lightly, and led her back toward the building. Wrapped in the thick sleeve of his coat, his arm seemed to be as big around as her waist.

"How's that head then? You feeling alright?"

Zelestina said nothing.

"Are you alright?" The man repeated.

Zelestina stared at him amazed. He seemed to be speaking without moving his mouth. He had a light brown moustache the hairs of which remained perfectly still even as he spoke. His lower lip was as thin as a wire and his upper lip, which Zelestina imagined must be equally as thin, was invisible under the moustache, which supported a layer of ice.

"Gonna be a change. Warming up a little, maybe have a good snow, been awful cold now for a few days." Then he stopped, as if waiting for her to speak.

"English is a funny tongue," Iñaki had explained to her, "as if people are only practicing for talking."

"You don't know."

"*Noski, badakit.*"

"And how is that you, who has never been farther from Arnegi than Banka and Donibane Garazi and who has never met anyone who speaks English, know this?"

"Maybe you don't know everything I've done." As if he'd gone to China with Marco Polo or crossed the Rocky Mountains to paddle down the Columbia River with Lewis and Clark. He paused for effect then took his sister's arm and led her to a chair, saying as he did so, "Hello, please sit down." But it sounded more like, "Yellow, police seat doan." Noticing the expression on Zelestina's face, Iñaki said again, "Yellow, police seat doan." Then, "*Ez kezkatu, amerikara zoaz, ez ilargira*—you're going to Amerika not the moon."

In Clearmont, Zelestina pushed her hand down into her pocket and pulled out the rumpled card she'd been showing people all across the continent. It read in English, "I am Zelestina Urza from Euskal Herria. I speak Basque and French, some Spanish. I do not speak English. I am going to Wolf, Wyoming where my employers Søren and Smylla Christiansen will greet me."

She handed this to the man. He looked at the card for a moment. This allowed him to avoid looking at her face. Then he pointed to a building down the street, pointed to himself, pointed to the door of the room where she had awakened, pointed to her, pointed to the card, said, "I'll be damned," and shook his head. Finally, he held his hands out palms facing her and waved them forward and back hoping she would understand that he meant to say, "Wait here." Then he left, returning in a few minutes with another man who held the card and was smiling. This second man extended his hand. Was he returning the card?

"Good afternoon, Miss Urza. I'm the Clearmont station-master. I helped you up when you fell getting off the train. Samuel here works with me. He doesn't read so he brought me your card. I'm sorry to tell you that I can't speak Basque, French or Spanish and, since you can't speak English, we're in kind of a pickle. Well, I'll go ahead and maybe you'll understand a little bit of what I say. I know the Christiansens. I can put you on the coach to them in Wolf. I'm sure there'll be someone there to help you. In the meantime, you can wait here till the coach comes."

Making that speech while keeping his eyes off the skirts that covered Zelestina's legs took a good deal of the stationmaster's strength. As Samuel had, he waved his hands around. He made big circles in the air to indicate rolling coach wheels then he wiggled his fingers, pointing first here then there as if she might be Lakota or Crow or Cheyenne rather than Basque and he might be an early fur trapper who knew sign language.

That hay merchant in Donibane saw something Potxo was blind to and the stationmaster saw it, too. So for reasons different from those of his companion Samuel's, the stationmaster did not look directly at Zelestina. In the end, he opened the door and gestured as if he might push her into the room without touching her.

Zelestina tried to smile. In the course of what had seemed to her to be a very long speech, she had understood three words—Wolf, Christiansen, and her name. Maybe the man had said, "I'm sorry but I've never heard of any Christiansens in Wolf." Or maybe he'd said, "Perhaps there is someone else who can help you—someone in a different town, a different country, a different galaxy." Or, "Oh, yes, I knew the Christiansens but I'm very sad to tell you that they died in a tragic accident." Or simply, "There are no Christiansens."

Zelestina stepped back into the room she had so recently left and sat down to wait, her hands folded in her lap. After a few minutes, she got up and began pacing in circles. When a knock came at the door, she jumped and very nearly cried out. Yet another man stood there motioning for her to come outside. Or was it the first man, the one with the thin lower lip and motionless moustache? Or the second man, the one who'd returned with her card and pointed everywhere and spoken for so long? These *Amerikanoak* waved their hands around like Frenchmen.

The snow had stopped. The new man moved quickly behind her, picked up her coat, mimicked putting it on, then handed it to her. After that, he went inside and got her bags. A closed coach drawn by six horses stood in the street. The horses stamped their hooves, causing bits of snow to swirl up into the air. When they threw their heads back, Zelestina could hear the twist of cold leather, the dry rattle of metal rings against wood. Clouds of breath billowed around the horses' heads.

It was late afternoon and the pearl light had flattened to gray. The clouds hanging over the distant mountains obscured the sun so Zelestina saw no sunset. The day was dissolving into twilight. And then it would be night.

The man threw the two bags up on the back of the coach and opened the door. Zelestina didn't move. Once again, the man pointed, indicating that this was her coach. She climbed in and the door closed behind her as if by its own volition. There were two small bench seats facing each other. At the ends of each bench there were openings for windows. There were also openings for windows in the doors on both sides of the coach. There was no glass in any of the window frames. Heavy canvas curtains were pulled down to cover the openings. Now and again these curtains flapped and bits of snow drifted into the compartment. There were no other passengers.

Zelestina lifted a flap and looked out. There was a lurch and the coach rolled forward. A light whirring sound came from the iron-rimmed wheels as they rolled through the newly fallen snow.

"'Bout thirty miles to Wolf, Ma'am. Give or take a mile or so," a voice shouted from above her. "Wouldn't normally go in the dark like this but had some problems today so we're late and it's a nice enough night—still early, snow's pretty much stopped, temperature come up twenty degrees, maybe more, since this morning, no wind, big moon, and the horses know the way. We'll be there before sunrise." There was a pause. "Hyeah." And the snap of a whip. "I guess there's no sense telling you all this, you not speaking English." Then, as if he should apologize for knowing this fact about her, the driver explained, "I mean they told me you don't know no English. Well, you'll be alright." He tried to smile in a comforting way, but quickly realized that she could not see him from inside the coach. He finished by saying only, "Don't fret."

Gibberish. As she'd done a few minutes earlier, in fact, as she'd done all the way across the continent, Zelestina imagined the words. Could be the man said, "We just go up here a ways then lift off for outer space—oughta reach the moon in about sixty-seven years. Well, give or take a year. I ain't total sure."

She heard the whip snap again and leaned back in the center of the coach as far from the window openings as possible. It wasn't long before it was clear to her that she would freeze to death if she kept sitting there. She stuck her arm out the window closest to the front of the coach and banged on the wood.

"*Itxaron pixkatean.*" Wait a minute, she called.

The coach rolled on.

"*Itxaron!*" She shouted again.

When the coach didn't stop, she opened the door and looked down—a meter at most to the ground, the horses moving at a steady walk. She stepped down, hanging onto the door handle as she did, careful about how and where she placed her feet. Then she ran next to the coach for a few steps until the driver noticed her and stopped. The bottom of her coat dragged along the ground and grew heavy from snow clinging to it.

The driver stopped and climbed down from his seat. His head was covered by a greasy wool hat with another wide-brimmed hat over that. A wool muffler was wrapped around his face so that only his eyes showed. He wore a full-length coat with a fur collar. From the ends of the sleeves came not hands but paws, huge and mute. Leather mittens covered wool liners. He smelled like coal.

"Yes, ma'am?"

Zelestina slapped her hands against her arms and stamped her feet. She pantomimed exaggerated shivering and pressed the edge of her coat between her fingers to show how thin the material was. She waved both hands in front of her in a gesture of no and pointed at the interior of the coach. She shook the snow off the hem of her dress and began to run along the road.

"Hey, wait there, where d'ya think yer going?"

Zelestina kept running.

The driver followed, trying to catch her. When he did, he grabbed her arm and pulled her back. She wrenched the arm away and shook her head no, shouting, "*Ez, ez, hotza ari du.*" and going through the pantomime of cold again. She had no boots and so wore the light rope soled cotton shoes she'd worn in Arnegi. Sitting unmoving in the coach was impossible. She had to run to keep from getting frostbite. She imagined one toe freezing then the next until all ten toes dangled black and useless from the stumps of her feet. She stamped around in the snow and pointed at her feet. Then she ran in a tight circle and started off again—*hobe izango litzateke korrika egitea*.

Not a cruel man, the driver took off after her a second

time, grabbed her, and tried to offer her some of his winter clothing, tried to wrap her in his knowledge of the cold. But Zelestina would accept nothing. She made use of her inability to understand English, pretending she had no idea what the man meant when he tried to remove his coat and give it to her. She wanted to run; she would have wanted to run whatever the temperature. She needed to get wherever she was going on her own. She couldn't have explained this to the driver even had she known how to speak English.

Zelestina set off heading west toward the dark Bighorn Mountains. She walked or ran nearly half of the thirty miles from Clearmont to Wolf. She ran until she was exhausted then she sat in the coach until she could bear the cold and her own desire no longer, and she ran again. Sometime between midnight and dawn, she and the otherwise empty coach reached the town center of Wolf where there were no people in the street and no lights on in the buildings. The moon had set and the stars shone down on frozen mud.

The coach driver banged on the door of the Etxeko Hotel and the sound disappeared into silence. Zelestina felt momentarily hysterical and feared she might scream or throw up. She put one hand to her mouth and coughed to hide her feeling. There was a flutter in her chest. The fluttering was at first like the wing beats of a newborn songbird then it grew until it was more like the thrashing of an injured hawk.

Again, the driver banged on the hotel door. This time a voice called out, "Hold onto yer hat there, I'm coming." The door opened. The two men spoke and the driver climbed back up on the coach. The man from the hotel pulled Zelestina's bags into the cold lobby. When he saw that she didn't move, he came back and took her arm to lead her inside.

"Hello," he said and, directing her to a deep overstuffed chair, "please sit down."

She more collapsed than sat and in the moment just before losing consciousness, when it is too late to pull oneself back into waking, Zelestina realized that she was, for the first time in her life, alone. Her body jerked, her head fell forward, and she slept. The hotel clerk didn't have the heart to wake her so there she sat—a sixteen-year-old girl from the village of Arnegi, not far from Donibane Garazi, in Nafarroa Beherea, one of the three provinces of the Iparralde region of the nation known as Euskal Herria. She had spent weeks traveling on foot and by horse cart, by boat and train, across ocean, mountains, and plains to finally reach Wolf, Wyoming and pass her brief first night in that place.

3

Indianoak

The Basques are the Indians of Europe. That's what Zelestina always told me. At first I thought she was pulling my
leg—*adarra jotzen*—which means something like hitting the
horn of the bull. Hyperbolic hoo-hah like, yeah, yeah, the Indians of Europe.

There's that scene in the movie *The Commitments* when
Jimmy, the hustler who's trying to put together a soul band in
Ireland, tells the bass player Derek "Meat Man" Scully, and
the guitarist Outspan Foster, along with the rest of his embry-
onic imagined band why, of all musics, they should be playing
American Soul. With a videotape of a James Brown concert
playing behind him, Jimmy explains that, "The Irish are the
Blacks of Europe and Dubliners are the Blacks of Ireland and
North Dubliners are the Blacks of Dublin so say it loud, I'm
Black and I'm proud." Most of the pasty white band members
look a little queasy but then *The Commitments* is meant to be
comedy not social commentary.

It's not the same with Basques and Indians—the more I
learned about Basque people, the more I saw that my doubt

about the comparison was wrong. Raised American I was infected with irony—the way hip urbanites can embrace and discount something at the same time or the way nearly all Americans will make fun of something but not quite. Just too sophisticated to be sincere. Or maybe they are sincere.

With Zelestina you always knew what she felt and believed. And here she was laying out a strange truth—the Basques are the Native Europeans. Like Indians in North America no one knows where the Basques came from, when they got to their homeland, or how they got there. All we know is they were there first.

Academics like to say the Indians came across the Bering Straits when the ocean was frozen. This was maybe 15,000 years ago and those Indians who at the time were Asians set off walking toward a new land. Why an entire people would suddenly up and trek thousands of miles through ice and snow to an unknown land is unclear. I grant you the climate in Central Russia and Siberia is a little daunting. But if that was it, why take off walking across an ocean of ice?

Vine Deloria who wrote *Custer Died for Your Sins* says that the Bering Land Bridge theory is bullshit. He says Indians were always here, that if they'd come during the ice age that froze the strait they would have had to walk most of the way through narrow canyons of ice hundreds of meters high. You know those early Indians they call the Sheep Eaters? Maybe they should have been called the Ice Eaters.

On the first page of *A Brief History of Time*, Stephen Hawking tells the story of a famous scientist giving a public lecture on astronomy. The scientist explained how the earth revolves around the sun, and how the sun revolves around the collection of stars we call the galaxy. When he finished a little old lady—that's how Hawking wrote it, "little old lady." Funny kind of condescension toward aging from a man who suffered a lot of physical indignities of his own. Anyway, this little old lady stood up and said, "What you've told us is rubbish. The world is a flat plate supported on the back of a giant tortoise."

The scientist smiled and said, "If that's true, what's the tortoise standing on?"

And the woman said, "You're very clever, young man, but it's tortoises all the way down."

I heard this story long before Hawking put it in his book but the way I heard it the scientist was a theology professor at an academic conference on ontology and the little old lady was a tribal elder. The elder explained that the world, whether it was flat or round, rested on the back of a giant turtle. From that point on, the story's the same.

Some scholars say the Basques came from the Caucasus Mountains region of what's now Russia. One batch of Central Asians walked east to become American Indians, while another batch walked west to become Basques. But the Basques say this too is bullshit—*kaka zaharra*, they say, which is literally old excrement. Actually excrement is *gorotza*. You can read it on signs in the parks—pick up your dog's *gorotza*.

The Basques say that, like the Indians, they were always where they are. They note that the Garden of Eden was in the Pyrenees Mountains. Given the shift of tectonic plates and the slow movement of the magnetic poles, this is not a completely implausible notion. Also, the first human language was Basque—Euskara. Then the Tower of Babel with its human pride and God's paranoia ended that. Who knows how the Basques explained their origin before the Christians came—turtles all the way down.

I mentioned the poverty in Iparralde in the late nineteenth century. Poverty that emptied entire villages. Another factor is the Carlist wars—you can Google those at the same time you Google Gernika. These wars ended in the total defeat of the Basque people and the final end of the *foruak*, the laws and rights that governed the relationship between the Basque nation and its larger neighbors France and Spain. From the end of the Carlist Wars, the Basques were to be a vassal people.

Maybe I'm making too much of this but any Basque who thinks about life for more than about thirty seconds can see the parallels between Basque history and the more recent history of the American Indians. The difference is that the Basques have been struggling against outside colonizers for thousands of years. Maybe the tribal governments in Wyoming and the Dakotas ought to consider bringing Basques in as consultants on cultural survival in the face of implacably hostile imperial nations. Or at least for cooking workshops—that fry bread can taste pretty good but it's murder on the cholesterol count.

When Franco died, the Basques decided language was the key to their survival. They even have a phrase for a non-Basque person who learns to speak the language—*euskaldun berria*—a new Basque person. The same two words are used to describe a Basque who learns his native language in adulthood. *Euskaldun berria*.

The Basque writer Bernardo Atxaga, who has a keen sense of the centrality of a language to a people, once asked writers from the big languages—English, French, Spanish—to imagine what it would be like if you could read every novel ever published in your language. That's how it was when he started.

So the Basques decided they had to create a unified language in order to unify the people and give them a chance of surviving. This language was to be made of bits and pieces of the hundreds of dialects and would replace those dialects for national use. My father-in-law whose family was mostly, like Zelestina's, from Arnegi and Baigorri, said that he could hardly understand a word of what people from Bizkaia said. That was the problem. So now we've got one language—Batua—unified Basque—that's used on radio and TV, in the papers and magazines, and at school in every Basque province. The old people see teenagers talking Basque on the streets of Donostia and they are amazed, both because in Franco's time you went to jail for speaking Basque and because half the time the old people don't know what the young are talking about. Granted, that could be a non-linguistic problem.

Often jail meant torture and death. It's half a lifetime since Franco's death and the putative end of his fascist dictatorship in Spain but Basque political activists are still in prison and exile. If you travel around the southern Basque Country—Hegoalde—you will see hanging from thousands of balconies flags that show a map of Euskal Herria with arrows pointing in from outside and the words *PRESO ETA IHESLARIAK ETXE-RA*—bring the Basque prisoners and exiles home. The banners fly even in Iparralde where the French government has been brutal in a much more sophisticated way.

Here on the northern Plains it was the same—the little Indian kids stolen from their parents and sent to boarding schools like Carlyle or Phoenix Indian near where I grew up. My own school was half Chicano and half Anglo and we'd be sitting there in the stands for a basketball game with Phoenix Indian and when they came on the floor our little Chicano Anglo claque would start making those whoo whoo whoo whoo sounds Hollywood Indians made in the nineteen fifties when they were attacking the circled wagons. I guess the Chicano kids forgot they were Indian, too. There's no explaining the Anglos.

When they took Indian kids from their families and homelands and sent them to the boarding schools, they cut their hair—first thing—cut the hair. They took their animal skin clothes away and dressed them in cotton and wool. The kids got whipped for speaking Lakota or Arapaho or Cheyenne or Blackfoot or Navajo or Tohono-O'odham or you name it Indian language.

In Franco's day, Basque people often refused to teach their kids Euskara. They feared that a child, innocent and brave, or stupid, might speak aloud on the street in the hearing of some Spanish patriot or other fool and the next thing you know the Guardia Civil is at the door asking for the parents. A friend of mine—I'm talking in the year 2013—was overheard speaking Basque on the street and a Spaniard came up to him and demanded that he "Habla en cristiano." Speak Christian. That would be Spanish. This kind of lunacy forms the basis for what we like to call history.

4

The Messiah

Coffee Woman and Feather had been dancing. Everyone had been dancing. It was the Ghost Dance. The old people had come out of their lodges and danced small shuffling steps. The children had left the Northern Cheyenne mission school and danced wild child steps. No one had torn the ground open to plant crops as the government agent had explained to them they must. The bags of white man seeds had been flung skyward where they too danced in the northern plains wind.

The Ghost Dance had come to them from the Messiah, a Nevada Paiute named Wovoka, a holy man who had come to earth to save his children from the whites. When Coffee Woman and Feather went to Nevada to meet Wovoka, he had said only, "Go home. Begin the dancing among your people. If you dance, the white people will disappear. The slaughtered buffalo will rise up out of the earth and the grasses will wave again on the prairies. The dead will walk amongst us. It will be so by this time next year. Dance and all will be healed."

In hindsight it's pretty obvious Wovoka's advice was

ridiculous. Those Indians who listened to him were at best overly optimistic—grasping at straws. But at the time, I don't know, you had to try something. A Basque person would understand. How else can you face life if not with a big dose of unfounded hope? Otherwise we'd all slit our throats and gurgle out our last breaths.

I have to tell you about Coffee Woman and Feather in order to tell you about Yellow Bird Daughter in order to tell you about her meeting with Zelestina in order to tell about what they had to do to save both of their lives. And to get to that I have to wade through the mire of a man named Thomas Teague, a real son-of-a-bitch, not that I ever met him, thank God. My point is that this story is not a sidetrack. Or maybe everything is one long series of sidetracks. Well, one sidetrack at a time.

When Wovoka told the Indians to dance, Coffee Woman was pregnant. She loved Feather but he was Cheyenne and she was Arapaho so she wondered when she would see her family again now that she was a married woman. She didn't cry about this. She didn't cry about anything. It's like she was rehearsing the Indian future. You remember that scene in the movie *Smoke Signals* where Victor and Thomas are riding the bus from the Coeur d'Alene Reservation to Phoenix and Victor tells Thomas he's got to be careful "cause these white people will try to take advantage of you. You gotta look tough so they won't mess with you—you know, wipe that silly smile off your face. Come on Thomas, don't you know anything— Indians don't smile. Indians are stoic."

Victor felt that Thomas had to understand you can't give your feelings away to your enemy.

But that's not my favorite moment in the movie. There's a brief scene where a white woman whom Victor and Thomas have helped says, "You two are heroes. It's like you're the Lone Ranger and Tonto." And Thomas says, "Really, we're more like Tonto and Tonto." Or the two young Coeur d'Alene girls racing around the Rez in their car and the heavy gal who's driving says to the more fashionable one, "Give me a beer." And the fashionable one says, "We don't drink beer no more." And the heavy one answers, "Oh, yeah, well then give me a pop." The whole time she's leaning around looking over her right shoulder because the car's transmission is shot and they can only go in reverse. I guess in movies things have to be pretty obvious. Still, that's a good moment. Or the best of them all—Victor and Thomas singing the northern plains warrior song, "John Wayne's teeth, hey ya. John Wayne's teeth, hey ya, hey ya hey. Are they false, are they real, are they plastic, are they steel?"

All that fall, along with thousands of other Indians, Coffee Woman danced. When her back began to ache and her legs seemed to be collapsing, she danced. There had been something in Wovoka's eyes.

"I'm sure you can sit down to rest. We don't have to dance every minute," Feather told her.

"No. He said to dance. Everyone. All the time. That is the only way it can work."

Coffee Woman's labor began during The-Moon-When-The-Deer-Shed-Their-Horns. That's *Wanícokan Wí* in Lakota. I don't know what they called that time in Arapaho or Cheyenne. Maybe I should check on the internet—that's where I found the Lakota words. The words look more beautiful than November and December and maybe they sound better too though I don't actually know how to pronounce them so I can't say. But a metaphor is always more beautiful than an abstraction or an explanation and *Wanícokan Wí* follows *Waníyetu Wí*—The-Moon-Of-The-Rutting-Deer. The Lakota calendar was based on the cycles of the moon so each month was twenty-eight days long and there were thirteen months. Every third year the Lakota added another moon to the calendar. I don't get that since if there are thirteen moons of twenty-eight days then a year is 364 days so you wouldn't need another whole month every third year. I don't know—let's call it a metaphor about the artificiality of time. And I guess I should say the Lakota calendar is based on the cycles of the moon not was based.

The Basques call October *Urria*. In Euskal Herria it rains like crazy in October and the word for water is *ur* so *Urria* is The-Moon-Of-The-Falling-Water. Rain itself is called *euria* and that sounds like both *ur* and *Urria*. Of course it rains like crazy in November, December, January, February, and March, too. February is called simply *Otsaila* which sounds like *hotza*—cold—The-Moon-Of-Shivering-Dogs-And-Children. The temperature drops with the dark and waits. *Hotza egiten du* the people say—it's cold.

It was snowing. Feather, hurrying to get more firewood, fell in a drift and twisted his ankle. The wind chill made it seem even colder than it was—twenty-five below zero or thirty-five below. No one had a thermometer. Feather limped back with the wood. The winter light was slate colored. Coffee Woman's labor was slow.

"Come over here," she said to Feather. "It's cold."

"Yes, chilly, chilly, chilly. It'd be nice to have something hot to drink now, huh?"

"Burning hot coffee," Coffee Woman said and smiled. When she'd first tasted coffee as a child, she'd beamed and her grandfather had said they should change her name. "Falcon Walking is not right for her. Let's call her Coffee Girl. Better, Coffee Woman for when she grows up." The joke had stuck.

When Feather was trying to get up the nerve to speak to her, he traded a rifle to a white trapper for five pounds of coffee beans. Anyone could see he was in love for it was a many-shots rifle. A man wouldn't give that up for five pounds of coffee beans unless he had some powerful motive. Feather took the beans to Coffee Woman but he was so shy that when he presented his aromatic gift, he said only, "Coffee Beans" and held the bag out.

"Coffee Beans. That's a good name though strange. Like mine—Coffee Woman. Are we related?" Feather looked down, still holding the bag. He'd had to look away but it was not only from being embarrassed. He'd also had to hide his smile, his feeling of pleasure. She had almost asked him right out, "What is your name?"

Feather leaned toward his wife. He could smell her hair. "It's amazingly cold. You know how some of the people run across the line into Grandmother's land to escape Uncle Sam?"

"Yes?"

"They must be crazy. It's even colder up there. If you're going to run away, better to head for Mexico where you can spend your life sweating."

"Yes, or Florida."

"The Seminoles fought hard." He pressed the length of his body against hers. "I'll have to go out soon for more wood."

"Your ankle?"

"It's not so bad. I could even dance." He waved one leg around in the air.

Coffee Woman pulled her husband closer. Then, feeling a sharp pain, she clamped her jaws tightly together.

"Are you alright?" Feather asked. He wiped his wife's forehead. "Hey, you're sweating. I'll just look outside to make sure it's still winter. Or to get some wood for the fire anyway. I'll go now and check."

Hundreds of miles away, a Lakota chief named Big Foot had been taken prisoner by the United States government. Held in a temporary lodge and ill with pneumonia, Big Foot lay surrounded by the officers and men of the Seventh Cavalry. He was hemorrhaging and could barely speak. He couldn't make it to the bathroom on his own. There was no bathroom.

The day before, when his people had been captured in their flight from the Cheyenne River to the Badlands of the Pine Ridge Reservation, Big Foot had been unable to stay on a horse and was being carried in an open springless wagon.

As the soldiers approached, Big Foot pushed himself up on his elbow then struggled out of the wagon to his feet next to a white flag. His blankets were covered with blood from his splintered lungs.

In a harsh whisper, he said, "I am taking my people to Pine Ridge to protect them." Droplets of blood fell from his nose and froze as they hit the ground.

"No," the soldiers said.

Big Foot lay back down in the wagon. He stared at the undifferentiated mass of gray sky above him. The hundred braves and two hundred and fifty women and children with whom he was traveling looked up at the same sky.

"I ask you a second time to talk," Big Foot managed. From his position in the wagon, it was as if he were addressing God.

"No," the soldiers said again.

Big Foot let his head fall sideways and a thin line of blood ran onto his shoulder. These white men, they are not God, he thought, but neither are they quite human.

The Indians were taken to Wounded Knee—Chankpe Opi Wakpala—which in the early winter light seemed otherworldly, a vision place spun from ice crystals and sent shimmering darkly across the prairie. There was a United States Post Office and, at a distance, six or seven Indian homes littered along Wounded Knee Creek.

"Set the tipis up here," the soldiers ordered. The American in charge provided a tent warmed by a camp stove for Big Foot. As an Army doctor inspected the sick chief, four hundred and seventy soldiers were positioned around him. Four Hotchkiss guns were set up on a shallow rise to the northwest of the camp.

By eight o'clock the following morning, the doctor was gone, the soldiers were cold and tired, the guns were in position, and Coffee Woman's labor was growing stronger. Two of the Hotchkiss guns had been aimed down on the Indian encampment while two had been rolled back to be held in

reserve. The reserve guns had been turned so that they pointed northwest toward Coffee Woman. Of course I know that
was a coincidence but is it only a coincidence that there are
so many such coincidences?

The Lakota men emerged from their temporary lodges
and sat in a semicircle on the frozen ground. Big Foot, too ill
to stand for long, was dressed in a dark wool coat and wool
pants. A muffler was wrapped around his neck and his head
was covered by a piece of gray cloth, tied the way a person
might tie a bandage around his jaw when suffering from se-
vere toothache. His hands were bare and he kept blowing on
them and tucking them up in his armpits to keep them warm.

"You have slept well?" The American commander asked.

"I have passed the night."

"Good. Your people will move now, a score at a time, back
into the lodges and return with any weapons you may have.
These weapons will be piled here on the ground in front of us."

The first twenty Indians rose and stepped into the lodges.
They were gone a long time. The soldiers heard the whim-
pering cries of frightened children. In the dry wash behind
the lodges, the horses pawed at the frozen ground. When the
twenty men returned, they dropped two guns on the ground.

The American officers looked at these two battered single
shot rifles and began to speak quietly amongst themselves.
Troopers of Companies B and K were ordered forward.

"You will position yourselves approximately ten yards in
front of the seated hostiles, your weapons at ready."

Other American troopers were ordered to enter and
search the tipis.

Coffee Woman felt herself twisted in half by her contractions. She squeezed Feather's hand very hard. Her breath
froze inside her lungs. She gulped trying to keep the air moving in and out of her chest.

Inside the tipis, the soldiers overturned bedding, shook
out blankets and threw them aside, cut open pillows and

spilled buffalo fur on the ground. They ran their hands over shields and arrows, decorated bags and necklaces. Whatever was small enough, they put in their pockets. They grabbed at women and threatened children.

The whimpers turned to screams. The Lakota men looked at the soldiers surrounding them and began to fidget, a few rose to their feet. There were knives and clubs hidden under some of the men's shirts and in their pant legs.

The medicine man Yellow Bird began to walk about the encampment. He strolled along the line of soldiers blowing on an eagle bone whistle. "Stand and ready yourselves. The time to resist has come. Do not be afraid, for you wear the ghost shirts. No bullet will penetrate such garments. If the soldiers shoot, the bullets will lose their way, unsure who among us is living and who is dead, who is returning from another land, and who is disappearing back into that land. The prairie is large and the bullets must go roaming to find the few of us left alive."

Yellow Bird put his faith in magic clothing as Wovoka had put his in a dance marathon. It's hard to know how seriously the local Indians took all this. You get desperate. Like I said, you have to be optimistic. I already mentioned the movie *Smoke Signals*, and should say it's based on Sherman Alexie's book *The Lone Ranger and Tonto Fistfight in Heaven*. There are plenty more great scenes in the movie. In one, the young Victor is with his dad, a reformed drunk played by Gary Farmer. Farmer's driving in his battered pickup, drinking as he's not yet reformed at this point in the film. He's waving his arm around at his ten- or twelve-year-old angry and frightened son, and he says, "I can make everything disappear—poof, the post office is gone, and poof, the grocery, and poof, the rez, and poof, the white men." The father leans over, his beery face close to his son's—watch the road, Dad—and says, "And poof, me, I can make myself disappear."

It is a moment of aching sorrow and as a titular white man I suggest that the Americas be returned to their native inhabitants. "One day," Chief Seattle said, "they will try to sell us the very air we breathe." It doesn't matter that Chief Seattle's name wasn't really Seattle or that we don't know if he really said this or if you are white or Indian. You're buying your air all the same. And by the way, when we give America back to the Indians, we might consider giving the *Pirinioak* and the *Bizkaiko Golkoa* back to the Basques. How's that for unfounded optimism?

Yellow Bird smiled at the soldiers and blew the whistle again. The sound was an arrow in the cold air and the feathers hanging from the end of the whistle were the uncut hair of the dead. Walt Whitman said that about grass, the uncut hair of the dead waving across the northern plains. When Yellow Bird quit blowing the whistle and began to speak, his words fell like panes of glass, shattering as they hit the ground. If any of the soldiers spoke Lakota, they didn't let on.

Between contractions, Coffee Woman rested. She heard something in the distance and rose. Going to the tipi flap she pushed her head out into the cold. Feather woke and asked, "What are you doing?"

"Shhhh."

There was a songbird calling.

"A songbird?" Feather asked.

"Yes, poor thing."

"Poor thing? It must be sick or crazy to be here now."

Yellow Bird kept walking and talking and blowing the eagle bone whistle, all the time saying in his icy voice, "There is no need to fear. We will return in the spring and the whites will disappear. The earth will be reborn. We are wearing the ghost shirts. Do not fear."

"Look, there. You see it?"

"No, I don't. Where?"

"Between those two branches in the tree straight in front of us. Right there."

The bird lifted into the air and flew toward them fluttering around the tipi as if it might fly right in, sit down by the fire, and cock its head at the two people, maybe offer a little story of the bird people. It was twice the size of a chickadee, its breast feathers puffed up to give some warmth, and it had a white ring around its eyes, a heavy dark bill, and an upper body of olive green which made the yellow breast seem to glow even more brightly. It was a bird they saw in the summer along the watercourses.

Now the bird retreated and landed on a low branch of the same tree. From there, it leapt to the ground and began to drag one wing the way a mother pheasant will to feign injury so that a predator will follow it away from its hatchlings. It screamed a call like a crow's and flew straight up at Feather, giving him a sharp peck on the arm. The man was so startled he did nothing and the bird was gone leaving behind only a spot of blood.

When the soldiers returned from the tipis, they brought out forty rifles and laid them on top of the two that were already on the ground. They also brought axes, hatchets, knives, and tent stakes. These were thrown on the pile.

Still unsatisfied by what they saw, the American officers demanded that the seated Indians remove their blankets and submit to full body searches. Two rifles were found, one of them belonging to a young man the soldiers say was named either Black Coyote or Black Fox, though there is a great deal of difference between these two animals.

"This is my rifle which I paid many hides for," Black Coyote-or-Fox said, and raised the gun above his head.

The soldiers lunged for the gun. They grabbed Black Coyote-or-Fox and spun him round.

"This is my rifle."

The soldiers kept spinning him round and shouting. Not even at him really—just shouting the way people will. I have even shouted this way and telling this story I feel a kind of misery at my own blundering. I once got so angry with my girlfriend that I grabbed her arm and pulled her. She looked down at my hand squeezing her skin and went completely still. I released my grip and looked at my hand as if I didn't know how it got there on the end of my arm. That was it but the damage was done and there was no undoing it. What have we done on this earth with our human brothers and sisters besides fuck things up? Excuse me but maybe that's the only way to put it, the only word strong enough for our actions. And just as I know that falling asleep is not death, I also know that an argument with my girlfriend is not genocide.

One of the seated men leaned toward the man next to him and whispered, "Wolf's Nose is quite hard of hearing." So that was his name—Wolf's Nose not Black Coyote or Black Fox at all. The seated man went on to say, "They're shouting at him in English. He'll just think he's being threatened. Something bad is liable to happen."

"You mean later as opposed to now?"

That's when the first shot was fired.

"It was like the sound of a canvas tent flap tearing," Rough Feather said when interviewed as an old man. "Canvas not hide. Modern man-made material."

"More like the thunder that accompanies lightning," Afraid-of-the-Enemy said.

"He was crazy," Turning Hawk said of Wolf's Nose. "A bad influence on those around him and a nobody. It was as much his fault as the soldiers who, after all, were as frightened as young deer in the fall. Not that I'm very sympathetic, after all, they were murderers, but they were also a mostly unhappy bunch of kids who'd been fed a line about savages and American destiny. Then before they had time to grow up, they put their stupidity into action by trying to kill us."

Several hundred soldiers fired at once. The air was filled with powder and smoke. The first two Hotchkiss guns opened up as the second two were wheeled into position. Soon all four guns were firing, sending explosive two-inch projectiles into the camp.

Flying shrapnel shredded the tipis. Because they were firing from all sides of the encampment at once, many soldiers were killed by their own bullets. The Indian men seated on the ground leapt up and fought with whatever they had—knives, clubs, sticks, leaves, snow, dirt, the rifles they pulled from the hands of dead men, their own hands.

Coffee Woman moved slowly in a circle on her hands and knees. She squatted and pressed downward. She was sweating profusely and her body emitted the odor of sulfur. Feather sat against the tipi wall. Now and again he went to her, wiping the sweat from her skin and speaking quietly.

By three minutes past eight that morning, half the Indians at Wounded Knee were dead. The women and children ran toward whatever brush they could find. They hid in overhangs, in tiny caves, in holes they clawed into the frozen cutbank.

The soldiers followed them and pulled them out, wrenching arms and legs from their sockets. When they had brought these hidden Indians into the open, they shot them. After the shooting ended, the temperature dropped again and the sky had a heavy expectant look.

The soldiers walked up and down the draw, their boots splintering the crystals of ice that covered the ground. "It's all over," they shouted. "All over. You are safe now. Come out and we won't hurt you. Come out and we'll take you to Pine Ridge where you will have food and a place to rest."

Most of the people still alive remained hidden but a few small children came forward and some of the soldiers grabbed them, shot them, and butchered them the way they would wolves who'd gotten at their cattle.

The Lakota writer Joe Marshal says that the murderous rage white ranchers express toward wolves is a mask for the ongoing desire these men have to wipe out all Indians.

Maybe we shouldn't expect too much—take the hero Achilles at the end of *The Iliad*. He kills Hector and drags the dead body around the walls of Troy behind a chariot. Then he mutilates Hector's corpse and rapes Hector's wife. Finally, he takes the couple's infant baby by the leg, swings it around, and bashes its brains out against the same walls of Troy. That's classical Greece, the cradle of Western civilization.

At Wounded Knee, a man who was six winters old at the time of the massacre, reported seeing his father die: "The soldier shot my father then with the butt of the rifle struck him in the face. After that, the soldier grabbed my father's pony and jammed the rifle into its mouth. He fired and blood flew everywhere, on the pony's face, on the man. I ran toward the ravine."

As the boy ran, the soldier brought his rifle to his shoulder and took aim. A second soldier, who had been momentarily inhabited by an angel, dropped his rifle and threw himself at the first soldier, knocking the man to the ground. The boy disappeared and so did the angel, retreating back into the heavens.

"What the hell!" The first soldier shouted.

The second soldier picked up his rifle and swung it at the first, striking him broadside across the face. More blood flew and in this exchange, two lives were lost while several were saved. Even in the case of angels there is no unambiguous good.

At midday, the snow was falling still harder, and the wind continued to rise. The soldiers knew they had to get to Pine Ridge before the blizzard. Nearly as worn out as their victims, they hurriedly left with the survivors—four men and forty-seven women and children. That night at Pine Ridge in the deepening cold, the Indians waited in open wagons for several hours until the Episcopal Mission was opened. The pews were removed from the church and the raw wooden floor was covered with hay. The priest set out coal oil lamps which he lit giving the room the golden glow of an elementary school Nativity play.

Coffee Woman had given birth and now mother, father, and daughter slept on blankets and robes spread over the earth. In the middle of the night, Coffee Woman awoke and felt that she had returned safely from a long hard journey. She pressed her baby close to her breast and looked at Feather. His arm covered his forehead as if he had been brushing back a lock of hair at the moment he'd fallen asleep. Coffee Woman reached out and touched her husband's arm where the bird had struck at him.

At Wounded Knee, the dead lay frozen in the twisted shapes they'd assumed when they'd fallen. A teenaged boy sat leaning against his dead horse as if both were only resting or asleep. A woman's arms were locked around her infant baby. One man's hand rose above him like a claw. This last pose is documented in a famous photo that you can easily see on the internet or in an old book by Ralph Andrist called *The Long Death: The Last Days of the Plains Indians*. In death, these people had become no more than ill designed snow fences.

Coffee Woman rolled away, held her daughter, and waited for Feather to awake.

"Do you remember the bird?" She asked when he opened his eyes.

"Yes. Was it really here or was it a dream?"

"Of course it was here. Look at the mark on your arm."

Feather picked the baby up and held her in his arms. "Yellow Bird Daughter?" She drooled on him. "Yes, Yellow Bird Daughter."

It was a few days later when word arrived about the massacre of Big Foot's band. Everywhere, and almost immediately, the Ghost Dance ended. The magic ghost shirts were pulled off and thrown to the ground. In the wind they flew about like rags. People wondered how they could have been so deluded. In Nevada, the Messiah Wovoka announced that he had never actually been to Heaven, never gone anywhere, that he'd just had a dream without meaning, a fever, a vision that was a mirage. Maybe smallpox. He sent away those who came to see him.

"I am tired," he said. "I cannot help you. Go back to your land and try to farm like the white people tell us. There is nothing I can do."

Yellow Bird's eagle bone whistle lay buried under the snow.

Coffee Woman held her daughter up and stared into the baby's eyes. All the dead of Wounded Knee stared back at her. She felt the pain of that stare but, as it would be some days before word reached her about the massacre, she didn't know who might be there in her baby's eyes. She simply saw something she couldn't explain. Wovoka, without knowing what he was talking about, had been right. For better or worse, the dead do come back to life.

5

Marking Time

Game was scarce and the government rations were being cut. Portions of the assigned rations never arrived. There was no wood to make fires. Without irrigation water, those Cheyenne who agreed to try farming found it impossible to grow crops. The buffalo were gone, the deer nearly gone. It was sometimes necessary to kill one of the tasteless spotted white-man-buffalo to eat.

I know it's odd that I put it like that—the spotted white-man-buffalo—talking like I'm an Indian. I'm not. I know that. It's like the kid in the sci-fi satire *Galaxy Quest* who says to the captain of the NSEA Protector, "I just want to explain, I'm not a complete nutcase, I know the ship isn't real, I know it's a TV show..." and so on. Later of course it turns out the ship is real.

But that's television and postmodern irony. Me, I'm not even Basque—just married into a Basque family. My people came to America mostly from Norway though it's true that one of my grandmothers was Sami and another was a Sephardic Jew who fled the Mediterranean thinking there'd be fewer anti-Semites in the far north. All she found was fewer Jews.

Then of course there's Sweden ruling Norway like it was a vassal state. My great grandfather was a prosperous farmer who also edited a small town newspaper. For years, he wrote editorials calling for Norwegian independence and the creation of a socialist state. He ended up fleeing the country right before Norway did get its independence.

You don't have to go back very far to find that pretty much everyone's got a history of being enslaved by someone else. Still, it makes a difference if it happened to you and your parents versus your distant ancestors. You can't blame an individual for history but I understand why some people might blame all whites for what the European colonialists have done around the world. If you're white, it's embarrassing at best thinking about what's been done by other white people. At worst, well, it's way more than shameful.

If you can stand to feel a little of this bitterness colored by defiant hope and crazy comedy, read the half-breed Paiute poet Adrian C. Louis. He's got a poem called "Evil Corn." What could be more American Indian than corn? After all, it was from corn that God, hitchhiking through Guatemala, created human beings. First he used the dust in the tracks of the road but when it rained those dirt people melted. In Guatemala, God was like the captain in *Galaxy Quest*—never give up, never surrender—so he went back to work this time using corn as the first DNA.

Of Minnesota farming country Adrian wrote, "Left to the sun and rain, this land of quaint squares of dark soil sprouts a bright uniform green from road to road that murders anything natural. Gone are the tall grass prairies, vanished are the native trees, and corralled are the once-feathered Indians. Evil corn and its masters have murdered this land." *Pobrecito de Dios*, Adrian suggests though those first Guatemalans—corncobs glued together with spiritual spit—didn't speak Spanish.

Sometimes to feed his family a Cheyenne man might have to stoop to shooting some rancher's cow—the tasteless spotted white-man-buffalo. That or live on mice and weasels. Or maybe miller moths like grizzly bears do in Wyoming.

The land office in Miles City encouraged white settlers to file homestead claims on the Cheyenne reservation. The agents of the land office and many other whites assumed it was only a matter of time before the reservation would be abolished. Then the last acre of Indian land would be taken and opened for white settlement.

Those first reservation Indians would recognize their experience in the lives of Palestinians in refugee camps today. There are Palestinians who've lived for three generations in the camps. Maybe the big difference is that the Palestinians still have hope that at least some of their land will be returned to them.

It was on a day in early spring when Feather was out building fence that he decided they should leave. He picked up Yellow Bird Daughter, who was playing with a pile of sticks near him and asked, "You want to fly like the bird you are named for?"

"Yes," she said flapping her arms and running in circles. "Yes, yes."

Feather grabbed her as she passed and tossed her into the air. He took a step sideways then stepped back and caught her as she fell. Again and again he threw her into the air and neither father nor daughter mentioned how short the flights were.

It was a dreamy moment but not until several years later did Feather make up his mind to really leave Lame Deer. They were eating lunch and, as he looked at his daughter, it hit him that she was no longer an infant sitting on the ground near him and playing with sticks while he worked. She was a young woman. Things were no better than they'd ever been and there was no sign of improvement just around

the corner. And the farming, well, who was it who had decided the way to feed yourself was to rip your mother's flesh
apart and eat her insides?

When Feather asked Coffee Woman what she thought,
she looked at him with a kind of "it's-about-time" expression on her face and said, "I'm in." Maybe not exactly those
two words but that sentiment.

"You hear that?" Feather asked Yellow Bird Daughter.
"She's ready for us to go somewhere else and see what life
might bring. What about you?"

And like her mother, she too said, "I'm in."

"That's lucky. But we'll have to be careful. There are still
some wily foreign Indians hiding in the spaces the white men
haven't yet fenced and some of those Indians are your mother's relatives—the last real wild Indians. My grandmother always said never trust an Arapaho. Or maybe she said Shoshone. I'm not sure—they both live over there on the other side
of the mountains at Wind River. She probably said never trust
an Arapaho or a Shoshone."

Coffee Woman swatted at her husband. They would have
to walk a long way to get into the Bighorn Basin—upstream
along the Talking Waters, what the agent called Tongue River, then into the mountains, across the pass and back down.
After that there was still a long way across the Basin to Wind
River. It'd be cold in the high country and they'd have to cross
many fences.

Looking back on the posts stretching across the fields,
Feather could hear the voice of the agent at Lame Deer, "You
must fence your holdings properly." Then as a friend giving
advice, "White men admire fences. Fences give them a confident neighborly feeling. They know what's going to happen
and they can trust you."

Feather noticed about the agent what I'd noticed about
myself—he talked as if he weren't a white man, as if he were as
Indian as the next fellow. Both of us are like Father DeSmet,

the Belgian Jesuit who translated when the US government was negotiating the Fort Laramie Treaty. That was in the days of Feather's father and grandfather. "Negotiating" is not quite the right word.

Father DeSmet came to the Great Plains and Northern Rockies with passion and innocence. That's what the kindest of the white people had but as the British writer and spy Graham Greene said in his novel *The Quiet American*, it's the innocent ones who bring down a wall of suffering on everyone else. The innocent always think they're doing good while they go blithely along leaving a trail of destruction in their wake. And the guilty who don't give a shit often use the innocent to cause more destruction.

Though the only link is the problem of innocence, this reminds me of a scene in the musical *Hairspray*. Queen Latifah playing Motormouth Maybelle, the host of *Negro Day*, a television dance party show for teenagers on a local Baltimore station, sees that her son is in love with a sweet and attractive white girl named Penny played by Amanda Bynes. Motormouth looks at the young couple and says, "Oh, so this is love. Love is a gift. A lot of people don't remember that so you two better brace yourselves for a whole lot of ugly coming at you from a never ending parade of stupid."

Looking as calm as a just milked cow, the white girl says, "So you've met my mother." It's a fine moment in the history of film and I'm only sorry that Amanda Bynes has not lived up to the potential she showed here as an actress.

I admit not everyone agrees with me about Bynes or the movie. When I mentioned *Hairspray* to a young and terribly beautiful Greenland Inuit woman I know, she said with disgust, "It's a truly stupid movie." And a young Alabama friend—white and Catholic from Mobile—said he liked the film—it was funny—but the fantasy of teenage interracial love was ridiculous. "In the time and place—early 1960s, Baltimore," he says, "the young black man would like as not have been beaten to death by a crowd of white boys."

In his first yearly report to Washington, the Lame Deer agent had said that the northern Cheyenne were far in advance of white people in perceptive ability but far behind in intellectual capacity. Sounds like the same old same old—Indians are one with nature but don't ask them to design a rocket that can go to the moon.

Whatever—Father DeSmet had some perceptive ability, too. Unlike most of the innocent newcomers to America, he saw what was around him. He attended to the world and so he changed. Here was a place and a people neither his own life nor the church had prepared him for. He was soon caught up in a whirlwind of arguments with his fellow Black Robes about their mission to evangelize among the Red heathens. He even went toe-to-toe with the US Army arguing against its campaign to exterminate these Red heathens.

It got so bad the church sent Father DeSmet home or maybe he ran away because he couldn't stand what was being done in the name of Jesus Christ, who after all was about like any Indian in Montana or Wyoming. Not that Indians should be Christians. Just that Jesus would have picked up on the vibe.

Feather slammed another fencing staple into a post.

So what happened to DeSmet? Back in Belgium he built a sweat lodge in the middle of a Brussels boulevard and tried to live like an Indian. That is, he went crazy. Then he returned to the US where he died in St. Louis.

Feather noticed that while he'd hit the staple plenty hard enough, it had gone in off kilter. Unlike a nail, a fencing staple is shaped like a U so it has two points to drive into the wood. One of the points extends out farther than the other so if you don't hit the staple right, it goes in at a slant and won't hold the wire securely in place.

Sometimes the agent would watch for a few minutes then say, "Here, let me see that." He'd take the hammer and in one crisp set stroke and a second finishing stroke, the wire would be in place. Then he'd look at the finished line of fence—the barbed wire as straight and tight as a drumhead—and he'd smile. It wasn't pride. It was like he said—a white man loves a well-made fence. And in this regard he was a white man.

Feather grunted as he climbed another fence. It was a long walk to Wind River where Coffee Woman's people had been interned. They'd started into the Bighorns at the town of Wolf, but not wanting to be seen, they walked north of the buildings and up a series of ravines.

Meanwhile, back at the ranch, as they say in the cowboy movies, Zelestina was down in Wolf working her ass off for Søren and Smylla Christiansen, a Danish couple who were members of the Evangelical Lutheran Church and who understood it to be their responsibility to free the Basque immigrant girl from the Hellish influence of the papists. Until she came to Wolf, Zelestina had never met a Lutheran.

Twice a day, Zelestina put a pan of nearly frozen water on the coal stove in the back of the tack room. When the water was warm, she carried it to the unheated shed where she washed the udders and teats of three milk cows. She did the milking then carried the cooling milk back to the Christiansen's house. Through that first winter and into the cold season that passed for spring, steam rose both from the bucket of wash water and from the bucket now filled with milk. What Zelestina liked best was sitting on the stool, the side of her face pressed against a cow's flank, the smell of the animal and the sound of the milk splashing into the bucket.

Less appealing were the pigs. For months she hauled kitchen waste to them in the same bucket she'd filled with milk. Then there was the butchering, the way a pig would stand before dying, its short legs spread and its narrow eyes fastened on her, and after death, the way the intestines rolled out like thread from a spool and steamed in the cold air. Having cleaned the pig, she made cured pork, lard, sausages, and ham.

It seemed that there was more butchering in Wolf than in Iparralde. More blood on her hands. She collected eggs from the chickens but then it was time to kill them, too. She'd grab a rooster by the legs and haul it squawking out into the yard where she held it down on a wide chopping block, and with a bright hatchet, would sever its head from its body. She'd hang the headless bird upside down on the clothesline until the blood had drained into the earth. Sometimes a bird got away from her and ran, blood pumping from its severed neck until it keeled over in the dirty snow. She made chicken soup, roast chicken, fried chicken. She learned to make chicken and dumplings. She liked to say the word out loud—dumplings. I like it, too—dumplings—and remember my own mother cooking chicken and dumplings, the doughy balls floating atop the bubbling hot water.

Even vegetables you have to kill. She ripped them out of the ground or twisted them off their stems—beans, carrots, tomatoes, cabbage, turnips, rutabaga. In the fall, she collected baskets of windfall apples, dug the worms out of them, and made applesauce.

Søren and Smylla Christiansen spoke no Basque and Zelestina no Danish. None of the three spoke more than a few words of English. In the absence of a shared language, each person's inner life remained intact. The Christiansens were limited to giving orders and Zelestina was reduced to receiving them. Struggling to communicate, she had the opportunity to invent phrases such as, "I now going buy shop," which made it sound as if she would soon be an independent businesswoman. Or, "Fire for little sticks needs has, I am." I yam what I yam is how Popeye put it.

At the end of the day, Zelestina nodded and said, "Good night" to the Christiansens. They said, "Good night" back.

Then Zelestina left the house, closing the door quietly behind her, and walked in the dark to her room in the Bighorn Hotel. In the cold her fingers turned blue. If she was lonely, she understood that she was not the only one.

It occurs to me that I've told you a lot of things that you wouldn't think I'd know—like about Potxo's behavior on the day of his daughter's birth or about Wovoka's advice to Yellow Bird Daughter's parents or about the sexual fantasies of the hay merchant and the stationmaster when they first saw Zelestina. Maybe the best thing is to say that while it's as much a surprise to me as it would have been to my father, I was once a graduate student in folklore and I came to Wolf to complete an oral history project on Basque immigration in the intermountain west as part of my PhD dissertation. I know—B.S. means bullshit, M.S. means more of the same, and PhD means pile it higher and deeper. I guess in this last acronym you have to assume pile-it is one word. Anyway, I won't argue with you about this view of academia. In my own defense, I can only say that I did manage to drop out of the PhD program without getting a degree.

The point is that I was a grad student in folklore and as a student of the folk I interviewed about half of the population of Wolf, including Zelestina. Then I went back and interviewed many of them a second time. With Zelestina, I went back for a third and fourth interview. I didn't want to be a folklorist. I wanted to be a folk.

There was something about Zelestina—that little spark we feel in the presence of some people as if they are just a tad more alive than the rest of us. It's got nothing to do with how important they are in the world or with what they've done or not done. I think it's connected to what the sociologist Max Weber called charisma. Weber didn't coin that term until the 1920s but Zelestina had charisma in 1902. I admit it's connected to sex appeal. Zelestina was old when I met her and I was awfully young but she had physical energy and she moved quickly and easily. Grace. If we were closer in age, I would have wanted to date her. Given the difference, we became friends. That meant we spent a lot of time sitting together talking.

I got to speak with Yellow Bird Daughter a number of times too even though she had gone back to Lame Deer long before I got to Wolf. With both Yellow Bird Daughter and Zelestina I admit I've made some things up but I've tried to stick to the truth of their inner lives. I'm not so concerned with what people rather cavalierly call the facts though mostly even my facts are accurate.

Feather, Coffee Woman, and Yellow Bird Daughter followed Lost Creek past the place where Frank's Creek enters it. They went on climbing, hoping they might find a place near the pass to spend the night. But they had gone slower than they'd expected and it would soon be dark. The air was cooling as the sun began to drop below the mountain's edge. The billowing clouds crossed the sky, rushing away not so much to a better place as to just another place.

It was impossible to go any higher in the dark. There was a layer of hard crusty snow under the trees. Looking for a patch of bare ground, Feather stopped on a shelf high above the creek where the wind had blown the snow back into the sky. Coffee Woman broke dead branches from several trees and, with the brittle wood, started a fire. Yellow Bird Daughter collected pine needles in her pouch. Making several trips, she carried these needles to the campsite and made three beds that would be soft and warm on the cold ground.

Unable to sleep, Yellow Bird Daughter listened. The sighs she heard could have been the cries of children or they could have been the wind. The stars had disappeared behind the ceiling of fog. The weather shifted again. The fog became icy and hard chunks of snow began to fall. It warmed up a little and the flakes grew larger and wetter. The snow shifted to rain then to ice then back to snow. Typical spring. The sleepers were awakened by stinging blows to their faces.

Though it remained dark, it was early morning. They decided to get up and head over the peaks, stopping later to eat. In the snow, they could barely see the outlines of the trees around them. The wind constantly changed directions so that it seemed to come from everywhere at once. A wall of snow raced upward like a plume of fire then tumbled back to earth in splintery shards only to be picked up by another gust of wind. It was stupid to go on so they turned and moved back toward the shelf where they'd slept. From there they could get their bearings and head down the mountain until the snow let up.

"Something's wrong," Coffee Woman said and stopped. Feather slowed and stepped carefully across a field of loose rock. It sloped steeply down and Feather found himself sliding off into space. He reached out his hand. Coffee Woman leapt toward him, ignoring the loose rock. She managed to grab onto him but when she tried to pull him back, she too lost her footing. Unaware of what was before them, husband and wife, mother and father, rolled forward and over the side of a narrow canyon.

Yellow Bird Daughter stood in the echo of everything falling. She heard the words "Don't move," coming toward her through the trees and over the rocks. The branches swayed, bending toward the drop-off then away from it. "Don't move." Yellow Bird Daughter heard again—don't move, don't move, don't move. Then it was quiet.

She wrapped her arms over her stomach and tucked her head down in her coat to see if her heart was still beating. Like the branches of the trees, she swayed while the apparently oblivious rocks slowly exhaled and the obviously indifferent clouds crossed the sky.

6

Hunting Trip

Though it was the last week of May, it had snowed the night before and on into the day. Thomas Teague, who'd set out hunting two mornings before, had spent the night shivering in his camp above Wolf.

"God damn country," he said to himself. "Never changes." By that he meant that it was always changing. "It was spring two days ago. Then snow again. It never gets any better. Nearly June and I'm trying to walk around in this slop. Just my luck I'll run into some old sow bear and her cub, mad as hell about the weather." He picked up his rifle and sighted down the barrel as if the sow bear stood there on two legs staring at him. "Just you wait," he shouted, "might be ninety tomorrow. Not worth trying to farm or ranch. Hunting's miserable. May as well pick berries. Not worth anything. Pick goddam berries like a goddam bear."

Again, he shivered in the early morning cold, then took a step toward the imagined bear and, unable to see the crust below the newly fallen snow, broke through and sank to his knees. He fell forward and landed on his chest with his rifle beneath him in the snow. "Shit. Barrel'll be full of water."

That's when he noticed the girl. Half hidden in the snow and with her back to him, he saw only that she was thin. She didn't move and, had he not fallen, he might have passed without seeing her. It was as if she were invisible. Anyway, the light was bad.

"Hey!" Teague shouted. At the sound of his voice, the girl turned. "Hey!" Teague called out again, "What're you doing here? You lost?"

As if awakened from sleep, the girl—really a young woman—jumped and took off running down the mountain. Teague noticed how fast she ran even when her feet were flailing in the heavy wet snow. To avoid that, she ran as much as possible along the trunks of downed trees or across exposed rock.

Teague gave chase and, almost on her, yelled a third time, "Hey" and "Stop." The girl did stop, then turned and leapt at Teague. Before he'd thought to move, she slammed her small fist into his gut. The breath sucked from him, he nearly fainted. When he looked up, the girl was gone. He tried to shout but what came out was an unrecognizable croak.

He caught his breath and started after the already distant figure. Girl, woman—better said, animal. Running, he heard the labored breathing of his father—Thomas Senior— behind him, waving his fists and shouting. "You little bastard." Well, why not—being a bastard would have been better than being his father's son. Huffing and puffing, Thomas Senior couldn't run more than fifty feet. Teague didn't know how his mother had gotten his father on a boat and across the Atlantic from Ireland to America. Poured the asshole on through a sieve, Teague guessed. The man couldn't hold a job over a week— first Friday payday he drank up his wages and didn't show up for work the next Monday.

Once, late on a Saturday, Thomas Senior showed up drunk as a skunk. He had a woman with him. She was drunk, too. Thomas introduced his lady companion to his wife and took the new woman into the room where the family slept. He awakened his son by kicking him in the ribs while shouting, "Get out!"

Young Thomas sat outside the door listening to his father's grunting, imagining ways to kill him, ashamed for his mother who said and did nothing. When the visitor left, Thomas Senior's wife got ready for bed and joined her husband. That was when Teague knew he had to run away.

"Son of a bitch," Teague said, and picked up a rock. He threw it, and struck the girl—alright girl, let's call her a girl—on the left shoulder blade. She jerked and flailed as if in a parody of dance. Then she fell to the snow and lay still.

"Well, let's see what we've got here." He wasn't ten paces away when the girl leapt up, reared back, and threw what must have been the same rock Teague had thrown at her. He hopped to one side not quite fast enough and the rock hit him on the elbow sending a jolt of pain through his arm.

"What?" Teague was so stunned that he stood still for a moment. His own mother would never have returned a blow. What would his father have done if she had—beaten her to death or burst into drunken tears and begged for forgiveness? The girl had started running the moment she released the stone and she was again a good distance away before Teague got his bearings.

Would the old man really have asked for forgiveness? Forgiveness is just another kind of weakness and Thomas Junior swore off weakness the day he left. Not for him to ask for or offer forgiveness.

It took him the better part of thirty minutes slogging down slope over deadfalls and boulders through slushy snow then mud to catch the girl. When he finally grabbed her, she was panting raggedly and her hair was soaked. She bit and kicked at him, jamming the heel of one foot into his groin. When he bent slightly to catch his breath, she clamped down on his wrist with her teeth.

He could be as fierce as any savage though and so in spite of the bites and kicks, he held the girl's hands tightly, pulling her wrists together then pinning her to him. Though she was clearly undernourished, he could feel a nicely rounded ass and two also nicely rounded tits. How old was she—thirteen? Could be sixteen, maybe even older. Who knows with these people? He pressed his hand harder against her. Just a little more weight would be good but who wants a fat woman.

He pulled his hand away and gave her a stern thump on the head. Just to warn her. He half dragged and half carried her to his camp where he decided to take her home with him. He untied the horse but couldn't think how to saddle it without letting the girl go. "I'll just ride bareback," he thought, "come back for the gear later." He yanked the girl up in front of him. Her arm felt loose in the socket. Again holding her tightly to him, he rode down out of the last of the snow. The rattle of breath from man, girl, and horse echoed off the unseasonably cold trees.

It was late afternoon when they got down off the mountain. Teague locked the girl in the pantry and went to sit for a minute in the kitchen. He took off his boots and banged them together, knocking mud and snow to the floor. He rolled his shirt up and looked at the purple bruise above his elbow. It throbbed.

Maybe he should have stayed and tried to help his mother but goddam it she wouldn't help herself. There's only so much a man can do and then he's got to look out for himself. "I'm tired," he said aloud to no one, "bone tired." And shuddered. Wrapping his arms around himself, he stood up and walked to the washbasin into which he spat.

"Damn dirty snow's melting. I should get a broom to sweep it up before the floor is a pool of water." As he went to hunt for the broom, he heard tearing and banging sounds from the closed pantry. "What the hell is going on?"

Teague fumbled around for a minute with the latch then

pulled the pantry door open. The girl had knocked everything she could reach to the floor—beans and flour, sugar, coffee, several jars of canned tomatoes and apples his neighbor had traded him for splitting wood. As Teague opened the door, the girl was struggling to pull a fifty-pound sack of potatoes off the lower shelf.

"Put that down. What are you trying to do? Hell, you can't even pick that up."

Without seeming to hear the man, the girl made a huge effort and, grunting, pulled the sack off the shelf. Potatoes spilled out and rolled across the floor. Then the girl grabbed one of the jars of tomatoes and, just as she had on the mountain, reared back. With both hands, she flung the jar at Teague.

"Christ," he shouted and leaned to the left. The jar sailed past him and crashed against the kitchen wall. The pantry floor and walls were covered with a red paste made from flour and tomatoes. The girl pulled another jar from the shelf and was getting ready to throw again when Teague knocked her down. The jar landed next to her, breaking and sending more tomato and glass flying.

Teague pulled the girl up by the arm and hauled her out of the pantry into the kitchen where he slammed her down into a chair. She leapt away and ran again. He lurched after her, managing to grab her by the hair and drag her back. This time when he sat her down, he held onto her. He could see that the red on her face was blood not tomato and that splinters of glass were embedded in her right cheek. He grabbed her chin and turned her head. "Let me look at you."

She wrenched her face from his hand but now made no attempt to run. Instead, she stared into his eyes. When he'd first come West, he'd decided he would be a trapper and he remembered being taught how to kill an animal without damaging the pelt—he was to give it a stern blow on the nose to knock it out then snap its neck. He'd caught a wolverine and when he bent toward the trap, the animal looked up at him. It was the same look in this girl's eyes, the look of a creature that will not be tamed, a creature that, given enough time, will chew off its own leg to escape the trap. You'd think it might have occurred to him that he'd be better off not trying to keep such an animal in his house.

"Hold still," Teague ordered. "You'll see what happens if you don't." He lifted the girl from the chair and hauled her toward the washbasin. He opened a drawer, took out a rag and continued pulling her, this time toward a cupboard. She wasn't resisting him now but neither was she helping. At the cupboard he took out a bottle of Mercurochrome. He went back to the table with his supplies then returned to the drawer for tweezers.

When the two were finally seated more or less together, Teague began to slowly pick the splinters of glass out of the girl's face. She jerked around a few times and Teague very nearly pushed a piece of glass into her eye.

He wondered if he could quit holding onto her long enough to fill the basin with water. He thought he might try, thought better of it and, again, pulled her with him while he lifted the basin and placed it beneath the pump. He leaned hard several times to get the water flowing. When he had enough, he went to the stove, started a fire, and set the water on to warm.

This should have taken five minutes but with only one arm free to work, everything was complicated—opening the box of matches, splitting kindling, setting the fire in the stove. Time passed and the glass remained embedded in the girl's cheek. The last gray light of day settled into blackness and Teague got up, still dragging the girl after him as he lit lamps.

He placed a coal oil lantern on the kitchen table then sat back down holding the girl's face close to the light from the flame. He daubed roughly at her cheek with a rag soaked in hot water. He brought her face even closer to the lamp and poked at her skin with his forefinger to see if he could feel any remaining bits of glass. If glass were left stuck in her flesh, the skin would heal over it and the wound would fester. Later, there'd be an infection and the oozing pus to deal with.

He knew about that. Once he'd been running—not from his father but from a fruit and vegetable vendor from whom he'd stolen two bananas. He'd leapt a fence and the man, old and deciding it wasn't worth the effort for two bananas, gave up the chase. Teague had found a back lane where he sat down and began to eat. Only then had he noticed the pain in his ankle, cut somehow getting over the fence. Later, it became infected. He didn't tell either his mother or father. Finally, he cut the wound open and drained it then heated a piece of iron to burn the rotten flesh.

Teague looked at the girl again in the lamplight. He leaned back in his chair and let the tweezers fall from his hand. He sighed and looked down at his lap. Tits and ass, but really she was still a child. Or something between child and woman. He hadn't touched a child since he'd been one. And he'd only rarely touched a woman without money coming into the matter.

Maybe he'd never been out hunting at all, maybe he'd hunkered down like the bear he feared and gone to sleep for the winter and he was asleep now and this Indian girl was a dream. Funny dream—dried and canned foods thrown everywhere, glass and blood, tweezers. Who would have a dream like that? He began to sweat then was wracked by chills.

The girl stroked his arm and smiled. He was holding her tighter now and he could again feel her breasts through her clothing—smaller and harder than he'd first thought. He looked at her—prominent cheekbones, straight jaw, flat wide chin. Her hair was parted in the middle and fell over her shoulders in thick black strands. Her deeply set eyes were so dark as to seem black and the outside edge of each eye seemed to rest on the point of her cheeks. She was the perfect Indian.

And how would she describe him? Sandy hair and long

face, reddish mottled skin, but not so bad. It's true his beard was untrimmed and his clothes stank a little but it was only the stink of human, after all. Had she noticed the shape of his fingers as he plucked glass from her face?

Maybe he could do something differently than he had before. It's like that song in the *The Commitments*—"Oh, she may be weary, and young girls they do get weary, wearing that same old shaggy dress, but when she gets weary, try a little tenderness…"

In this fevered reverie, long before anyone dreamed of Motown music, Teague's grip loosened and the girl was up and off again. She shoved Teague's chair and he went over backwards, hitting his head on the floor and for a moment blacking out.

She had her hand on the door when he shouted, "Damned savage." No reverie now. She turned and hesitated. He leapt up, bounded across the room, and wrestled her back into the kitchen, slipping on the not quite congealed canned tomatoes and sliding to a stop against the wall.

When he fell, her face slammed into his chest. She pulled back and Teague slapped her hard with the back of his hand. It was the second time he'd hit her, well, the third time if throwing the stone counted. He hadn't planned to hit her so much. She slumped against the wall and closed her eyes.

Now, as though he were working on a dead body, Teague finished the chore of cleaning her up. He heated more water, took off her clothes and wiped her clean as he might have wiped his rifle clean after it had fallen into the muddy snow. He dressed her in one of his shirts, laid her in his bed, and began to haul everything else out of the room—the rough plank table and chair, the second coal oil lamp, the trunk with almost nothing in it, the clothes hanging on hooks along one wall, the formal hat he never wore. Each time he returned for another load, he glanced at the girl, still unconscious. Her chest rose and fell as she breathed and it seemed to him that with each breath her breasts grew a little larger, then smaller, then larger again as if she were doing a bizarre magic trick.

With everything out of the room, he closed the door and locked it. He went outside to bar the shutters on the bedroom windows. He returned to mop the tomato reddened flour paste off the kitchen floor.

There's Thomas Teague with his matted hair and a little blood spattered on his hands and shirt sleeves, thinking how tired he is and talking to the mop. Maybe he didn't talk to the mop. In fact, it's unlikely he had a mop. I'm just trying to fill in the blanks here. He might have cleaned up the floor with a rag made from an old shirt. If he was thinking, he might have tied the rag around the end of a stick. But maybe he never cleaned the floor. Just threw a pile of old horse blankets down on the drying stain and went to sleep. He could have slept in his bed with her but it occurred to him that she might pretend to sleep, that if he fell asleep she would try to kill him. Then there were the windows. What if she broke one and came at him with a shard of glass?

In the morning he finished cleaning the floor then got something to eat. He sat listening but no sound came from the locked bedroom. He walked to the door and pressed his ear against it. He imagined her doing the same thing and stepped away. Better to let her stew. He spent the day opening the shutters one at a time and removing the glass from the window frames. Closing the shutters. He never saw the girl. That night he slept on the floor again.

On the third day he worried she might be dead then he thought that was ridiculous. Nobody dies of glass splinters in her cheek. He waited one more day. At dusk, he lit the lamp and went to the bedroom. He rattled the doorknob then stepped back. The same silence. He put the key in the lock and turned it. When he opened the door, she knocked him backward and the lamp flew from his hand. This time it wasn't canned tomatoes but fire that flashed across the floor.

Teague knocked the girl down as he ran past her to grab the blankets off the bed. He threw the blankets over the flames. Before he could do more, the girl appeared and threw a washbasin of water over the blanket. "More," he said.

When the fire was out he could hear the girl breathing beside him. He pulled her into the bedroom and pushed her down on the bed. He bent over and brought his face close to hers. She turned her head away. He put his hands on her shoulders and held her down while with his left foot he pushed on the heel of his right boot and shoved it off. Same thing, other foot. He crouched over Yellow Bird Daughter, grabbed her wrists, and pulled them up next to her head.

"Hold still," he said. She tried to twist out from under him. "I said hold still." She kept twisting. He thought about it and slapped her—not as hard as he had before. He let her go, picked up his boots and left the room, locking the door behind him. The next day he began leaving food for her, opening the door, sliding the food in, and closing the door again. Oatmeal, a piece of deer meat, bread, sometimes an apple.

It makes me think of my own father. When he was eight, he was quarantined for several months with scarlet fever. He told me he could never leave the room they put him in and that no one ever came in. There was a little hinged opening like a dog door in the wall next to the real door. It had a latch on the outside so he couldn't open it and try to crawl out. Someone would open that dog door and shove food in. He saw the person's hands but never anything else. For months, he said, he was completely alone. As a kid, I never understood if he was bragging about his strength or explaining some aspect of his personality that he thought I should understand. It seemed strange that the doctors and nurses and his parents would leave an eight year old alone for months. How did he wash? Was there a toilet in the room? Maybe my father made the whole thing up.

I never asked my grandmother about this and I don't

know why I didn't, as she would have explained. When I was sixteen, she asked me to come into her room. She sat down on the carefully made bed and patted the spot next to her. When I sat down, she said, "Your father is my baby who never grew up so now you have to be the grown-up. You have to understand this."

What about Teague—not so much the baby who never grew up but the baby who grew up to be not quite a monster, but not quite a person either. He went about his business—a little hunting, a little fishing, a little carpentry. He never mentioned the girl to anyone. Summer passed and in the fall he worked building fence for a Basque rancher who'd bought four sections of land east of town along the Middle Fork. The weather got colder and the work was miserable which meant the pay was better than for most fencing jobs.

Each day when Teague left her locked in the room, Yellow Bird Daughter waited until the house was still. Then she rose. She checked the door, hoping or fearing that she would find it unlocked. If she fled, he would follow her. She knew that. Finding the door securely locked, she sat on the floor in the half-darkness—the empty window frames still shuttered. Sometimes she lay down. Never on the bed. She ate and when she finished, she set the plate down by the door. In the late afternoon, the door opened, the empty plate was removed, and a full one was left in its place. She stayed out of sight behind the bed. After a time, Teague began to leave a basin of water along with the food. She could drink it or wash with it or drown herself in it.

As the days grew shorter, Teague returned earlier in the day. Yellow Bird Daughter could hear him in the other rooms opening drawers, lighting the coal oil lamp. She could see the guttering lamp wick then the flames spreading across the floor. Often she daydreamed. There was one summer night when she was small and she'd gone east with her parents to a spot where a few Cheyenne lived among the

Lakota. They'd sat in the dark watching fireflies, the flashes of light in the dark.

In the day she repeated her dreams from the night before—saying them out loud to remember them, looking for messages. In one dream she was alone but aware that someone was watching her. That was obvious but in the dream she knew she was asleep and she would rise just to the point of waking then feel herself pressed back to sleep. Once, in the dream, she refused to be pressed down and opened her eyes. Boys dressed in deerskin shirts and pants, and girls in deerskin dresses surrounded her. The children all had blue circles tattooed on their foreheads. This was an Arapaho tradition she'd never experienced—the cuts in her skin, the ashes and bits of sand rubbed into the cuts making them heal as ridged bluish scar lines. Her mother and father had decided she would be better off without such marks, better off in the world that was to come. When she woke from the dream, she wondered if the dream children had been angels. She'd never seen an angel but the sisters at the Lame Deer Mission School had explained that they were real.

One morning the door opened and a dress was thrown into the room. A second dress followed. They lay on the floor side by side like two deflated human beings. Yellow Bird Daughter poked at the dresses with her foot then picked them up and laid them down on the bed where she left them for several days. Finally, she put one on. She wore it for six days then took it off and washed it in the basin of water Teague now left. She wrung it out and hung it over the headboard of the bed. She put on the second dress.

When she hung the damp dress over the headboard, it seemed she was hanging up herself. When she put the second dress on, she pulled it over an empty space. The dresses were slowly becoming the person who was slowly disappearing. The dress hanging up to dry was resting while the one being worn was growing used to having a soul.

One day in winter nearly finished with the fencing, Teague hit his thumb while hammering a stretch of barbed wire to a post while another man stretched the wire tight.

"Damn."

"Yup. Damn. Could be worse."

Teague looked at the man with whom he'd never spoken.

"I said could be worse." The man waited and when Teague said nothing, went on, "Could be forty below insteada zero. Coulda stepped in a hole, broke your ankle. Could be dead. Really—even what looks better might not be. Say it was summer. You wouldna been wearing those good gloves, hit your bare thumb and smash it bad."

Teague grunted.

"Or take these elections—looks bad but who knows, never can tell."

"What elections?"

"Town elections. You didn't vote?"

"I have no interest in politics."

"Well, it's not so much politics you know when it's all women taking over the town."

"Hand me that trenching shovel."

"Every council seat won by a woman—give 'em the vote and look at that—a few years go by and they get the smart idea of electing each other. People sure talking about it."

"People talk about a lot."

"Not just the council but the mayor, too, and the county sheriff—her name's Ruby Hoop. Like as bust out laughing saying that—'Evening Sheriff Hoop.' Or do you call a woman sheriff by her first name—'Evening Sheriff Ruby.' You know Violet Delaney? She got more votes than her own husband. It's true he's a scoundrel but that's dangerous having a woman beat her own husband in a election. I wouldn't wanta go home to supper in the Delaney house."

"Delaney?"

"Yeah, that's right." The man released another turn on the roll of wire and took a step to the next post.

Teague seemed interested now. "You think women won't be able to run the town?"

"Of course they won't. What do women know about running a town?"

"I don't know. You think they're stupid."

"No, I never said women was stupid. They're smart enough alright but they're devious. That's the problem. Never know when they're telling ya the truth. Can't run a town like that."

"You think all women are alike?"

"Alike enough."

"I'd guess they might be different from each other. Men are different from each other."

"That's fer damned sure."

"What about a woman you know? Your sister, say."

"I don't have no sister."

"Your mother then, or better, a stranger, a woman you see on the street and you tip your hat and say good day like you would to the sheriff. Then you come upon another woman."

"What other woman?"

"Any woman—and you think how she's different. For example, an Indian woman."

"That'd be different from a lady sheriff."

"Of course, an Indian woman and a white woman, surely they wouldn't think alike."

"No, they wouldn't but that's got nothing to do with women or sheriffs, that's Indians."

Teague nodded and said no more. The two men worked in silence watching the clouds of breath appear before their faces and disappear. When they finished, Teague's partner said, "G'night then."

"Yes, good night," then uncharacteristically, "I need to start work late tomorrow. Can you wait for me?"

"Sure. You gonna go down to the town hall and make a complaint to the new council?" Teague didn't answer and the man laughed then went on, "Like I said, sure, I can wait on ya, give it a little time to warm up not that it'll warm up all that much. What time d'ya wanta start?"

"Eleven o'clock."

"Eleven o'clock." Then, unable to resist, he added, "That's gonna be some complaint."

"I've got some business, that's all."

At home, Teague opened the bedroom door, and stepped in. The girl was nowhere in sight so he stepped to the far side of the bed where he found her on the floor. He leaned over, picked the girl up and put her down on the bed. He hesitated, wondering if it might be possible to civilize an Indian. He could keep her locked up forever. He could break her legs then open the door. The Chinese bound the feet of their little girls so when they were grown women they couldn't run. They could hardly walk, just hobble around on their scrunched up twisted feet. What about sending the girl to one of the Indian boarding schools? They'd hammer some sense into her.

During the Indian Wars, they talked some chiefs into riding the iron horse back east to see the President. But when they got to Washington, those chiefs never saw anyone. They got ushered into some secretary's office where everybody bowed pretending the chiefs were visiting dignitaries. The secretary smiled, pretended to be the president, and talked to the Indians like he was talking to fellow heads of state. When the visit was over, all the men in the room bowed again to the Indians, thanked them for coming, and showed them out. That's all it took to settle those old chiefs down—choochoo cha-boogie, the little train that could, only it was the little train full of Indians that couldn't. Let the Indians ride across the vast sweep of this nation, let them look at the cities and towns along the way—St. Louis, Cincinnati—the factories and warehouses, the well made fences, the tree-lined boulevards of the District of Columbia, and everywhere more white people than they'd ever seen before or thought existed. Those chiefs figured out pretty quick that there was no point in resisting.

There was also saving the girl's soul. Teague knew that Indians had souls and we have to save those souls. Some people said the only way to save an Indian was to kill him. Or her. They didn't mean literally with a bullet. They meant kill the Indian inside to release the man. Or woman. There was a general who said all it would take to destroy the Indian would be to destroy the horse and the buffalo. In that case there might be Red Men still walking the earth but they wouldn't be Indians.

Teague pushed his mouth against the girl's. It's unclear if he considered this an act of affection or of branding. When he pulled back from her, he said, "I've decided we should get married." He watched as the girl lifted one hand and drew it across her mouth as if wiping off a fungal film. She closed her eyes and turned away.

This act of denial was more enraging than her former resistance. It was the moment Teague cracked. Sometimes you read in the paper about a person who has been locked in a closet for twenty years, the victim of some other person. Often sexual abuse is part of the picture and again and again we read that the abuser rose from a childhood of being abused. I can see it sometimes in another person's eyes, both the abused one and the abuser.

Right at the edge of victory Teague felt himself defeated. And by what—the girl's passivity? What does it mean to be passive? A woman turns her face away and whatever happens, it's not happening to her. Or it is but she has taken herself away to some other place and one day perhaps she will be able to return. It's like those early astronauts who looked down on the earth from their tiny capsules and felt awe in the face of such beauty, a beauty no human had seen before.

Only Yellow Bird Daughter looked down on a planet turned to ash. When she'd bitten and scratched Teague, or thrown canned tomatoes at him, he'd allowed himself to imagine that he had a relationship with her. They say women like to play hard to get. Maybe their relationship was a kind of dancing. Yes, they'd been dancing all along but now there was a void.

He wondered if he might put his hand right through her. He clenched and unclenched his fists for a moment then hit her hard in the center of her chest. He'd thought about this blow and, in being planned, it felt better than the other blows he'd given her, more gratifying. Anyway, his hand stung a little and so it was clear there was someone there inside the dress.

In 1946 the boxer Joe Louis was asked how he planned to deal with his opponent Billy Conn. This may seem off the subject but wait. Conn who had been the World Light Heavyweight champion was to fight Heavyweight champion Joe Louis for the title. Conn said he had no plans to gain weight. Instead he would pursue a hit and run strategy. Louis famously answered, "He can run but he can't hide." Through the first twelve rounds of the fight Conn was clearly ahead on points but in the thirteenth round he got ambitious and decided to go for a knockout rather than playing it cagey and winning on points. He didn't get the knockout though and with two seconds left in the round Louis knocked Conn out. After the fight, Conn said, "I lost my head and a million bucks." And when pressed as to why he made such a stupid move, he said, "What's the use of being Irish if you can't be thick."

You can see why I thought of this boxing match when I saw Teague there raping Yellow Bird Daughter. I felt rage along with a kind of weird, "what am I doing?" sensation. Two things touch this. One is that long ago a friend told me to pay attention to what bugs me—people I don't like, behaviors that seem wrong. My friend claimed that we are driven craziest by what we most bury in ourselves, by the parts of ourselves we pretend don't exist. By this logic, the madder I am about Teague's rape of Yellow Bird Daughter, the more I am burying a secret rapist within myself.

There's a scene in the Disney movie *Aladdin* where the genie is about to free Aladdin from the cave underground where he's been trapped. The genie calls to the Magic Carpet—"Yo, Rug Man"—who flies in and hovers a foot or so above the ground. Sit right up here and watch your step. Then the genie becomes a massively overweight United Airlines cabin attendant in a little 1960s cabin attendant hat and dress and says, "There are emergency exits here, here, here, and here" while waving multiple blue arms hither and yon. There's no emergency exit in life—there's Yellow Bird Daughter under Thomas Teague. There's Zelestina thousands of miles from home forever.

Another big moment comes when Aladdin finally gets it that the genie thing is true. "You can grant me any wish?" He asks. "Yes, yes, yes, and yes." Then in a mock Peter Lorre horror movie voice, the genie backtracks, saying, "I can't bring people back from the dead. Don't ask me to do it. It's not a pretty sight." So to some degree the granting of wishes apparently follows the physical laws of the universe. And no book will bring Zelestina back to life.

There is no getting around the next thirty minutes in the life of Yellow Bird Daughter. If there really was a God whose son Christ came body and blood into this world, that Christ might have taken a moment out of his infinite number of moments to help a young woman in distress. And if ever there was a story made of fictional elements, it's the Jesus one. Don't tell me you can put your face up to the window here and watch the rape and then go to church on Sunday and thank God for his infinite wisdom and compassion. I'm not blaming God, just saying he's got nothing much to do with this world. Busy counting up the Heavenly Host.

The thing about infinity is there is no time. So you don't have to worry about whether God can get around to all the things needing his attention. All he has to do is go from one chore to the next and over the course of infinity he can get to everything. But no, here's the girl again. How many women have violently raped men? You tell me. And why is God a man? All right, enough, I'm through for now.

Given Thomas Teague's omnipotence, what might Yellow Bird Daughter remember—the color and texture of the hair that covered his arms and legs? Or the scar that ran along his left thigh, the turn of his nose as he pressed his head into her shoulder blade, his right ear crumpled against her and the solidity of his hands and feet, the feel of his palms pressing into her, the feel of his sex tearing at her. Or maybe none of this stays with her, maybe she can throw it all away and go on as if nothing happened. A lot of us do that in a lot of circumstances but we know we're pretending.

You may be familiar with the Vulcan Federation Starship Commander Spock in the Star Trek movies. Vulcans are awfully like humans except that Vulcans are rational. They don't experience emotion. No feeling. But Spock is different—half Vulcan and half human he sorta kinda maybe can feel and it gets him in trouble. When he saw his entire planet destroyed and nearly every living thing dead, he experienced emotion that was unbearable and he never wants to feel that again so he's chosen not to feel. "How do you do that," his friend Federation Starship Captain James Kirk asks, "how do you decide not to feel?"

If you're interested in this, you can go see the movie but it's not really worth your time. It's a stupid spectacle made of special effects and explosions and when the emotions come into the story, they're second hand. Still, the question is real.

Why might a person decide not to feel? Then how to do it? That's what a woman who's been raped might have to do—decide not to feel. But of course the real non-feeling person was Teague since to commit the rape you must have no human feeling.

I have to insert another warning here as I'm again extrapolating from the most basic information—Zelestina never told me these details and I can't say if Yellow Bird Daughter told them to her. Maybe it's wrong of me to make this all up. Maybe it would be simpler and clearer to say that Teague raped the girl. *Eta kitto*—done. But I can't help imagining what it must have been like for her. She was completely on her own—parents dead, old way of life gone. And she'd been locked in a room alone for months.

I said that Teague had cracked and gone over some edge. It's clear he was never coming back. And for a time the girl gave up. She closed her eyes again and again traveled far away. The Oglala shaman Black Elk, who at thirteen was present at the Battle of the Little Big Horn and who later survived the Wounded Knee massacre, told the writer John Neihardt that the hoop of the nation was broken.

Even Mother Goose knows that once a hoop is broken, there's not much can be done. When Humpty Dumpty fell off the wall and broke, yolk and white oozing away, all the king's horses and all the king's men couldn't put Humpty Dumpty together again. I understand that he was an egg not a hoop but it's all the same.

Maybe Yellow Bird Daughter could have bitten the man's ear off. Maybe he would have killed her then. Anyway, she didn't bite his ear off. What about Teague's mother? He'd thought to defend her at one point in his life. You'd think he'd notice the contradictions and stop. Hell, I don't know shit about what goes on in the mind of the rapist though as I said at least one old friend would question my confidence on this subject.

I see I've told this story twice. Do you get it? Everybody

has a hard life with ups and downs but everybody doesn't get kidnapped, locked up, and held prisoner for months then raped. My mother used to say, "Thank your lucky stars for what you've got. A lot of people have it a lot worse." I know some of the bad that happened to my mother at the hands of my father. When Zelestina told me this story, she too had a be-thankful view, be thankful for the things that don't happen to you.

Finished, Teague got up and left the room. As he opened the door, he said, "I'll be back in the morning and we'll go down to the courthouse. You'll need to be cleaned up for the wedding. It doesn't matter which dress you wear. I'll give you a coat when we leave. There'll be nobody there but the justice of the peace, a witness, and the two of us. We'll get somebody who works in the clerk's office to be the witness."

As he'd promised, Teague returned in the morning. He wore a dark suit with an equally dark hat and tie. His hair was combed flat against his scalp and he'd trimmed his beard. He gave the appearance of a man on the way to attend the funeral of a moderately important civil servant. Yellow Bird Daughter was on the floor behind the bed. Naked.

"You can't go to the courthouse like that." Teague picked up one of the two dresses and tossed it toward her. "Put this on." She didn't move. He went to her, grabbed her by the neck and lifted her, muscling the dress on over her head. Then he led her out of the house. The cold sun struck her head like a hammer and she sank to the ground. "No," he said. But this time he didn't hit her with his fists. He removed his belt and, lifting her, struck her across the back of the legs. "I've got to go to work after the ceremony and we've got no more time to waste."

Yellow Bird Daughter, after the rush of air from her lungs, inhaled carefully. For a moment she felt as if all the dead children of Wounded Knee were inside her jostling to be reborn. She threw up but then she stood and walked next to Teague.

I'd say that for many people it is not possibility that determines the conduct of a life. We all know the *Sophie's Choice* story in which a Jewish mother and her two children are facing the Nazi death camp guard who tells her she must choose one child to live and one to die. If she refuses to choose, both children will die. She picks her son to live and her daughter to die.

I'm going to say fuck for the second time here. It's like some kind of game in Philosophy 101—the impossible choice. What would you do? We go along with our lives and one day it hits us that something as simple as a decision to buy or not buy a particular brand of canned goods may mean life or death for a person thousands of miles from us. But we buy the product anyway thinking it's not us causing the death. That's how it was in Vietnam for the B-52 bomber pilots. They dropped bombs from thousands of feet above the earth and never saw the faces of the people they killed.

I had two friends—a married couple. The husband was a B-52 pilot. The wife was an antiwar activist. The two muddled along until the husband was promoted to colonel. That was a big deal and involved a ceremony that wives attended. The newly promoted officers were called bird colonels because their insignia was an image of an eagle. Each wife pinned the metal eagle on her husband's uniform. Only in this case the wife was at a demonstration at the SAC base in Omaha, Nebraska. Who pins the eagle on a new bird colonel whose wife is protesting the war her husband is charged to fight? The marriage ended in divorce. And Sophie's life ended in suicide.

How does a person maintain human dignity when all such dignity has been taken away? That's the question I'm asking when I report that Yellow Bird Daughter did go to the courthouse with Thomas Teague. She walked beside him up the steps and into the building. She could have committed suicide. She could have kept resisting till Teague killed her.

As they stepped into the clerk's office Teague said, "You see that it was correct to dress formally. This is important and so formality is, too." He held the door for his bride.

"I'm sorry, Mr. Teague," the clerk said while looking at the girl. "Justice hasn't come in today."

"I'm a busy man," Teague told the clerk.

"Yes, sir, I can see that."

"When will he be in?"

The clerk turned and stepped into another room. When he returned, he said, "Justice won't be in today at all. He's got business in Fetterman City. You could come back tomorrow."

"The justice of the peace isn't in."

"That's right. He'll be gone all day."

"You're certain."

"Yes, sir."

Teague turned and walked toward the door, pulling Yellow Bird Daughter behind him. The clerk looked down and, as if studying an unusual document, said, "Strange." Annoyed that he'd been unable to register the marriage and suspecting that the word "strange" had been meant for him, Teague turned back to the man whose head was bent over a pile of papers. Then he rushed toward the door and flung it open. When he pushed Yellow Bird Daughter out of the building, she slid forward and stumbled on the stair step. As she began to fall, she felt a sudden and intense abdominal cramping. It pulled her over. To keep from falling, she spread her feet and put one hand down to brace herself on the earth. But there was no earth below, just another step. Where her hand should have hit ground, it hit air. When she realized what was happening, she straightened up, jerking herself backwards. Her left foot was still sliding forward. She twisted around and looked up the steps trying to find something to grab onto. Teague reached toward her but when she saw his hands, she let her arms fall to her sides. Teague leaned over and grabbed her shoulder. The two reeled on the steps like a pair of novice figure skaters, spinning sloppily until Teague lost his balance and they sailed out into space. An observer might have thought they were momentarily weightless, their arms and legs flapping around oblivious to the force of gravity. When their brief flight ended, Yellow Bird Daughter lay at the base of the stairs tangled up with Thomas Teague who was, as he'd dreamed, lying on top of her.

In Basque the word for a rape is *bortxaketa* and the verb to rape is *bortxatu*. I learned those words not in the dictionary but from Zelestina.

7

Goddamn You

There's a three-holed bone fipple flute that was found in a cave—the Laminazilo Kobazuloa of Izturitze in Nafarroa Beherea. Using Carbon 14 dating which is said to be accurate up to about 50,000 years, scientists tell us that this flute is 25,000 years old though the guidebooks at the cave gift shop say 31,000. The flute, made from the ulna of a vulture, looks very like the three-holed *txistu* flute played in the Basque Country today.

Picture a proto Basque or whatever they like to call such an ancient person sitting there in the Laminazilo Kobazuloa inside the Gaztelu hill playing the flute and then for whatever reason, leaving the cave, leaving the flute behind, and never returning.

Some people believe that in those long ago days human beings shared caves with tigers and that from time to time a tiger killed and ate a human being. The theory is that the humans were making a conscious trade—the cave protected them from weather and non-tiger marauding animals or fellow humans but now and again a life was lost to their tiger hosts.

How did a tiger choose which person to eat? Maybe the humans picked the victim—ritual sacrifice with the *txistu* players doing honor to the ones who gave up their lives. Maybe they put the *txistus* down and played best two out of three Rock-Paper-Scissors. Or maybe they drew straws—*txotx ala motx* in Basque.

Or an old person might have stepped forward—self-sacrifice for the good of the group. It's been known to happen.

Or someone who'd been injured. You're out hunting and you step in a prairie dog hole and break your ankle. You'd be a drain on the whole clan and maybe it'd be you who was eaten by the tiger.

They don't and didn't have prairie dogs in the Pyrenees. I'm just using the prairie dog hole as an example of a hole you could stumble into and hurt yourself. I could have said Alpine Marmot which is in the same family as prairie dogs. The Alpine Marmot disappeared in the Pyrenees in the late Pleistocene, say 13,000 years ago but that gives plenty of time when humans and marmots shared the same space. A person in the Pyrenees could step in a marmot hole as easily as a person in Wyoming could step in a prairie dog hole. After their late Pleistocene disappearance there were no Alpine Marmots in the Pyrenees until humans reintroduced the species in 1948. Now there are marmots. But no tigers.

The last possibility is that they ignored the tiger. It came padding up out of the darkness in the silence of the night. Everyone was asleep or, if not, then pretending. In the morning someone would be gone and the tiger would be resting in the back of the cave. The even grimmer last possibility was that one night the tigers couldn't resist the temptation of all those sleeping humans. Any tiger thoughts of the future flew out the mouth of the cave and everybody got eaten at once. *Txistu* lying on the floor.

The cave at Izturitze is nearly 400 feet long by 150 feet wide. In some places the ceiling is 50 feet high. For 10,000 years it appears to have been home not to tigers but to bears. When the bears left, the humans moved back in. The cave walls are covered with images of reindeer, goats, a horse with what appears to be a halter—so those early people rode horses and maybe played the flute while riding. Unless the bears did it.

There's a piece of stone shaped like a loaf of bread. One side shows a man kneeling or maybe crawling forward. You can only see his upper body. His right arm is extended and his hand is open. He's trying to grab the ass of a woman reclining on her stomach in front of him. Wearing only a necklace, bracelets, and anklets, the woman looks very strong. Also, she's covered with hair. There's an arrow in her thigh marking the man's conquest. The other side of the stone shows the same event but that the protagonists are bears. There's no arrow in the female bear's thigh but the male bear is, like his human brother, reaching for the female's ass.

It's strange feeling the past as present, the flute player in the dark cave. A *txistu* has an intense penetrating sound. Depending on the size and shape of the fipple, the sound may be heard a mile away. Even with the traffic roaring, I hear my neighbor playing from across the street. But so much has changed, too. The Atlantic Ocean, for example, is about eighteen miles from Izturitze but in the time of the cave dwelling flute players it was thirty miles away, sea level being a hundred yards lower then, so much water locked up in ice.

I keep wondering why the player didn't take the *txistu* with him when he left the cave. Even if he were running away, wouldn't he take his flute? If my house burned down, the first thing I'd grab would be the flute. I don't care what they tell you about leaving everything behind. Maybe it was a woman who played the flute. Would a woman be more inclined to leave the flute behind or take it with her?

The abandoned flute is mixed up with the confusion Zelestina felt during her first years in Wyoming. When I asked

Zelestina about her parents, she told me almost nothing. I had to make up nearly all of what I know about Arnegi and Zelestina's birth. I do know that she never saw her parents again after coming to Wyoming. Surely that would have been difficult especially since the Basques have lived for so long in one place. Only the aboriginal peoples of Australia have lived in the same place longer. Maybe the American Indians, too but that's a big debate. There's no debate on the Aboriginals or Basques. So a long time in one place and then suddenly in the past few hundred years, lots of Basques leaving their homeland.

Another big thing is religion. Zelestina's parents were not particularly observant Catholics. Potxo would make the same joke he always made—if the Lord's really a loving father, he would send a labor contractor not more babies.

In Wolf, Zelestina needed something to hold onto and she found herself attending Mass most mornings. The more confused she felt, the more often she attended. Sometimes she wondered if God had planned her transportation to Wyoming as a punishment, as if Wyoming were Hell and she had been damned. It was more likely that if there was Hell on Earth, it was in France or Spain. Wyoming would be, as it is in real life, Purgatory, a place passed through on the way to somewhere else.

Hell or purgatory, what sin could she have committed in her first sixteen years to warrant transportation to either one? Maybe no sin at all. In Dante's *The Divine Comedy*, the Roman poet Virgil is Dante's guide on his journey through the three realms of the dead—the Inferno, Purgatory, and Paradise. Both Dante and God agree that Virgil is a decent man of high ethical standing and wisdom. It is God who chose Virgil as Dante's guide. But Virgil will guide Dante only through Hell and Purgatory. In Heaven, Dante's girlfriend Beatrice will serve as guide.

Virgil can't step into Heaven. He has been condemned to Purgatory for being born before the invention of Christianity. The Mormons solve this problem of temporality in the spiritual realm by combing the genealogical records to find all their forbears. They then baptize these dead people as Latter Day Saints and voilà off to Heaven they fly—or in the case of Mormon men off to the celestial planet they will rule in the afterlife.

It's odd to think of the Basques as Christians. Odder yet to think it's not odd. There are Christians everywhere on earth. The medieval and Renaissance Christian armies and priests spread over the entire world telling people their heathen beliefs were in error and explaining that it is necessary to accept Jesus Christ or be doomed to the fiery pit for eternity. And that's the best you could expect. More often, the arrival of the Christians meant torture and death. If it had been the Nazis, we'd call it genocide. Not that I mean to bring the Nazis into the discussion but did you Google Gernika yet?

So, that Izturitze flute is somewhere between 25,000 and 31,000 years old while Christianity is slightly less than 2000 years old. The first Christians got to the Basque Country four hundred years after Christ's death but like most visitors to Euskal Herria over the millennia they didn't mean to stay. It wasn't until the sixth century that there were permanent resident Christians—hermit monks living in caves. I wonder if a brother ever found one of those vulture bone flutes, played it and, in the end, abandoned his Lord to go native.

Even before the hermit monks came, the Romans built the garrison town of Iruña that was to serve as a bishop's seat. That made Iruña the buttocks of a church father. The newcomers made no attempt to Romanize the Basques, being content to collect taxes and go on home leave. It's not clear if the Bishop ever saw the surrounding countryside.

The Romans were way easy going compared to their descendants—the French and Spanish. By the twelfth century, these remnants of the Roman Empire had set up shop in earnest and were going to town trying to convert the locals to the one true God. Which they did though it took some time—let's say another century or two before the terrain was completely pacified. That means Basques have been largely Christian for seven or eight hundred years out of the past 25,000.

Before Christ there was Mari. Mari had separate apartments in two mountains and every seven years she traveled from one mountain home to the other. Her travels made the weather. Her boyfriend, or consort as the comparative mythologists would have it, was named Sugar or Sugaar. *Su* means fire, *sugar* means flames. So the boyfriend was a passionate guy. But maybe there was a transcription error and Sugar's name came not from *su* but from *suge* which means snake. The Basques believe the Garden of Eden was in the Pyrenees. That would make Sugar the first temptress of Eve aka Mari. Mari never appears in Genesis. I believe she was deleted because God was ashamed about how much desire he felt for her. And I believe that God changed his and Mari's names to throw us off the track. There is somewhere in a distant galaxy God's first wife and children and they don't know he's gone for good.

It's a bit like the man who lived in suburban Bizkaia in a typical Basque apartment building—twelve floors with six apartments per floor. This guy had two wives. He lived with one during the week and the other on weekends. His weekend wife believed he had a five-day a week job that required being away from home while the weekday wife believed her husband had a weekend job. Simple. The man, committed above all else to his own comfort, decided it would be way easier for him if both wives lived in the same building. Neither had ever seen the other so it seemed pretty safe.

One Friday, the man knotted his tie, zipped up his rolling suitcase, kissed his wife goodbye, and left for the weekend, taking the elevator down two floors. There he opened the door, called out a cheery, "Honey I'm home" and walked in. His wife smiled and told him to take off his tie. She gave him a nice glass of wine, and said dinner would be ready in a minute. They ate, then got into their pajamas and were watching television when the wife sighed.

"What's the matter?"

"I just realized I forgot to take the garbage and recycling out this afternoon."

"The truck won't have been here yet. I'll just take it now."

"You're so sweet." And she gave him a congratulatory little peck on the cheek.

So the man got up, put on his slippers, picked up the kitchen trash can along with the bag of recycle plastic and glass, and padded off to the elevator.

Here comes the part that's like that radio show *This American Life* only it's *This Basque Life*. Coming back up the elevator the man passed his floor and without thinking stopped at his weekday apartment. When he got there and found the door locked, he realized he'd forgotten his key so rang the bell. The door opened and his wife looked at him like he was an alien just landed from another planet wearing a space suit that looked exactly like earthling pjs. Maybe the trashcan was some kind of advanced technology breathing device. The wife was speechless. It's important to emphasize that this really happened. Many things that seem beyond belief actually happen.

Long before the apartment mix-up, Sugar and Mari had invented ethics. More important was their role as co-equal creator and destroyer of the world. Once it was set in motion, Mari and Sugar were able to relax and watch things unfold. Or unwind. They had enough down time to be able to meet every Friday night in the high mountain caves of the Pyrenees. These meetings were felt in the valleys as volcanic tremors and blustery rainstorms. Sugar and Mari were a happy couple.

These Basque gods dismayed the newly arrived Christians who, with their pens and swords, claimed there never
was a Mari, that she was actually a Navarrese princess in a low
cut dress who had married a Catholic priest. It was another
link in a long chain of condemnation of uppity women.

And it was nothing new—the Greek writer Strabo, who
traveled around the Mediterranean during Christ's lifetime,
wrote in his seventeen volume *Geographica* that the Basques
practiced "a sort of woman-rule." Strabo considered such
woman-rule to be inconsistent with civilization. He noted
that Basque women could inherit and control property and
that they could officiate in the churches. I don't know what
churches he meant. Maybe some runaway Christian subgroup
had fled the empire then started a congregation in a mountain village. If so, they were apparently influenced enough by
Basque beliefs to let women handle the body and the blood
and so officiate at the Eucharist.

Sixteen hundred years after Strabo's death the Spanish
Inquisition began another in a long series of witch hunts in
Nafarroa and Hegoalde. Armed with letters of Grace which
would pardon all those who admitted to witchcraft and named
their fellow witches, junior inquisitor Alonso Salazar Frías
spent 1611 traveling around the region near Zugarramur-
di where the witches met. One meeting place was a stream
called Infernuko Erreka—Hell's Creek. Duh. Of course the
witches met there. And what about that word *infernuko*? Sure
looks like Latin to me and since we know that Basque pre-
dates Latin by thousands of years the Infernu—Hell—has to be
a loan word in Basque. Mari might scare the living daylights
out of people but she'd never send anyone to hell.

Frías gathered 2,000 confessions, around 1,400 from
children between the ages of seven and fourteen. These
2,000 witches implicated 5,000 others. A number that large
must have been worrisome to at least some in the church
though we all know how much an empire needs an enemy so

maybe the more witches the better. The Inquisition opened up branch offices in a number of Basque towns including Irun and Hendaia.

If you're ever in Hendaia, you should visit a little restaurant bar coffeehouse called Ipar Haizea—North Wind—run by a hard working barista, waitress, and cook named Vikki. Vikki is one of the kindest people on earth and the food she makes is great. She offers two dishes each day based on what's at the market and on the docks from the daily catch. After eating, you can hang out for coffee and desserts that Vikki also makes. Ipar Haizea—it's about thirty minutes' walk from the last stop on the Euskotren—the *topo*—in Irun where the Inquisition went devil hunting.

In both Irun and Hendaia the Devil appeared in his favorite seventeenth-century form—lanky handsome he-goat with polished shoes hiding cloven hooves. The interesting thing is that the Devil summoned his followers in Basque and discoursed to them in that language. That of course is impossible.

Zelestina explained to me that the reason Basques were such good Christians was because their language was too difficult for the Devil to learn. Long before the Christians, Deabrua arrived to convert the Basque people but after seven years he could only say *bai* and *ez*—yes and no—and left in disgust for France and Spain where the languages were easier to learn and the people more easily tempted. *Deabru*—devil—is, like *Infernu*, a loan word from Latin.

"The devil came before the Christians?" I asked her.

"Of course. The Devil is why Christianity was invented."

"Invented?"

"What's your question?"

Recognizing my blank look, Zelestina waved her arm in the manner of a teenage girl on a television sitcom and said, "Whatever." She loved to do this.

So one day Zelestina was coming out of Our Lady of the Bighorns Church after morning Mass and she decided to walk a bit, to clear her head and think. She was restless and uneasy—*mal dans sa peau*, as the French say. She went around the block twice then stepped back into the church and sat for fifteen minutes in the stillness to stop the merry-go-round of the material world. The church reminds us there is something beyond this moment, something we feel but cannot name or explain—the mystery of being. That's what's beautiful in the church and that's why even I, who just spent several paragraphs blasting the Christian imperialists, love the church.

Zelestina left Our Lady of the Bighorns for the second time and walked toward the Christiansen's. If the answer wasn't in the church, the other place to look was in work. As she passed the county courthouse, she heard the door bang at the top of the stairs. The courthouse sat on a rise above the street so that elected officials could look out the windows and survey their kingdom stretched below. A man and a woman stood on the top steps; then the woman appeared to leap into space where she hovered for a few moments before falling back to the steps where she leaned precariously backwards. The man too had leapt into space and when he touched down again on the step above the woman, he reached out for her but somehow the two didn't make contact and they tumbled down the steps, arms and legs tangled up like overdone spaghetti noodles. They landed not twenty-five feet from where Zelestina stood, mouth open, staring. Wham, the man and woman like one four-armed four-legged alien creature.

"Mother of God," Zelestina said and ran toward them. Both were silent and motionless. Zelestina tried as gently as possible to separate the two. When she'd done this, she pressed her ear to the woman's chest. She could both hear and feel the heartbeat but before she had time to register relief, the man groaned. One of his arms was bent at a funny angle and his pant leg was torn revealing a gash below his right knee. Blood stained his trousers and the wooden sidewalk. He groaned again then spoke but his voice was a scraping whisper Zelestina couldn't make out. She turned her head to press her ear close to his mouth. When the man spoke a second time, Zelestina lifted her head and said, "I can't understand you."

He twisted his mouth as if he were chewing on a piece of gristle and, struggling to lift his head, said, "Goddam you."

When they hauled the two bodies off to the doctor's, Zelestina went along, hoping she might somehow help. How, she didn't know. She'd never seen Thomas Teague or Yellow Bird Daughter before. Still, she followed the doctor and offered to serve as a nurse's assistant.

Though Teague's injuries weren't life threatening, he'd been pretty banged up—a broken arm, multiple bruises and contusions, a long gash on his left thigh that required seventeen stitches, and a knot on his head the size of a lemon. Just to be safe, the doctor asked Teague to stay at the clinic to make sure there would be no infection around the stitches.

"I'll just leave you with the paper," the doctor said. "It's the Denver one—something to fill the time a little. I know it'll be dull lying here doing nothing but you'll be more comfortable and if you stay here I can make sure everything is going to heal well. Not that you'll really be comfortable."

"Fine," Teague said.

The doctor cleared his throat. "The young woman who also fell down the stairs. Forgive me for saying this, but it is your good fortune that you landed to some degree on top of her as she cushioned your fall. She, on the other hand, was not so lucky. She has a broken ankle, broken arm, three broken ribs, and a knot on her head larger than the one you have. More importantly, she has not regained consciousness. I'm reluctant to say she is in a coma but we will see. Can you give me her name?"

When Teague didn't answer, the doctor changed subjects. "There is another woman—a local Basque named Zelestina Urza. She insisted on coming along. She's sitting with the injured woman now. Miss Urza says she doesn't know the young woman." Teague remained quiet. The doctor watched him for a moment then said, "Well, I'm sure you feel very tired. Perhaps you'll remember later. I'll check in on you from time to time."

When the doctor finally left, Teague looked around the room and saw the paper folded open to the police pages. A headline read, FIREPLACE POKER AND PISTOL USED IN KILLING. The story noted that Mrs. Rodric Alton, after a marriage of many years during which her husband had repeatedly lifted his hand against her, departed her home. With two other women she rented an efficiency suite at the Excelsior Hotel. After some weeks, Mr. Alton went to the hotel in the early hours of the morning. He knocked on the door, awakening the three women. His wife opened the door and after a short discussion, let her estranged husband in whereupon he demanded that she return home with him. When she refused, he drew a revolver and threatened to shoot her.

While Mr. Alton was occupied with threatening his wife, one of the other women picked up a fireplace poker and struck the man on the head. He dropped the gun and Mrs. Alton picked it up. She told her husband to get out and leave her in peace. When he ignored her request and stepped toward her, she fired twice. The first bullet passed through Mr. Alton's heart, the second through his head. He died immediately. The widow is in custody pending the results of an investigation.

Served him right being such a fool, Teague thought. Anyway, it's Denver and cities are full of craziness. His leg throbbed and his arm felt swollen tight against the cast. Below the story of the Altons was a brief article on the experience of a Mrs. John Peckham who had left her husband and was living temporarily in the home of a lady friend. Mr. Peckham went to the lady friend's residence and demanded that his wife return home. When Mrs. Peckham refused, her husband displayed a small caliber pistol with which he shot his wife once in the right shoulder. She fell back stunned.

Attempting to intercede on Mrs. Peckham's behalf, the lady friend reached her hand out toward Mr. Peckham and he shot again, this bullet passing through the good lady's wrist. She fainted and fell into Mr. Peckham's arms. Mrs. Peckham, holding her shoulder, was leaving the room. Mr. Peckham set the wounded lady down and told his wife once again to return home. When she kept walking, he fired a third bullet which passed through his wife's bicep and caused her to fall to the floor. Seeing her lying motionless, Mr. Peckham gasped, turned the pistol on himself, and fired for the fourth and last time. The bullet entered his brain and he died immediately. Mrs. Peckham and her wounded lady friend were reported in good condition after the removal of the bullets.

Teague threw the paper across the bed. One heard about such stories now and again and so what. There was that case of a Mrs. Potter or Palmer who'd cut her husband's throat with his own razor. That was down in Casper. And in Cheyenne there'd been that accident with John Stanton who was president of Wyoming Beef Ranchers. Stanton was chasing his wife off the porch of their house when he stumbled, hit his head on the corner of a step, and died.

Teague sat up but felt woozy and lay back down. He took some of the pain reliever the doctor had left him and fell asleep. The next morning he woke early, put on the clothes he'd worn to the courthouse, and walked out of the doctor's offices.

Three days after Teague disappeared, Yellow Bird Daughter woke. She hurt everywhere. When she opened her eyes, the light came in like knife blades. She saw Zelestina only as a dark figure sitting by her bed. "Where am I?"

"The doctor's office. You fell. Do you remember?"

"I was standing on a prairie. There was a mountain lion. It

was the same dusty tan color as the grasses so it must have been late fall. I was walking toward the mountain lion and I don't know why because the animal smell was so strong I thought I would vomit. Still, I kept walking closer. It had scars on its face and along its flanks—scars from the teeth and claws of other animals. I stopped and the mountain lion flicked its tail then leapt forward running full speed toward me. That's what I thought but when it reached me it kept running. I turned and there was Thomas Teague—that's the man who fell.

"He's gone."

"Gone?"

"Yes, he was here at the doctor's but he disappeared."

"He was in my dream. He stood alone in the field but now the grasses were tall and green as in summer before the white man buffalo were brought here. Where Teague stood the grass had been cut or animals had eaten it. There were no clouds in the sky and it kept getting hotter. I could feel sweat dripping down my face. I saw that Teague was swatting at the grass, tearing it up by the roots, making it easier for the mountain lion to see him. And the animal was running faster and the smell was getting stronger.

"Finally noticing it, Teague dropped a handful of grass and stood. He turned and started to run but after a step or two he stumbled and fell. He got back up and limped forward into the grass, which melted away to reveal a great cliff. He was at the edge with nowhere to go. Heat waves rose shimmering in the air. He would have to jump like a buffalo driven to a cliff by hunters or else he would have to turn and face the mountain lion."

"What happened?"

Yellow Bird Daughter blinked. "Neither of those two things. He turned away from the cliff and the mountain lion and toward me as if I'd been the one chasing him. He said, 'Goddamn you,' and I woke up."

Part Two

8

Disappeared

In grade school, I loved maps. Maps assured me that there was a world beyond the one where I lived—a possible escape from the life I was living. The countries were laid out in bright blats of color—pink and green and fire engine red and the oceans were blue and the borders were smooth black lines and no one ever mentioned the fact that there were men like my father at the borders, only those men carried machine guns instead of belts. At age nine I was an idealist.

I wanted to go anywhere away from where I was. I'm not suggesting such was the case for Zelestina. I know how poor the Basque Country was in the late nineteenth and early twentieth century so while Zelestina may have been an adventurer she was also a refugee. Her case is a mass of contradictions—excited to go, desolated to leave. She came from a happy home, her father being the cheery goofball of Arnegi and her mother the type who was always telling her husband to behave while smiling and kissing him.

About half the countries on earth didn't exist when I was born and half of the ones that existed then don't anymore.

Then there are places like Euskal Herria—the Basque Country—places that have been countries for thousands of years but are not recognized as such and can't be found on maps.

Once after I'd escaped from home I was in Euskal Herria only I didn't know it. It was before I'd come to Wolf, before I'd met Zelestina and heard her stories. I imagined I was in Spain. It was long before Franco's death and there were soldiers with machine guns everywhere. I was bicycle touring in southern Nafarroa—long stretches of plains, hot and dry with almost no towns. I came upon a tiny village and rolled along the dusty main street. There were no signs on anything so there was no way to tell what might be a hotel, a grocery, a hardware store, a radio and TV repair shop. The buildings were the same color as the dirt of the streets.

There was an open doorway with a black curtain hanging across it. People were talking inside and though their voices were so low I couldn't understand them, I felt confident that I could ask them where to find a grocery. I spoke Spanish after all. I got off the bike, leaned it against the wall, and stepped toward the door. But when I got closer and could hear the voices more clearly, I still couldn't understand a word. I was sure I was in Spain. Unless the curtain was the entry into a *Twilight Zone* episode.

As a kid I loved it when Rod Serling came on and told us that we are surrounded by strange things, things we can't explain or understand. I knew this meant that there were other worlds even if in the case of *The Twilight Zone* they were mostly unpleasant ones. I preferred *The Twilight Zone* to *Outer Limits* though I loved the latter's opening with the music going doo-doo doo-doo, doo-doo doo-doo and then the voice that said, "There is nothing wrong with your television set. Do not attempt to adjust the picture. We are controlling transmission."

I put my hand out toward the curtain but didn't pull it aside. Instead I stood and listened for a moment. They may as well have been speaking Martian. When I finally pulled the curtain aside, there was an old woman wearing a floor length black bag of a dress and, next to her, two middle aged men, both with skin the texture of lizards. The three looked at me and immediately began speaking Spanish. It turned out this was a grocery and I was able to buy a half-kilo bag of rice, an onion, and a tiny paper container of drinkable yogurt—no refrigeration necessary. When I stepped back onto the empty street, the three immediately switched back to speaking Martian.

Maps promise there is somewhere else and in that somewhere else people lead other lives. On the map, everything is still and calm. The map is never on fire. The people are content, have enough to eat, and do not fear their families or their neighbors. I should have been a mapmaker myself. I could have made a map of happiness or at least a map toward happiness.

There's a novel by the English writer Russell Hoban called *The Lion of Boaz-Jachin and Jachin-Boaz*. They are father and son. Jachin-Boaz was a trader in maps. He bought and sold maps to anywhere. If the map hadn't been made, he made it himself and traded that. Jachin-Boaz could sell a young man a map to where a young girl would be at a certain time of day. He sold husband maps to wives and wife maps to husbands. Poets could buy maps showing where to find acuity and clarity. Thieves could buy money and jewel maps and the police could buy maps to find thieves. Holy men could buy miracle maps and the pope could buy scandal containment maps. Pirates could buy any number of treasure maps and junk dealers could buy maps to foreclosure auctions though Hoban does not mention that map. Actually, he doesn't mention the pope map or the pirate map, either. You can find the list of maps on page ten of Hoban's novel but you will have to find a map to the novel because it's out of print. Used book dealers of course have all sorts of maps.

The maps remind me of another novel I love. By Diana Darling, it's called *The Painted Alphabet*. It's set in Bali but it's a Bali you won't find on the maps in geography books, a Bali where Hanuman the monkey king is still bringing a mountain of herbs down from the Himalayas to save the lives of Rama and Lakshmana. He's carrying these herbs in a battered rolling suitcase and he's riding a diesel bus chugging its way up and down the narrow passes. Across the aisle is a man reading the *Delhi Times* with the headline BUS PLUNGES INTO GORGE—FIFTY DEAD. Hanuman gets off and hitchhikes across the subcontinent and somehow in the end he's racing across Indonesia on a Honda 125 motorcycle with no fenders and the suitcase is strapped onto a wooden rack with rope made of jute. I don't even know what jute is.

Long ago in another lifetime I had the good fortune to meet a very famous literary editor who worked at a publishing house where I hoped someday a book I had written might be published. I know I've explained that I'm writing a book but I feel a compulsion to emphasize this. When I told the famous editor that I loved Diana Darling's *The Painted Alphabet*, she said, "You and twenty-six other people."

"Don't you mean me and twenty-five other people—twenty-six letters in the alphabet and all?"

"You know what I mean."

She was drinking a gin and tonic from a plastic glass. I felt bad but now I don't care. Neither about whether she liked the book nor about how sad it is that we go to these writers' conferences where people jockey for position while having to drink gin and tonics from plastic glasses.

Darling's story begins, "Once upon a time, deep in the heart of Bali...when life was still quiet and all things were in some way holy..." and I realize that is how this book should have begun. But it is never too late to change and this is the beginning of part two of Zelestina's story so once upon a time a man named Thomas Teague disappeared. It was as though

time had run backwards and sucked Teague into the place before being.

When Yellow Bird Daughter and Zelestina moved into
what had been Teague's house, the first thing was to haul everything outside and separate it into two piles—one to burn
and one to bury. They dug a hole first, pushed the to-bury
things in and covered them with dirt. Then they put the to-
burn things on that pile of dirt and lit the mound. When the
oily smoke had cleared, they stood near the charred ground
and watched, a little fearful that somehow Teague's still buried property would come surging to the surface. They planted
rye and they crossed their fingers.

Nature is both hardy and resilient and I hope we too
can be hardy and resilient. On the news they reported that
for forty years a group of scientists has been studying plastic
garbage on the ocean floor in the north Atlantic. The scientists want to learn where the plastic comes from, how much
there is, what effect it has on ocean life. One scientist noticed
that in the past several years though the total production of
plastic has gone up such that one would assume the quantity of plastic on the ocean floor would go up correspondingly,
that hasn't happened. Then the scientist noticed tiny beads
of something floating on the ocean's surface. He scooped
some of these up, put them under a microscope and found
they were plastic. More interestingly, they were plastic that
showed signs of being eaten and when looked at even closer
he saw the beads were covered with living microbes.

The point is that there are now tiny creatures on the
north Atlantic floor that eat plastic. Petroleum derived plastic has become biodegradable. Everyone felt good thinking
how nature had evolved to solve our plastic waste problem.
It was especially exciting because scientists had thought the
north Atlantic floor's water was too cold to allow for this kind
of metabolic activity. Then it occurred to some scientist that
if they can eat plastic, what else might they eat? And if they

can evolve that fast, what else might they evolve to do, or what other organism might evolve into something that eats us or more reasonably gives us an illness for which we have no immunity.

There are a lot of depraved men in the world and Teague was by no means the worst though what it actually means to talk about degrees of depravity I don't know. How can I compare Teague to say Papa Doc and Baby Doc Duvalier? How can I compare them to each other? Ask a Haitian. How about those generals in Argentina kidnapping people, torturing and drugging them then flying them up over the ocean in helicopters and pushing them out?

Disappear is *desaparecer* in Spanish. And from that we get the word *desaparecido*—a noun meaning a person who has been disappeared and the brand new transitive use of the verb *desaparecer*—they disappeared her. Now Los Desaparecidos exist in all the languages of the world.

Perhaps you have heard the music of the Chilean guitarist and singer Victor Jara. In his song "El Lazo," Jara speaks of a person's hands—old but strong. When the generals made their coup in Chile and overthrew the government they rounded up 5000 of their enemies and marched them into the Estadio Chile in Santiago, Victor Jara among them. The generals knew the famous folksinger for freedom and to remind everyone who now ran Chile they broke all the fingers in Jara's hands. The soldiers laughed and asked Jara what he might play for them now. An officer put one bullet in his pistol, spun the cylinder, put the gun to Jara's head, and pulled the trigger. No bullet. The officer played this game several times until there was a bullet and Victor fell. The officer ordered conscript soldiers to finish the job and Jara was machine gunned to death.

In the few moments before his death, Victor Jara wrote a poem that another prisoner hid in his shoe. The untitled poem survived and is known now as "Estadio Chile." The

American poet Jorie Graham said that, "For every lie we're told by advertisers and politicians, we need one poem to balance it." And I'd say that for every murder committed by those who would silence Victor Jara, we need 10,000 poems, tumbling as the drops of water in a river do over a waterfall and into a deep pool below. We should all swim naked in that pool. Maybe I'm kidding myself about wanting justice. Maybe I just want us all to get naked and go swimming.

Once upon a time there was a fire, a huge fire whose flames rose from earth all the way to heaven. And when God smelled the stink from what was burning he turned away, afraid to look down and see just what was going on in his creation. But Yellow Bird Daughter and Zelestina didn't turn away. They kept shoveling the material evidence of Teague's life into the flames and when the sun went down and the air cooled they warmed their hands on the man's disappearance.

9

The Basque Picnic

"August fifteenth soon," Zelestina said to me. It was blistering as it often is in early August. The fifteenth though is the day when summer collides with fall. That means a hailstorm. The overheated sky spits out balls of ice that destroy the second planting of lettuce and spinach, the peppers, basil, and parsley. The wind blows hard enough to knock the six-foot tall corn stalks down. Now and again there's a heavy wet snow and the trees, still thick with leaves, bend to the earth. On the other hand, it may just stay hot.

"It's the Assumption," Zelestina went on. "Do you know what the Assumption celebrates?"

"Yes, sure."

"You do?"

"Yes, I said I did." Maybe the heat was making me cranky.

"What does it celebrate then?"

"The observed fact of Mary being taken up to Heaven in both body and soul. A surprising event and as far as we know the only one of its kind."

When she looked at me suspiciously as if I might be

making fun, I said, "My father was a Belgian Catholic and my mother a Norwegian Lutheran. One grandmother was a Sephardic Jew who married into the Belgian family—try explaining that at Seder or Mass—and the other was Sami. She never believed any of what she called the God and Jesus cults. She said that weather and trees and snow and migrating reindeer were spiritual forces worthy of veneration. To me, the differences between religions don't seem all that big and the religions themselves feel like party gags. I'm not making fun of Catholic beliefs, just saying it's not necessary to be so attached to any idea."

Zelestina shook her head and said, "Fine. Go ahead and explain it to me the way you see it."

"In one version of Mary's story, she dies and is buried in a tomb. Three days later, Saint Thomas opens the tomb. Why, I don't know. In those days the saint was just plain Thomas or Tom or Tomasito. But it's hard to back up to the days before canonization. So what does Saint Thomas find in the tomb? Mary's clothes but no Mary. The story actually says he found Mary's 'girdle' and while I know that the language has changed and that girdle in those days meant an encircling sash or garment—I looked it up—I can't help but think of it in the more modern sense, the way my mother would have used it to mean the one-piece elastic body armor that held in her stomach and hips to make her appear slimmer and, as a result, more attractive. But my mother was a good looking woman whatever way you looked at her and I've always imagined Mary was good looking, too."

"Ok, I see what you mean," Zelestina said. By now she'd begun to smile. Not that she agreed with me but that she liked this way of looking at life as if who knows what might happen or be true.

I have a young neighbor who would like to have children—not with me—but she's worried that pregnancy and nursing will ruin her body, which I admit is rather beautiful.

I tell her to get pregnant the way Mary did and she'll have no worries on that front. "Wait," I say, "I'm mixed up, it's not having sex that makes your body go to pieces, it's the nursing—gravity's deleterious effect on milk engorged breasts. But your breasts are small so gravity won't have such a big effect." My neighbor was raised a Baptist but she just laughs and tells me I'm terrible.

I went on explaining the Assumption to Zelestina, saying, "In another version of the story, Saint Thomas opens the tomb and finds neither Mary nor her girdle. He hears someone calling and when he steps out of the tomb, he looks up and there's Mary in the sky dropping her clothes down to show she has been taken up in body as well as soul. That means she's hanging naked above Saint Thomas who, if he notices the size of her breasts, doesn't let on. I find that one of the marks of a saint is to hold your cards close to the chest."

Zelestina said only, "Go on. I'm listening."

"Ok, we don't really know what Thomas felt. We do know that people started celebrating the Assumption pretty soon after Mary's death but it wasn't until 1950 that Pope Pius XII declared that the Assumption was in fact a fact. He made this declaration in his state of papal infallibility. Now there is a surprising idea—a man is a man—sort of—and then a bunch of other men vote and say he's the pope and the moment he's named pope he becomes infallible. Named infallible by the fallible, he can't make a mistake."

"That is a little odd," Zelestina said. "But then a woman can't be a priest in the Church."

"You think the two are related?"

"Well, since you have to be a cardinal to be elected pope, it means a woman can never be the pope so a woman can never be infallible."

"Except Mary."

"She was without sin not infallible."

"You mean a person can make a mistake that isn't a sin."

"A thousand times a day."

"My dad once told me that any Catholic male can be elected pope. You don't have to be a cardinal. Then my dad laughed and said, 'fat chance. The last pope who wasn't a cardinal before being elected was Urban VI. He was elected in 1379.' I was amazed my dad knew that and always suspected it wasn't true."

"You could go to the library and look it up."

"Okay. But here's another strange fact about infallibility—I learned this one from my dad too so maybe it's also untrue. Papal infallibility wasn't made official until the First Vatican Council of 1869–70."

Zelestina put her hand to her cheek and said, "That means the popes could make mistakes until sixteen years before I was born."

"Yes sirree, those early popes could make all the mistakes they wanted but nowadays that's impossible—they can rob a bank and now it's the right thing to do and the only difference is when they were born."

"I don't know who the pope was when I was born."

"And what if infallibility was announced while a pope was already in office. Most days the man wakes up capable of being wrong and then one day he wakes up and he can never be wrong again."

She screwed up her face and said, "What about Mary?"

"Some people think Mary was taken up while still alive which blows the tomb story to pieces whatever version we believe. And in the Eastern Orthodox Church Mary was taken up while sleeping."

"Are you sure about that?"

"Yes, I know that one is true."

"It's awfully hot today," Zelestina said and we both looked up at the sky.

The August fifteenth that Zelestina told me about was many years before I met her. It was before I was born. On that long ago day, it seemed that the Heavens would be in accord with the plans of the Basque people of Wolf—it looked as if the weather would be perfect for the sheepherders' mountain picnic celebrating the feast of the Assumption.

The Assumption is a Holy Day of Obligation—you have to participate in the Mass and abstain from words or actions that hinder the worship one should render to God or that hinder the joy that is proper to the Lord's day, or the relaxation of the mind and body. Hence a picnic.

Zelestina and Yellow Bird Daughter headed up the mountain along with nearly every other Basque in Wolf. From the 8000 feet high meadow where the picnic was to be held, the Basque dancers stood a chance of reaching Heaven not too long after Mary.

Trying to explain the holiday to Yellow Bird Daughter, Zelestina said, "It is very important, this day, because it is when the Mother of God was taken to Heaven."

"Yes, I know—the missionary at Lame Deer told us that the soul of each person lives forever in Heaven or Hell. But only the soul—the body rots to nothing. Except Mary's. But I don't think this is right. Why do we have bodies if they are to be thrown away?"

"Well, we all die. I mean our bodies die. We don't."

Yellow Bird Daughter said nothing and Zelestina went on, "I have wondered though. When the body is gone there must be some other part of us that is gone, too. Otherwise we'd be only spirit and if we were only spirit why would we be given a body at all?"

I had heard Zelestina talk this way and knew that this was the point when she always stopped, the point when she had no answer for her own question. I loved that about her—that she would ask questions for which she had no answer. I always thought the answer was that God is a sadistic bastard who delights in torturing his creation. I never said this to Zelestina, though now I'm sure I could have.

"That's not what the missionary told us," Yellow Bird Daughter said. "He said it's because of sin. Sin is the action of the body, the first sin and every sin that has followed—we are all living in sin and must be redeemed. But Mary was born in grace with no sin and committed no sin in life so her body can go to Heaven with her spirit."

"You remember all this?"

"I listened closely when the missionaries talked. I wondered if maybe they were right, if maybe their God was better than ours. The blue-coated Christian soldiers had killed many of us and put others on reservations. Maybe they were right and we were wrong."

I don't know if this was the beginning of doubt for Zelestina but I know that she reported this conversation to me and that for her the experience of the Northern Plains Indian woman who was now her friend was as unusual as the experience of a Martian would be for me.

"Maybe it's better not to pay attention," Zelestina said.

The Mass was scheduled for 3:00 PM but when 2:00 came and went and Father Stephen Jameson, bishop of the Wyoming Diocese had not appeared, some began to worry. It was a three hundred mile trip from Cheyenne to Wolf, then seven miles up the dirt road to the turn and five more rough miles to the meadow. Father Jameson had left Cheyenne the day before, taking the train from the Union Pacific depot on the south side of the state capitol to Casper and from there, traveling by automobile to Wolf and up the mountain.

The bishop might have broken down on route. Or perhaps he'd arrived in Wolf and started up the mountain and the car's radiator had boiled over, or a tire had been punctured by a piece of sharp willow. While an automobile could easily negotiate the dirt road, the way from the turn was passable only with great caution and under the direction of an experienced driver. Sometimes it's better to walk.

Wolf's own priest, Father Homer Aristides and three other men, including Father Martin Amezagoira, the priest who had come from Iparralde seven years ago as the Vatican's envoy to the Basque people of the American West, went back down the mountain in search of Bishop Jameson. They found him a few miles away, walking, and though he was of good cheer, tired. The car had stalled and he couldn't start it again. When the entire party arrived back at the meadow at 3:30, clouds already filled the sky and there was a gusty wind from the southeast.

Bishop Jameson walked across the meadow with one arm raised in beatific greeting. He was late. His black shoes were covered with a film of red dust, as were his pants and jacket. When he walked, tiny clouds of dust rose from the cuffs of his pant legs. His face looked a little drawn and his thin graying hair had been blown around so that it stuck out in several places while at the same time it fell haphazardly over the bishop's large bald spot.

Though his journey had been difficult, he smiled a broad smile that revealed large crooked teeth yellowed by nicotine. When he raised his hand in greeting he was Saint Stephen, patron saint of dangling cigarettes, displaying the yellowed fingers of his outstretched hand. Still, he was smiling and people standing nearby couldn't help smiling with him. His human foibles made him seem to the Basques not ridiculous and, consequently, less priestly but vulnerable, ordinarily human as Mary was. It is the human Mary, after all, rather than the God Jesus whom the Basque people love.

The bishop smiled again and shouted, "*Egun On!* How is everyone? I can speak Basque a little." Then he walked around the meadow, shaking hands and saying, "*Egun on!*" a hundred times. He stood before Zelestina and Yellow Bird Daughter. "Yes, hello, how are you? *Egun on!*" He boomed. His smile became even more infectious. Yellow Bird Daughter covered her mouth to hide her own smile. When the priest left, she turned to Zelestina and laughed out loud, "He spoke Basque to me."

"He doesn't know you. He thinks you're Basque."

"But I am not," Yellow Bird Daughter said, serious again.

"For all the bishop knows, anybody might be Basque. And you heard him, how proud he is to say 'good day.' 'I know some Basque,' he says, 'a little. *Egun on*' to you and '*egun on*' to me and '*egun on*' to everyone." Zelestina pointed to the people around them and said, "to you and you and you."

This was way before the musical *The Sound of Music* had been written but there they were in the high mountain mead- ow with the bishop nearly singing "to you and you and you…" and in only a few moments we will all be free.

As Bishop Jameson crossed the meadow, the wind blew harder. In the dust and grit, his eyes began to water and he blinked and rubbed the tears away with the edge of his sleeve.

"Here we are, Father." The voice of Father Aristides boomed across the meadow as he motioned to the temporary altar that had been set up under a large canvas tent. In front of the altar, hay bales had been laid out in long curving rows. These would serve as pews. Worshipping, the parishioners would kneel directly on the dusty ground, on the grasses that were burnt to a late summer brown.

As the three holy men walked in and out among the bales of hay, Father Amezagoira casually pulled a comb from his pocket and discretely handed it to the bishop. He smiled and lifted his eyebrows first in the direction of the altar then in the direction of the bishop's unruly hair. The tent, designed to protect two hundred people from the effects of sun or rain, was packed with over three hundred Basques.

"Yes, welcome, everyone. *Ongi etorri*." Father Aristides was known for the rich tone and great volume of his voice. "Come along. *Eser zaitezte*. Bishop Jameson has arrived so we can begin." Because many of Father Aristides' flock spoke little or no English, there was a lot of translating of his call to Mass. Father Aristides waved his arms broadly and kept looking at the roof of the tent rising and falling in the wind. It was as if the huge sheet of canvas were being sucked up into space then released to come crashing down with a mighty whoomph. The tent poles had been hammered into the rocky soil of the meadow and tied down with guy ropes. Now they were being whipped about like reeds. Each time the tent roof was sucked upward, the poles vibrated and threatened to pull out of the ground. The aspen trees that surrounded the meadow were waving furiously, their leaves fluttering on their stems.

Father Jameson took the *makulu*—the crozier—that had been presented to him by the Basques of Wolf. In the wind, the strips of red, white, and green cloth that decorated this shepherd's staff slapped the bishop in the face and he kept turning away as if someone had called his name.

"*Egun on*," he said one last time then began. Midway through the Mass, he spoke personally to the worshipers, "We are grateful to celebrate this Holy Mass in such a beautiful location here in the Bighorn Mountains. It means so much to honor God and the Blessed Virgin in this spot. These beautiful mountains are a reflection of the grandeur of God's creation. And it is so impressive to stand before such a large assembly seated, as you are, humbly, on rough bales of hay. I'm reminded of the great importance of the Basque people to our church. Remember all the saints and fathers of the church who were Basque—Ignatius Loyola, Ferminus, Martin of the Ascension, and Francis Xavier. They were all Basque."

Bishop Jameson stopped. He had a slightly stunned look on his face. "Yes, all Basque, why not even the Irish have as many saints, you know." Amidst a smattering of laughter from the English speakers, the bishop went on. "I was late for Mass today and so want to talk about my journey here to be with you and about what it means to us when God presents us with difficulties."

Before Bishop Jameson could continue, the wind picked up another notch and thunder began to roll across the high peaks. Lightning crashed and the tent poles lifted, as they'd been threatening to, out of the ground. Several men leapt up and grabbed the poles, hoping to hold the tent in place until the Mass was completed.

"Let it go," someone called out. "The wind is too strong."

Bishop Jameson had stopped and was looking around as if unsure how to integrate this blast of wind into his talk. Finally, he said, "Blessed Mother Mary is calling each of us to the glory of Heaven with her," then realized that the violence of the heavens was perhaps not the best metaphor for his talk.

"*Korrika egin! Azkar—azkar. Kanpadenda erortzen ari da,*" Father Amezagoira shouted. "Run!" As his words were the first that many people understood, everyone fled.

The thunder came rolling in across the peaks and it began to hail. The hailstones were at first small, like bb's, then they grew larger until they were the size of marbles. Babies cried as the frozen pellets hammered their heads.

"Here, Father," someone shouted, opening a car door, "get in." The bishop and the few who'd driven huddled together inside their automobiles. Most people threw themselves under the wagons they'd arrived in.

When the tent collapsed, the expanse of canvas lay like a tablecloth over the bales of hay and the men and older boys who'd been holding the poles found that they could now rest comfortably on the dry ground, the tent roof a foot above their faces. In the closed space, the smell of the hay was rich and strong. For at least one boy, being trapped under the tarp in the storm was a great adventure and the smell of timothy and alfalfa would forever after make him feel ready to burst from happiness. There he was, years later, a middle aged man out haying, and he'd find himself falling to his knees in the field to give thanks.

After about fifteen minutes the hail stopped, the wind dropped, the clouds disappeared, and the sun blazed down once again. The meadow steamed as the hailstones began to melt. Children ran scooping up the last of the hail and throwing it at the adults who shouted in mock surprise and took off after the kids.

"Our Holy Mass is not finished," Bishop Jameson said. "Let us begin again where we left off."

At the same time Father Amezagoira shouted, "*Berandu da. Etor zaitezte jaunartzera.*" Hailstones in their hair, the adults formed two lines. One would receive Communion from Fathers Aristides and Amezagoira, the other from Bishop Jameson assisted by Ardene Ysursa. Father Amezagoira smiled at the bishop who, thinking that the Basque priest had translated his words, began to move back toward the original temporary altar. But when he saw no one moving to lift the canvas, he turned. People were lining up as the other priests prepared the host.

Ardene Ysursa waved at the bishop, who at first didn't notice her. She called out, "*Begira hona, aita. Ia-ia prest gaude.*" When the bishop finally looked her way, she continued, shouting, "*Itxaroten ari dira. Oraintxe bertan.*" She spoke in a clipped telegraphic way as if this might help him to understand. Anyway, he could see the people waiting in line.

Bishop Jameson stopped and stared, as if at Ardene's words—"like crows swallowing stones and spitting them up again," he said to himself as he walked toward her.

When Communion was finished, everyone realized there'd been no collection. Three boys passed among the worshipers, each boy holding out a cowboy hat turned upside down. As soon as the collection had been made, the tent was lifted from the bales of hay and pulled off to one side of the meadow. The bales were set out to form a circle and the altar was torn down and replaced by a full cash bar. The transformation, begun by nature, was completed by man in slightly more than thirty minutes.

Large pits had been dug into the ground at the edge of the meadow and several men were already roasting hundreds of pounds of beef and lamb. A group of women was chopping cabbage and carrots. Near the bar there were several tables covered by wheels of bleu cheese and bowls filled with roasted garlic, platters stacked high with hard white flour rolls, and more platters filled with spicy *lukainka* sausages. In the center of one table was a wooden bowl filled with garbanzo beans in a scorched sweet tomato sauce. Men sauntered up to the bar for red wine or bourbon while women chopped and basted and cut.

In the center of the field where the bales had been placed in a circle Goiene Intxerria began playing the "Hegi" on a two-row button accordion. Men who had wandered off to inspect the grass and wonder about how long they might yet graze sheep in this area heard the sound of the *trikitixa* and started back. Several people carried the plates and drinks over close to Goiene who shifted from the "Hegi" to an unnamed march.

The circle opened up to let a group of young men and women dance in from the aspen trees. The young men looked straight ahead, their upper bodies still, their hands hanging at their sides. They wore white pants with red and green piping down the legs, white shirts with red neckerchiefs and black berets. The young women also looked straight ahead and held their upper bodies still, but their arms were bent, their hands on their hips. The women wore white blouses with black vests and red skirts with small black aprons. Both men and women wore soft cotton shoes.

The dancers began the "Agur." They saluted the bishop, dancing only a few feet in front of him. With each leap they rapidly crossed their feet at the ankles, almost fluttering. They danced to the left then back to the right always facing the bishop. When they made their turns, they went only part way around so that their backs were never to the priest.

Bishop Jameson, who didn't know the dance was being done to honor him, began to walk toward a group of people standing nearby. He always enjoyed chatting with his flock after Mass, thanking them for coming and giving them a few words of spiritual encouragement. As the bishop moved away, the dancers followed. Though it was difficult, they managed to stay in front of him and move in the direction he was walking.

After the "Agur," there were hoop dances—"Uztai Handia" and "Uztai Txikia." The "Uztai Handia" hoops reached from the ground and up over the dancers' heads so that it took two people to hold a single hoop. The smaller "Uztai Txikia" hoops could be carried by individual dancers. These small hoops were clacked together during the dance. After the hoop dances, the even louder stick and sword dances were presented.

The bishop turned toward the sound of sticks and swords slapping in the air. He approached Father Amezagoira and, leaning down to the shorter man, said, "I'm very fond of this. It calls to mind the primitive warring times of our Basque people before the teachings of the church were given to them."

"Perhaps," Father Amezagoira said, "but these dances are not based on themes of battle."

"No?"

"No. For centuries farmers did these dances in the late winter and early spring. Some still do. The sticks are struck against each other and against the earth. The noise and the act of striking the earth awaken the soil after the sleep of winter. And drive away evil spirits, too. When metalsmithing was discovered, swords often replaced sticks. They're louder. If the earth is very tired, she might sleep through the sound of sticks, but not swords. And swords are also more frightening than sticks to evil spirits. In some ways this is much more than a dance."

"I see."

"Oh, but you must watch closely this next dance," Father Amezagoira went on. "It is the 'Zahagi Dantza.' You see that man carrying the large bag over his shoulder? That is the *zahagi* filled with wine, the fruit of the earth. I hope you will not find me lacking in orthodoxy if I tell you that I've wondered about this bag of wine as large as a bloated sheep. How is it related to the wine that is the blood of our Savior? There is enough wine to make every man here drunk for two days. May I tell you that I've read about the Sufi metaphor of drunkenness—being drunk on the love of the Lord?"

"Sufi?"

The man carrying the *zahagi* on his back lurched past, bumping the bishop as he passed. "*Barkatu, Aita*, Sorry, Father," he said. Men with sticks ran in circles around both priests and after the *zahagi*.

"Now they will beat him with the sticks. See there."

Struck especially hard by two sticks at once, the man fell but when he hit the ground, he only laughed and got up running madly back toward the dancers trying to escape the men waving their sticks.

"Well, what does it mean?" Bishop Jameson asked.

Father Amezagoira smiled. "I must tell you later. They are about to start the most beautiful dance of all, the 'Godalet'— the dance of the wine glass. Here come the principal characters. Each is one of the band of *gorriak*—the forces of good—of moral order, cleanliness, dignity, and manners. There is another band—the *beltzak*—that represents the forces of chaos and disarray, evil and obscenity. *Gorri* means red and *beltz* means black. I've never known how red came to be associated with good and black with evil. In any case I do not think we will see the *beltzak* today but of course one never knows. The *gorriak* are not only what is good and orderly but they are the traditions that guarantee this. The *beltzak* remind us how precarious order is and how important is tradition. It is like temptation. How can we call a man good if he has never had to resist the temptation to do wrong?"

The Bishop smiled in a pained way, wondering if all Basques might be Jesuits.

"I hope I am not lecturing too much. When I was young I did these dances as most young men do." He lifted his hands above his head and snapped his fingers. "I'm sure I could still do most of them though the 'Godalet,' that would take some practice."

A figure in a black military style uniform with a white tunic stood holding what appeared to be a large pair of crossed lengths of metal.

"*Sorgin-guraizeak*—witch's scissors, cat's claws."

The dancer moved quickly left and right, dancing around a glass of red wine that had been placed on the ground. Suddenly, he leapt into the air and came down almost standing on his toes, both feet balanced on the rim of the small glass. He stood for several seconds perched there then leapt back into the air. The glass shook slightly but no wine was spilled. The crowd of watchers cheered and laughed, shouting at the dancer.

A second man danced forward. He wore a similar black uniform with white tunic but around his waist was a stiff oblong hoop extending three feet or so in front of and behind him. The hoop had skirting that fell nearly to the ground so that only the dancer's feet could be seen. From the front of the hoop rose an arched curve of wood.

"A horse," Bishop Jameson said.

"The *zamaltzain*," Father Amezagoira said. "He is the most important figure in the dance—the keeper of the horse, the groom. Some people say the *zamaltzain* is a muleteer but a mule is a *mando*. Well, a horse is a *zaldi*. Our language can be very confusing. My grandparents believed the horse represented the freedom of the Basque people but I cannot say."

The *zamaltzain* moved rapidly around the glass in a tightening circle then he leapt over it, side to side, front to back. Finally, he made a high leap and, like the dancer with the scissors, came down balancing with both feet on the rim of the glass. The horse's skirt waved for a moment and the crowd was still. When the dancer leapt again into the air, the glass remained standing.

Father Amezagoira smiled. "That is very good. He didn't spill a drop and it is much harder for him as he can't see his feet. All dancers are not as skilled as this man so sometimes a glass is knocked over. When that happens there is a momentary opening for the *beltzak*. Quickly, the glass is refilled and the dancer takes a swallow then puts the still partially filled glass back on the ground. Of course, each time you knock the glass over you must drink. If you knock the glass over enough times, you risk becoming drunk and the drunker you become the more likely you are to knock the glass over and become still drunker and knock the glass over again and *beltzak* everywhere. Some dancers put a hole through the hoop skirting so they can look down to see their feet but I consider this a little bit cheating. You understand this is my personal interpretation of history."

The bishop looked at the priest with what in books is called a searching glance.

"You must excuse me for how I am putting it but I am serious. This dance re-enacts or stands for or metaphorically explains temptation and the ways that we can open the doors to forces we are ill prepared to confront. But as I said this is a rather idiosyncratic view I take and I'm not certain every dancer would agree with me."

After an hour during which dances were presented from the villages of Arnegi, Banka, Baigorri, and Irulegi, Goiene

Intxerria announced that he would play a fandango and arin-arin to which everyone was invited to dance.

"Ah, it is too bad," Father Amezagoira said to Bishop Jameson.

"Too bad? But I thought the fandango was the Basque dance."

"Oh, yes, it's not that. Only that we are not going to see one of my favorite of the *uztai* dances. Well, next time. Please excuse me as I will play the *txistu* to accompany Goiene."

The bishop nodded, "Of course."

"It is time for all of us to dance," Father Amezagoira called over his shoulder to the bishop. "You, too." By the time the priest crossed the field Goiene had already started the fandango.

By now everyone had eaten and the food tables were nearly cleared. "Come," Zelestina said to Yellow Bird Daughter. "Fandangoa."

The dancers formed a circle facing in with their arms above their bodies and out to the sides of their heads. Someone began the *irrintzi* and Yellow Bird Daughter jumped. It was like screams she'd heard in childhood—a warble, a loud mocking laugh that rose in pitch, intensity, and speed, like a train picking up momentum. Several people shouted the *irrintzi* then, snapping their fingers and twirling, they leapt into the air where they hung weightless for a few moments before falling back to earth.

Yellow Bird Daughter remembered her mother describing the Ghost Dance, then her mother and father sliding out of sight over the cliff. She felt a chill and looked down. When she looked up, there was Teague among the dancers. Uncertain if this was a vision, she turned and saw Zelestina staring at him, too. He was real or else a double vision.

Yellow Bird Daughter tried to move away but stumbled. Someone took her arm and she closed her eyes. As Teague approached, a young man, already slightly drunk, came down from a leap and turned his ankle. He cried out and grabbed Teague's leg. "*Lagundu, jauna, lagundu.*" He pulled himself up and was now practically hugging Teague as he tried to hobble away from the dancing. "I'm wounded," he cried, laughing.

"Let go of me," Teague demanded.

"I can't. You've got to help me." Using Teague as a crutch, the dancer hobbled over to a bale of hay where he sat down. Someone put a glass of red wine in the young man's hand. Another glass appeared in front of Teague.

"I don't want this," Teague said and thrust the wine away.

Before the cup could fall the young man grabbed it and said, "That's what I need, not one but two glasses of wine." He lifted his rapidly swelling ankle up on a second bale of hay and began to drink. "I don't feel a thing."

Back among the dancers, Teague grabbed Yellow Bird Daughter's arm and pulled, forcing her to follow him. Zelestina shuddered.

When Goiene stopped playing, the dancers stopped dancing and in the sudden quiet, everyone could hear Teague clearly when he said, "Did you think I wouldn't come back for you? I'm not the kind of man who would abandon his wife."

A stranger stepped forward and asked, "And just what kind of man are you?"

This is another point at which I wonder how much Zelestina embellished what she told me. I mean, come on, "And just what kind of man are you?" That's a good line even if it sounds scripted for the kind of Western movie John Ford would have directed. And to top it off, it turns out the man wasn't quite a stranger. It was the stationmaster, the man who'd been hypnotized by the sight of Zelestina's undergarments when she fell stepping down from the train onto a patch of ice. Whoosh. I shouldn't make fun as it appears that the stationmaster's initial infatuation had ripened into a secret love.

Between Teague and the stationmaster, we've got about all the Deus ex Machina type events we can stand. Any more coincidences pop up at this picnic we may as well call it a Mexican telenovela—*El Viento del Otoño*, say—The Wind of Autumn. In episode nine Teague returns after some undetermined time missing and presumed gone, then the stationmaster, who is not Basque, turns up at the Basque picnic and will in a few minutes reveal himself as a self taught Japanese jujitsu master hiding in the remnants of the mountains of Oaxaca. Or at least the mountains of Wyoming.

That's the TV show but as usual the real story is plainer and simpler. The stationmaster had a number of Basque friends and one of them invited him to the picnic. And Zelestina had spoken to him a number of times on the street. But the word "stranger" gives the scene its proper tone. The stationmaster came hoping to see Zelestina. She was happy to see him and in a moment there would be some heroic action. Stereotypes are, after all, based on something.

Still holding Yellow Bird Daughter by the arm, Teague started to run. "Drunken Basques," he called and spat. While it would be unfair to say that Teague struck Zelestina when he began his flight, he did push her out of the way and she fell as he ran through the crowd with the stationmaster close behind.

When he caught Teague, the stationmaster struck him on the elbow with a piece of pipe. Don't ask me how he just happened to have a piece of pipe in his pocket. There was a cracking sound, a grunt, and the release of Yellow Bird Daughter who took off like a terrified trooper at the Battle of the Greasy Grass—the Little Bighorn.

"I'd say the best thing would be to leave," the stationmaster said. "Look around—you can see what I mean."

Teague stepped back as if giving this advice serious consideration then he rushed the stationmaster who, at the last moment, stepped aside, turned, and pushed Teague from behind. Unable to check his momentum, Teague slammed face first into the ground. He got to his feet and made a second try with the same results. After the second fall, he got halfway to his feet and passed out. Without the stationmaster's helping hand, Teague's third fall seemed to be in slow motion. When he hit the earth there was an audible thud and dust rose then fell like a shroud over the still body.

Four men picked Teague up and carried him across the meadow where they threw him down in the back of a wagon. Several hours later he awoke in the dark. Shivering in the late summer evening's mountain coolness, he pulled himself over the wagon's sideboards and looked into the darkness. His head was spinning and when he took a step, he felt the collected acid in his stomach rising into his throat. He coughed convulsively, and threw up.

It's too bad that a person can't throw up all the garbage that he is and start life again as someone else. But I suppose the job of creating that kind of rebirth belongs to the Church or to psychiatry.

After Teague had been stashed in the wagon, Goiene Incherria, who'd decided playing some more would be a good idea, started a polka—the happiest of European dances. In a moment the party was again in full swing. In every moment, life is recreated and reborn, but mostly we don't think of it. We dance a fandango and an arin or a waltz and a polka, sip a glass of red wine, comment on how well the lamb is cooked, tell the bishop about the *gorriak* and the *beltzak*. And all the time we go on as if nothing were happening, as if unaware of the sea change that occurs with every breath a human being takes.

Goiene Incherria grew tired and put down the accordion. Another man picked it up and played on. Anyone who tries can play a musical instrument. Soon a whole group of men were taking turns playing fandango after fandango, arguing about which tune and which musician was the best. When the exhausted dancers sank to the ground, the accordionists went on, quitting only when the wine ran out.

By then, almost everyone had thrown a bedroll down in the meadow. The bishop of Wyoming, who wasn't quite warm enough under his blanket, lay counting the stars in the hope that this would put him to sleep. The Basque priest, Father Amezagoira, stayed up all night talking to his friends about God and music. In the early morning hours, he sat playing unaccompanied melodies on the three-holed *txistu* flute. Several men leaned back against a log, smoking and listening. Lying with their eyes closed but no more able to sleep than the bishop, Zelestina and Yellow Bird Daughter listened, too.

A few young people who like Father Amezagoira had stayed up all night stumbled into the woods searching for the sunrise. The smell of eggs frying in bacon grease drifted across the meadow, eggs along with onions and garlic and thin strips of peppers whose seeds the Basques had brought with them from the slopes of the Pyrenees, unaware that peppers had come from America in the first place and now were simply going home in the suitcases of Basque immigrants.

A group of boys found one of their uncles wrapped in his coat sleeping beside a bale of hay. The boys hoisted the sleeping man into the air and began running toward the nearby creek. The grown man's aging mother saw the boys and took off after them waving a stick of firewood. When she saw she wasn't going to catch them, she threw the stick, managing to strike one boy on the shoulder. "Put me down," the uncle was shouting at the boys while looking behind himself at his mother running as fast as she could. "Put me down," he shouted again, between laughs. "Come on, *Ama*, save me."

At the creek, the boys tossed their uncle in then stood by to watch what would happen when he rose from the cold water. The uncle stood up in a dignified manner and walked carefully to land. At the bank, he whirled suddenly and grabbed two of the boys, hauling them back into the cold stream. "My dear mother," he said as the old woman lurched up to the creek, "thank you for your defense. If you'd been ten years younger, I know you would have caught these boys before they could treat me so shabbily." He pushed the two boys underwater at which point the other boys on shore leapt in shouting and splashing. When everyone came up for air, teeth chattering, the uncle said, "Now, let's go dry off and have some breakfast, something hot."

Here are the things people would remember from the August fifteenth party honoring the Assumption of Mary, mother of God: the sprained ankle and the collapsing tent, the bishop wandering around saying "*egun on*" through his nicotine stained teeth, the number of young men and women who got drunk and Lord knows what happened next, the weather—always the weather—the day starting out sunny and fair, then the wind and a violent hailstorm, the blue of the sky after the storm had passed, and, finally, the most surprising of all, the return of Thomas Teague and his attack on the woman he claimed was his wife.

There was a line of horses tethered in the trees at the edge of the meadow and to them Teague was no more important than the hailstones that had melted in their manes. As the sun rose, the sigh of the horses breathing filled the air and warmed it. Now and again a horse would shake its head or paw the ground. Grunt. Turn and blink into the light. It was soothing and Heaven and earth recognized themselves in each other's embrace.

10

An Umbrella and
Two Deaths

One day in June I was walking home from the grocery store with Zelestina. We each carried a paper bag of groceries. I said it looked like rain and she said, "Maybe," and cocked her head up to the sky. "Good if it rains. Always good."

In the Basque Country, Lord how it rained—day after day, week after week, month after month. One year when I was there in May there were two days of sunshine in the month. Everyone had an umbrella tucked away somewhere—in a briefcase, in the door pocket of the car, in a purse, a backpack, a bicycle saddlebag. The bars and coffeehouses all had umbrella stands at their doors. You wouldn't leave home without an umbrella anymore than you'd go out without wearing underwear. Not that some people don't skip putting on underwear on some days. Imagine how your mother would feel if you got in an accident and the EMT had to take off your pants.

On one of those two sunny days I walked into a key shop in Donostia to get a copy of the key for my bicycle lock. The lock had come with two keys but I'd lost one. What if I lost the other? Then I'd be in a pickle. So many keys we have to open all sorts of things—a chest of drawers, our house and car, the safety deposit box at the bank. So many things we keep locked up.

There was once a book of zen stories in which a hermit monk lived by the shore of a northern lake. His house was a one-room mud and wattle hut. There was a wooden table and a wooden platform on which he slept. He had a wool blanket; a tin cup, bowl, and spoon; and his well worn clothes although these included a beautiful pair of Gortex hiking boots that a rich pilgrim had left for him.

One day while the monk was out gathering wild onions, a burglar entered the hut only to see there was nothing to steal. Returning that night, the monk heard a rustling from the hut. He stopped and in the moonlight shining through the open door saw the burglar. Stepping inside, the monk apologized for the poverty of his circumstances, saying, "You've come a long way to visit and it would be inhospitable to send you away with nothing." Then the monk began taking off his clothes.

The burglar waved his hands no. Anyway, who would want those ratty old clothes? But the monk insisted. "Please," he said then noticing the burglar looking at the gortex hiking boots, he began taking them off, too.

"No, no," the burglar nearly shouted but the monk kept on and when he was naked he shoved both clothes and boots into the thief's hands. "Really, I insist." When the thief had gone, the monk stood in the doorway, his blanket wrapped around him, staring up at the night sky. "Poor fellow," he said. "If only I could have given him this moon."

That's a good story and even if the monk exists only in the imaginary doorway to the hut, I like to believe that there are people of such pure and great hearts. I've met one or two, Zelestina at least.

I've not forgotten the key and the sunny day in Donostia. When I walked into the shop, the clerk was in the back working at a metal cutting machine. I could hear the grinding and see sparks. When he came toward me, he held his hand up in front of his face and squinted into the light. It was as if he'd been living for years in a cave and the light was painful. After he'd adjusted, he smiled and said, "So that's what the sky looks like. My ama told me about it when I was a kid but I've never seen it before." Then he cut my key.

Zelestina and I were still walking home with our paper bags of groceries when the sky opened and the rain tumbled down. When we got to Zelestina's and shook the water out of our hair, I said, "Next time we'll have to bring umbrellas."

"I don't own an umbrella." She'd emptied a bag of sugar that had gotten wet and was spreading the soggy crystals out on two large cookie sheets.

"You don't own an umbrella?"

"No, why should I?"

"Well, it rained pretty hard today."

"And already it's over."

It was uncommon for her to express impatience or disdain or anger but all three were in her voice. I think that the rain was a stand-in for the Basque Country and she'd left there never to return. Maybe she felt some shame about abandoning both people and place so it didn't rain in Wyoming and it wouldn't rain in Wyoming and if it did rain in Wyoming then she would ignore that rain. Never own an umbrella again.

She'd finished spreading out the sugar and was licking her fingers. "Five days a year it rains. Maybe ten at most," she said then softened. "One afternoon when I was a little girl—I don't know how old but I had to be at least six or seven because I was coming from school—it started raining. Only a little at first then harder. Soaked, I was still pretty far from home. My dress was heavy where it had dragged in the mud and my wool coat, wet along the hem, smelled like sheep. It made me feel like a bum lamb. When a mother sheep loses her lamb, people skin the dead newborn then they take a lamb whose mother has died and they put the dead lamb's skin on the living orphan like it was a jacket. The mother who has lost her lamb will accept this new lamb as her own because of the smell. I'm sure some ewe would have accepted me."

"So you were excited to be disguised as a dead lamb."

"I was excited to be both sheep and girl for a few moments. I was standing there wet and happy when I saw a man coming along the muddy street toward me. It was Aitzibar Nexmendia. Everyone called him Nexmen. The adults said Nexmen was crazy. Then they'd say, 'crazy but not dangerous.'

"He was carrying an unopened umbrella. I ran to him and asked, 'If you're not going to use your umbrella Nexmen, may I? We can walk together and I'll give the umbrella back when we get to my house.'

"'Oh, Ume,' he said. He always called children *umeak* as if we were baby goats or ducklings—'oh, Ume, *barkatu*—I'm sorry but I'm afraid my umbrella won't help you. The cloth is torn so it won't keep the rain off anyone's head.'

"'If your umbrella is ripped and so no good, why do you carry it with you?'

'Well, this one day I didn't think it would rain.'"

Zelestina laughed and shook her head. The last drops of water flew around the room. Then she frowned.

"What?" I asked.

She waved her hand as if to brush away a stinging insect.

"What?" Again she waved me away and a third time I asked, "What?"

She sighed. Something had made her think of the time when she and Yellow Bird Daughter were living in the house Thomas Teague had abandoned. Nobody knew where he'd gone. Yellow Bird Daughter had shown Zelestina how to make a sage bundle and they'd smudged the house, the sweet sage smoke driving Teague's spirit away. The room where he'd locked Yellow Bird Daughter up, they smudged several times. Still, there was something not quite right.

Most people in Wolf figured that after what had happened

at the Basque picnic, Teague was gone for good. His cruelty toward the Indian girl was supposed to have been a secret but like a lot of secrets, everyone knew it. That's after all what a secret is—something everyone knows but agrees to pretend they don't. If everyone knows, we might ask, why don't they do something? That's a good question and like a lot of good questions it's yet to get a good answer.

It was in the middle of the night when the wind came up. You might think this is a little odd, this wind always coming up at dramatic moments but the truth is Wyoming is windy. My wife has a t-shirt that says WYOMING WIND FESTIVAL and below that the dates of the festival—*January 1 – December 31*. That night even with rags stuffed along the bottom of the doors you could feel the cold and see the curtains fluttering at the windows.

Thomas Teague had decided to check on his property. He walked around the house in the dark, sniffing like a hungry hound. He banged on one of the closed window shutters then walked around to the door and tried the doorknob. It was locked but he rattled it anyway. Perhaps it would change its mind if he impressed his intention on it. Nothing happened and he muttered, "My own house, for chrissake." He spat and looked into the darkness. He was about to slam his shoulder into the door when it opened as if an invisible hand had turned the latch and then the knob. "That's better," Teague told the door which of course had opened not for Teague but for the wind.

Zelestina rolled over in her sleep and in her dream she opened a door to see what was coming. She stared but the street was empty and when she turned to go back inside, she realized it was her family's house in Arnegi. When she closed the door she could hear the wind blowing raindrops against the wood.

Teague stepped in and the door swung back and forth on its hinges a few times then slammed shut. That's convenient, he thought. He wore the dark suit he'd worn to the courthouse for his wedding though now it was dirty and the cuffs frayed. There was also a hole in the cloth at his right shoulder and his shoulder hurt as if thinking of hitting the door had had the same effect as actually hitting it. He lifted his hand and brushed away the dust then rubbed the sore spot, struggling to remember how he'd hurt himself.

He stepped across the room into the kitchen and began looking for the pistol he kept in a drawer. Unable to find it, he moved steadily from drawer to drawer shoving aside wooden spatulas and spoons, a cast iron frying pan, and a pile of flower sacks that had been cut up and hemmed to serve as tea towels.

He opened the cupboards and pulled out more bits and pieces of domestic life—a ball of string, a hammer and pliers, a box of soap powder, gloves. "It's got to be here some place." He looked in the drawer farthest from the stove. "Unless some sonovabitch came in and stole it." Pulling the drawer completely out of its cabinet, he spilled the contents on the floor and both Zelestina and Yellow Bird Daughter jerked in their sleep.

There was the pistol. But when Teague picked it up and turned it over in his hand, it felt wrong. The balance and size were different, the finish shinier, the cylinder stiffer. No matter. He found a box of bullets in a cabinet on the other side of the room. What kind of a fool keeps the bullets separate from the gun? It'd be a nightmare if you were in a hurry. But again, no matter. After he'd loaded the gun, he held it up before him and turned it in his hand.

"It'll have to do," he said, and it took all his will to resist pulling the trigger to see how the gun fired. "Better not. Don't want to be giving anything away."

As he walked around the dark room, he noticed the furniture was different and his things were gone. There'd been a thief in the house. He lifted his arm and sighted down the barrel of the pistol but the gun was too heavy to hold up for more than a few moments. He set it down on the table, shook his arms, and rolled his shoulders like a boxer warming up. A sharp pain shot through him. He lunged at the pistol as though it might leap away and with both hands grabbed it. But it was so heavy.

"What the hell?" He said, and when he tried to squeeze the trigger it wouldn't move. He pulled as hard as he could and it felt like someone had cut the nerve ending in his finger. Even with both hands he couldn't hold it any longer and it fell to the floor with a bang.

This time Yellow Bird Daughter woke and sat up. She shook Zelestina who mumbled, "Must be the wind."

"The wind," Yellow Bird Daughter repeated and lay back down.

"Never felt so tired in all my life," Teague said. It was like he'd walked all day through wet gumbo and now could barely pull his feet free. Maybe it was for the best, as he had to get down on his hands and knees anyway to find the gun amidst the butter knives and strainers and wooden spoons. He slid his hands along in front of him pushing objects aside as he crawled forward. One knee came down on the tines of a fork and he stifled a groan.

This time when he found the pistol, he couldn't lift it. He lay on his stomach on the floor, his body aching all over as if he had the flu. He crawled forward and his hand came down on the sharp edge of a paring knife that had lodged between two floorboards.

Hearing a scream, both Zelestina and Yellow Bird Daughter woke and looked at each other with a "not the wind" look. When Teague heard the women's footsteps he pulled himself into the pantry, closed the door, and waited. He was like Gregor Samsa, the young man in the Franz Kafka story who wakes up one morning to find himself metamorphosed into a bug. The translators sometimes say "insect" or "beetle" or even "cockroach." One critic said it was a word more like "vermin" in Kafka's original German. What kind of writer imagines a petit bourgeois Czech twenty-something young man struggling with his job and family who goes to bed one night and when he wakes up he's a bug on his back under the sheets? But for his sister, no one recognized that the bug was Gregor and in the end even the sister abandoned her sadly transformed sibling who died in desiccated despair.

Zelestina and Yellow Bird Daughter had gone into the kitchen where they'd turned on the light—they'd had the house wired—and were picking up the contents of the spilled drawer. "Maybe a raccoon," Yellow Bird Daughter said.

"I think I heard a door open and close earlier," Zelestina said. "I thought it was a door in my dream but maybe it was a real door."

"It'd be like a raccoon to figure out how to open a door."

Teague thought the best thing would be to come crashing in from the pantry and surprise the women but he couldn't stand up. He pulled himself to a sitting position and pressed his eye to the keyhole. A shaft of light hit him like a needle and he pulled away. "I didn't notice there was electricity. I'll need to shoot out the bulb." But he'd left the pistol on the floor in the other room. Again, he pressed his eye to the keyhole.

There was no sign of a raccoon and in a few minutes the two women had picked up the spilled cutlery, turned out the light, and gone back to bed. In cleaning, they'd missed a fork under the edge of the oven and the pistol—of course the pistol—that had made its way under the pie safe when Teague scuttled out of the room.

He waited a long time gathering his strength. Finally, he was able to get up, open the door, and go back into the kitchen. The moon had risen—the same moon that the monk wanted to give to the thief—so that even with the lights out the room was bright. Teague stared around and saw the glint off the gun barrel. He crawled across the floor and laid his head down on one side to look under the edge of the pie safe. Pushing his arm into the opening he swept the pistol toward him. When he touched it he felt a surge of energy and stood but the sudden rise made him dizzy and he fell against the pie safe, which rocked away, hit the wall, and leapt back toward him. He was able to step aside as it fell but again the sudden motion was too much for him and he spun sideways, throwing his arms out to his sides and striking a window with the pistol. Glass flew everywhere, some of it cutting his face and hands.

Yellow Bird Daughter turned on the lights. Adrenaline pumping so that he felt a sudden strength, Teague extended his arm and took aim at her but it was too late. Zelestina had picked up a shoe and thrown it, striking Teague's arm and making the pistol fly into the air. It was like a pop-up to short left center with the second baseman, shortstop, and left fielder all converging on the ball. Teague took three large steps and leaned forward. Zelestina, who had jumped to one side when she saw the pistol, collided with the table and fell, hitting Teague as she went down. She was immediately up and slammed her full weight into the man again. Both of them went down and, as they fell, Teague's hand found the pistol. There was an explosion, a scream, and Zelestina lay still. Not waiting to see if she'd get up, he turned and was hit in the already injured shoulder by an iron pot. He didn't drop the gun but now he couldn't hold his arm up so that when he fired a second shot the bullet drove itself harmlessly through the floorboards. He toppled backwards and his third shot went through the ceiling.

Teague looked confused for a moment as if he had forgotten why he was here. When he saw Yellow Bird Daughter, he remembered and stood. He lifted the pistol with his good hand and she held her hands up like a soldier surrendering. Teague took a step toward her. She stepped back and he took another step. With her next step back, he jumped at her. Just as the stationmaster had at the picnic, Yellow Bird Daughter stepped aside at the last second so that Teague missed her, slammed into the wall, and bloodied his nose. When he lifted his hand to wipe the blood away an electric jolt ran through his arm. He shook it violently as if he would shake the pain away then swung around full circle thinking to knock Yellow Bird Daughter down but, as he couldn't fully extend his arm, she remained out of reach.

Now the injured arm had no feeling at all. The pistol clattered to the ground. Thinking of him weak, bleeding, driven crazy by anger, I'm surprised that I feel so little sympathy. They say that when you write a story you need to have some human feeling for every character.

Ok, Teague had a rotten childhood. So did a lot of people, so what. It would have been better if Teague had fled with his mother to another town in Ireland. It would have been better if Yellow Bird Daughter's parents hadn't fallen off a cliff. It would have been better if the Europeans had never come to America and the American Indians had never found themselves herded onto reservations. It would have been better if the Roman Empire had never existed, France and Spain had never come into being, and the Basques had remained fishermen and farmers left to their own devices. Of course, if all these ifs had come to pass, Zelestina would not have come to Wolf and might have found herself not so many years later facing a pistol held by a fascist supporter of General Franco—someone who was a better shot than Teague.

The attack in the kitchen was a replay of the Basque picnic. Sometimes I think we all repeat our worst behavior and, in this, Teague was like everyone else. My father was a laborer—aluminum extrusion mill assembly line, pulp mill, janitor, sweatshop cabinetmaker. He was an angry and bitter man who hated his work and resented his large family—there were six of us kids. He could be violent and so all of us just tried to stay out of the way. Maybe I should make the effort to understand Teague better but I think I got away from my family without turning into some kind of psychopathic rapist nutcase so Teague could have, too.

I was the oldest of the six and I took off from home as soon as I could. Years after I was gone, my youngest brother wrote to me about a night at home. He was in high school and I was already in Wolf hearing Zelestina's stories. My father was still working and still hating it. Each night he came home from work and collapsed on the couch in front of the television—by now the family had television. One night the Alfred Hitchcock film *The Birds* was on and my kid brother begged to see it. My father wanted to watch some situation comedy—*My Three Sons* or *Hogan's Heroes* or *I Dream of Jeanie*. But the kid kept begging. I'm sure he knew what he was doing. My father relented. That's the biggest surprise in the story because he never relented. A few minutes into the film, my father got up and grabbed my brother by the shirt, lifted him out of his chair and started screaming, "I work hard all day to put food on the table for you and when I come home I want to relax. I want to be entertained. I don't want to see some goddamned nightmare." He whacked my brother a couple of times and turned the television to the comedies.

"You should have seen the look in Dad's eyes," my brother wrote. "He might really have killed me." The kid sounded proud that he'd driven the old man that far.

My wife and I were talking about my childhood, about my father's violence. One of my sisters had never really gotten over what had happened and she wanted an explanation. She asked our mother why she hadn't protected us. Our mother said she'd done the best she could. My sister said, "The best you could is not enough. If your husband is abusing your children then you must take them and leave, get away from the man." I can't imagine saying anything like that to our mother. Not that it isn't another good question, the good answer to which we are still seeking.

This sister asked our mother why she'd married our father and our mother answered, "I felt sorry for him."

"Why didn't you divorce him?"

"You make your bed and you lie in it."

This all came up again when a neighbor of ours was suffering estrangement from her young adult daughter. Our friend's experience was like my sister's and mine in that she'd had an unhappy childhood and she'd cut herself off from her mother. Now the neighbor's daughter was cutting herself off from her mother. There was a son, too, but this boy seemed fine with his mother. They'd fought all through his childhood but he just shrugged it off—like water off a duck's back they say.

That's what I'd done, too. Shrugged it off. This world's a shitty one, let's ignore it and find another world. And I found other worlds in books. Once I was reading and my father was yelling at me to do something. I didn't hear him as I was totally absorbed in the book—probably science fiction. I could do that as a child—read and everything around me disappeared. The room might be full of people talking or laughing or shouting or crying and I'd hear nothing. My father could barely read and he didn't believe a person could be so engrossed in a book. He figured I was ignoring him, pretending I didn't hear what he was saying. He walked up and slammed his fist into the book making it bounce off me and fly into the air. When I heard him screaming, I dropped the book and ran.

I told my wife the ability to ignore the psychological reality of our lives is one of the advantages of being male. We are insensitive and so things that would bother better people don't bother us. It seems a good tactic but the flip side is the male abuser—as insensitive to the pain he inflicts as he thought he was to the pain he experienced. I should be a psychologist. Or at least I should finish telling what Zelestina told me.

Teague's arm fell like a stone and he stumbled to one side. Yellow Bird Daughter saw another fork on the floor and thought how lucky it was they'd missed it. She picked up the fork and stabbed Teague, driving the tines into his forearm. It was like the day he'd found her—the stone, the horse, the flour, the canned tomatoes, the broken glass. But now she was stronger. He threw one leg out and hooked it around one of hers as if he might begin some elegant tango. As they had at the courthouse, they tumbled down, this time to the floor. Teague landed face first with Yellow Bird Daughter on his back, his injured arm caught under his body. The fork drove itself deeper into his flesh.

At this point Yellow Bird Daughter bit Teague, breaking the skin and tearing at the muscle underneath. He screamed and pushed her away but she kept her mouth clamped onto him so when he broke free a chunk of his flesh stayed in her mouth and there was a silver dollar sized hole in his forearm. He lurched up throwing Yellow Bird Daughter against the wall. She slid down and lay unconscious.

In the quiet Teague heard his own ragged breathing. Gotta get a hold of yourself. Inhale, exhale, and so on. Yellow Bird Daughter was going nowhere but where was the Basque woman? Teague whirled like a top looking for her. There was more clattering from the kitchen—someone rummaging again through the household utensils and tools. What did she think she'd find—a colander, an apple peeler that could be mounted on the end of a counter, a meat grinder that also mounted like the apple peeler, wooden boxes filled with assorted sizes of nails and screws, the usual tarnished knives, forks, and spoons, and a broken screwdriver that he'd kept to pry open stuck windows.

Well, no, she wouldn't find that would she? They'd gotten rid of his stuff. Even his pistol. He couldn't fathom why they'd thrown it out only to buy the nearly useless thing he now held.

But he wasn't holding the pistol. He turned his hand over as if the missing gun might magically reappear.

What if she found his meat cleaver? He pictured the hefty knife with its ten-inch long, six-inch tall blade, a blade even a woman could use for breaking the leg bone of an elk and cracking apart its rib cage.

Teague reached Zelestina and they both pulled on one of the drawers at the same moment. It flew out and they fell backwards. Zelestina felt so weak from the bullet lodged between two ribs below her right lung that she was uncertain if she could stand.

The wind shuddered and blew the front door open again. The cruel wind that had let Teague in. Maybe it had now suffered second thoughts and opened the door hoping Teague might take the cue and flee.

"Which is crueler, I wonder—Nature or God?" I once asked Zelestina.

"Think about the time God planned to destroy four cities because of the sinfulness of their citizens," she said. "Confronted by Abraham, God hesitated."

"Yes."

"Nature never hesitates," she said.

Abraham asked God if he would murder an entire population for lack of fifty good men. "If you destroy the cities to kill the sinners, you'll kill the good decent folk, too."

God smiled and said, "Well, no, I suppose I wouldn't murder the fifty along with the hundreds or perhaps thousands of sinners in town. You find me fifty good men and I'll spare the cities."

But Abraham wasn't through. "Right," he said, "but what if there were forty good men? If you could only find forty, surely you wouldn't kill everyone for the lack of ten good men, would you?"

This time God was a little surprised. He thought how disheartening it was that Eve had chosen to eat of the tree of the knowledge of good and evil. Abraham was Eve's son that's for sure. It hit him that every man is Eve's son and every woman Eve's daughter. "Very clever," is all he said.

On it went down to thirty, twenty, ten. In the end Abraham couldn't find even ten good men though it's unclear how much time God gave him or if maybe he did find the ten but the Lord ignored the deal he'd made. Often it feels that talking with the Lord is an exercise in futility. The result which we knew before Abraham began his pleading is that God killed the entire population but for a man named Lot and his family—wife, daughters, daughters' fiancés—fiancés who are the model for the advantageous marriage.

What if you were a rat? No one loves a rat but surely in this case the rat was as innocent as an angel who happened to be in town on the day of destruction. What if you were a child's beloved pet cat or a man's loyal hunting hound? How about a mockingbird in the branches of a mulberry tree, a grizzly bear rambling across a meadow in the Bighorn Mountains chasing miller moths? It's silly to go on. The Lord in his majesty killed them all. He set those four cities on fire and he watched them burn and when Lot's wife turned, wondering perhaps what had become of the women she met at the fountain where they drew water for their households, the Lord turned her into a pillar of salt.

I looked at Zelestina and said, "So God hesitated when Abraham challenged him and nature never hesitates. But in the end God killed them all. That seems even crueler."

When the wind opened the door the second time, a porcupine strolled in like a superhero in a comic book. Imagine a superhero called Porcupine Man. Threatened, he turns his ass to the bad guy and lets the needles fly. I vote we turn our asses to the Lord and smite him. There's no other way to get justice in this world. But the porcupine is more rational than I am and recognizes that a given force—the Lord, say—is too big to deal with. It's better to put your effort where you can have some impact on the outcome.

The stout little animal did a shuffling two-step, turned around, and presented his backside not to the Lord but to Thomas Teague.

When the first quills hit Teague's leg he involuntarily reached down and the next volley hit his hand and arm. Zelestina had found her umbrella in the rubble on the floor and she extended it until she managed to hook the handle around Teague's leg and pull so that he fell. If this man goes up and down anymore, we're going to have to call him an elevator. When he hit the floor he landed on the pistol which went off again.

"And then the porcupine did a slow fandango out the door as cool as a cucumber," Zelestina told me. Cool as a cucumber. Easy as pie. A piece of cake. You can't get blood out of an onion. If life presents you with lemons, make lemonade. She loved these English figures of speech. I guess that's what you'd call them. She watched the porcupine leave then she passed out.

"After it was all over I had the best night's sleep I ever had. It was all dreams of flying to distant planets—no porcupines, no Teague, no knives, no guns."

Maybe this is the way we should think about the stories of the Lord. We are fueled by doubt to seek what's true. Saint Thomas, who as I've mentioned was in those days just plain Tom, was out of town when Mary was taken physically up to Heaven. When he got home and was told what had happened he laughed and said, "No way." So Mary had to throw down her girdle and smack him in the eyes with her bodily presence.

On the earlier occasion of Christ's resurrection, Tom had expressed the same kind of doubt. He was again out of town, got back, and learned from the other Apostles that their Lord was risen. "Really, it's true," they said. "We went to the tomb on the third day after the Crucifixion and the stone had been rolled away."

That was a heavy stone. A man couldn't move that alone, especially a man who'd been weakened to near death from hanging on the cross then shut up in a cave for three days with no food or water. It was an unlikely feat of physical strength.

The Apostles went on. "We stood around like a bunch of kids scared to go in an abandoned Roman guardhouse until somebody stepped forward, leaned in, and said, 'He's gone.' Then of course we rushed the place and sure enough the tomb was empty."

One of the Apostles looked at Thomas and spelled it, "E-M-P-T-Y" though that was showing off as most of Christ's followers were illiterate and so couldn't spell.

"Listen," someone else said, "we all saw Jesus dead. He was dead and now he is risen. The way I see it, he got up, walked to the tomb entrance in the pitch black, rolled the stone away, and stepped out into the light of day. So, like I said, there we were standing around with our hands in the pockets of our robes thinking I don't know what, mostly not thinking at all, just dumbfounded when we heard someone walk up behind us and sure enough it was Jesus. Lord Christ, I nearly jumped out of my skin. But what I noticed right away was that his halo was gone. It was like he'd thrown it away to prove once and for all that he was a real flesh and blood man. Like he was Pinocchio, you know, the wooden puppet that wanted to be a real boy. A man carves a puppet and the puppet wants to be the man." The apostle shrugged and went on, "When Jesus came toward us smiling that big open smile of his and flinging his arms up as if he were a mother welcoming her sons home from war, I nearly cried. Then I noticed the strain around his eyes—the dark circles from lack of sleep—and the blood oozing from the nail holes in his ankles and wrists, and of course that big hole in his rib cage."

Thomas looked around to see if they were joking, saw they weren't and asked, "Then what?"

"He walked away."

"What do you mean he walked away? Why didn't you stop him?" The men shrugged and looked sheepish. "No way," Thomas said.

"But it's true, it's just like we've told you."

Thomas remained incredulous but, recognizing the seriousness of the situation, said, "Except I shall see in his hands, and put my finger into the print of the nails, and thrust my hand into his side, I will not believe."

A week later Jesus showed up again and Thomas asked if he might examine the wounds, the proof of Christ's suffering and death and more to the point the proof that this man was indeed that same Christ who had died on the cross and was now, some claimed, miraculously resurrected.

"Yes, you may touch the wounds."

Thomas came forward and carefully lifted the flap of skin below Christ's right nipple to press his finger into the Lord's damaged flesh. Doing this, he called out, "My Lord and My God, it is so and it is you."

Jesus said, "Thomas, I'm glad that in seeing me this way you have come to believe that it is really I who stand before you. It is good to see and believe but I want to remind you blessed are those that have not seen and yet believe."

When Zelestina and I had this conversation, I asked her, "How can a man be judged inferior because he wants evidence? You can't expect people to accept anything so fantastic on faith alone. There must be thinking and questioning or we abandon our title as human. Thinking for ourselves is what makes us human."

Zelestina shrugged, "They used to say it's our opposable thumb that makes us human. With the thumb we can be toolmakers and users but many animals make tools and then use them. And monkeys have opposable thumbs. Then they said it's language or even music but animals talk and whales compose songs for their yearly migrations."

I could hear the motor on that winch lowering Zelestina's coffin into the earth and her voice—"Thinking, yes, and questioning. But don't animals do these things, too?"

It wasn't long before Yellow Bird Daughter came around and went to Zelestina who like Christ rose from the dead and walked again on the earth. In Zelestina's case, the walk was to a doctor in town, a man who, like Saint Thomas, lifted a flap of skin on his patient's ribcage and probed around. Unlike Thomas, the doctor used a stainless steel tool much like a pair of needle nose pliers to poke around in the wound. Slightly below Zelestina's lung, he found the bullet, which he removed. When he dropped it into a small metal bowl the clanging sound made his pet dog awaken and yawn broadly.

11

A Coffin

The next day while Zelestina lay dozing fitfully, her side throbbing, Yellow Bird Daughter explained to the doctor just enough to make it clear—not just Teague's shooting of Zelestina and then himself, but the back story so the doctor would know why Teague had come to the house. The doctor nodded and said nothing. Of course, he already had a pretty good idea of what was what, secrets, as I've said, being things we agree to pretend we don't know.

The two women and the doctor walked back to Teague's, going slowly as Zelestina felt weak. When they got there, the house was empty. "I heard the shot," Zelestina said. "He fell forward with the gun below him so the bullet must have gone through his chest."

"Maybe, but there's no one here now."

In all trashy murder mystery stories, when you come back to the house and the body is gone something bad is going to happen.

As he was leaving, the doctor advised the two women to keep him informed. He opened the front door, stepped out, and Teague fell from the porch roof, planning, I guess, to make his last attack. But he missed the doctor, hit his head on the edge of the porch, and was still. When the doctor bent and pressed his fingers against Teague's throat, he felt an immediate deep sorrow. However monstrous Teague had been in life, in death he was merely dead and like all the dead deserving of sympathy. The doctor covered Teague's face with a flour sack tea towel Yellow Bird Daughter gave him. He returned to town, arranged for the body to be taken to the undertaker, and, two days later, set off to see Zelestina and Yellow Bird Daughter again.

"I thought I'd check on you," he said to Zelestina. "Make sure there's no infection." He inspected the wound then said, "Good, it looks good. You're very lucky."

"Yes, I am lucky."

"Well, I guess there's nothing more I need do here. You should clean the dressing morning and evening and let me know if there's any build up of fluid, any yellowish pus beginning to develop. I'll check again in a week. By then you should be pretty well on the way to complete recovery. The bullet lodged in nothing vital."

"Yes, I will do as you say."

The doctor hesitated. "There is one more thing. Excuse my frankness but the body of Thomas Teague is still at the undertaker's."

Neither woman spoke.

"There is no one to make funeral arrangements."

Still they didn't speak.

"I know that this was his house and I wonder if you could help. I know this can only be repugnant to you but I know of no one else."

"Can't you make the arrangements?" Zelestina asked.

"I'm sorry but I must leave for Cheyenne tomorrow. I know you have your reasons to say no, good reasons. But truly, there is no one else." He looked around the room. No one spoke for a long time.

"You must excuse us for being impolite," Yellow Bird Daughter finally said. "We were about to have dinner when you arrived. Can you stay and eat with us?"

"Yes, thank you."

There was lamb, mashed turnips, and dried apples. Holding her side, Zelestina went to the pantry and was about to take down a quart of canned haricot beans when she changed her mind and reached for corn. Americans loved corn and the doctor was American. Then she changed her mind again and took the haricot beans. As most Basques did, she believed corn was suitable only as animal feed.

In the middle of the meal, Yellow Bird Daughter fainted and slid off her chair. When she opened her eyes, the doctor was leaning over her and his mouth was moving but it was Teague's voice she heard.

"I've got to go somewhere and it may as well be here. I never knew it was so crowded in the afterlife."

"How do you feel?" The doctor asked. "You fainted."

"My stomach."

"I'll give you something that will help then I'll be on my way. Thank you for dinner. And thank you for considering my request."

That night Yellow Bird daughter slept fitfully and woke exhausted. "I feel good," she heard Teague say, his voice almost gleeful. "Better than I have in years."

Yellow Bird Daughter spent the next day in bed and for a second night slept fitfully. On the following morning she apologized to Zelestina. "You have been shot and now you are caring for me."

"Yes, but you are ill. You should stay in bed."

"No, I feel much better today and I've decided the doctor is right. Really, I am the only one. I must make arrangements for Thomas Teague's funeral." She sat up and slid her legs off the bed. When she rose, she nearly fell. Zelestina ran to her and held her arm.

"I'm alright. I'll just do this last thing then it'll be over. He's dead."

It's like that moment in *The Wizard of Oz* when the witch has put a match to the scarecrow and he's leaping around batting at the flames and Dorothy picks up a bucket of water that just happens to be sitting there waiting for the cleaning lady who scrubs the floor every Tuesday. She throws the water hitting both the scarecrow and the witch and the witch begins to dissolve, crying, "You cursed rat, look what you've done. I'm melting…melting. Ohhh, my world, my world. Who would have thought a good little girl like you could destroy my beautiful wickedness."

In a few moments there's nothing left but a puddle of dark water. Dorothy's little terrier Toto sniffs at it then one of the witch's flying monkeys steps up to examine the remains. The monkey looks up in awe at Dorothy and the captain of the witch's guard says, "She's dead. You've killed her."

Dorothy says, "I didn't mean to kill her. Really, I didn't. It's just that he was on fire."

And again the captain of the guard, "Hail to Dorothy. The wicked witch is dead."

The evil minions, who, of course, have been enslaved by the witch and aren't evil at all, fall to their knees and cry loudly, "Hail. Hail to Dorothy. The wicked witch is dead." Can you be a good minion?

As the two women walked slowly to the undertaker's, a voice said, "Where are we going?"

"What do you mean where are we going?" Zelestina asked.

"I didn't say anything," Yellow Bird Daughter answered.

They went on without speaking then the voice again, "I have a right to know."

"You're talking to yourself," Zelestina said. "Are you sure you can do this?"

Yellow Bird Daughter tried to smile and nodded. "I can walk."

Teague was working himself into another of his frenzies. He began to shout and careen around inside Yellow Bird Daughter. She stumbled and nearly fell.

Now here's where the story gets even weirder and remember I'm only reporting what Zelestina told me. It turns out that Teague wasn't the only spirit who'd taken up residence inside Yellow Bird Daughter. The children who'd been killed at Wounded Knee had been inside her all along. Stunned by the violence of Teague's feelings, they saw the time had come for spiritual activism. They shifted a bit so that Yellow Bird Daughter didn't fall. They sat on Teague, holding him down while they stuffed rags in his mouth so he couldn't speak. Don't ask me where they got the rags.

"Maybe we should go home," Zelestina said. "You're not well and I'm not so strong to help. We can go tomorrow."

"No, no, I'm better now, really, just some kind of spell. I'm sure I'll be alright."

The two women climbed the steps at the undertaker's. French doors opened onto the waiting area. Tacked to the wall beside the doors was a handwritten note, "Please ring." Yellow Bird Daughter was too distracted to notice, Zelestina couldn't read English and Thomas Teague was suspicious. "What've they got to hide?" he tried to say, but with the dead children pressing their hands over the rags filling his mouth, all that came out was a muffled growl—mmrphgh—which might have been mistaken for a person passing gas.

"Excuse me," Yellow Bird Daughter said.

Inside, the women wiped their feet on the woolen doormat and looked around. Dark wainscoting covered the walls and five straight-backed wooden chairs filled the tiny vestibule. On the opposite side of the vestibule from the entry was another set of double wide French doors.

"Here," Zelestina said, and opened the door to the display area. Lined up in the center of the room were five coffins. Two were open to reveal interiors of shining satin. Zelestina leaned over to look in. She shook her head.

Behind the five full size coffins were several smaller models. Maybe they were for women or the wizened old, or youths who had not yet attained their full stature. Finally, there were two coffins so small as to be toys, coffins for infants.

Stepping back from these smallest coffins, Zelestina bumped into one of the large adult models. Open, it rocked briefly on its stand. Zelestina whirled, caught the lid as it was falling and lifted it back into its open position. The interior of the coffin was lined with an ivory colored satin. She'd never seen material so shiny. She put her hand inside to touch. Her winter and work-dried skin caught on the smooth cloth like the barbs of many small fishhooks.

"The hinges are coated so that they will not rust even underground."

Zelestina and Yellow Bird Daughter both jumped.

"I'm sorry, I didn't mean to startle you." The man was annoyed that the women had not rung the bell. Then he put on his sympathetic face and continued, "That is a very good model. The action of the hinges is very smooth. And the satin is silk not the less durable cotton."

Yellow Bird Daughter felt a wave of nausea and put one hand over her stomach as she turned. "We've come to purchase a coffin," she said. "For a man who has died."

"Yes, of course. Allow me to serve you in any way I can. May I ask who the deceased party may be?"

Neither woman spoke. The salesman was accustomed to the tongue-tied recently bereaved and went on, trying to be soothing. "Whether you come on behalf of a friend or family member, it is difficult making these arrangements, and there are often unexpected losses."

"It's a Mr. Thomas Teague. We've come because he has died. He wasn't a family member."

Yellow Bird Daughter could hear Teague shouting that he damned well wasn't ready to be dead yet. "And what other family do you have besides me?" he added.

"May I sit down?" she asked.

"Yes, of course, please forgive me for not offering you a chair sooner."

"Thank you," Yellow Bird Daughter said. As she sat, she arched her back slightly, hoping this would relieve some of the pain in her stomach and abdomen.

In that moment, the children of Wounded Knee grabbed Teague and, before he had time to resist, pushed him out into the atmosphere. Not that there was an actual person to push. And not a spirit in the way we understand that word. He was only a wisp, a shock of dirty wind. Anyway, the children pushed and Teague found himself rotating like a damaged helicopter, his arms and legs spinning like the rotors, his head twisting this way and that. As he flew across the room, he collided with the open lid of one of the small children's coffins. The lid was thrown back on its hinges and in an inevitable reaction fell, pushing Teague downward. Before he knew what had happened the lid slammed shut trapping him in the tiny satin lined box.

"What the hell!"

Now it was the undertaker's turn to jump. He looked at the coffin and said, "How did that happen? Excuse me just a moment." He walked to the coffin intending to prop the lid open again but the hinges were latched and locked. He looked at the two women. "Did you...?"

"What?"

"Nothing. May I get you a glass of water? Perhaps you'd like to return later."

Yellow Bird Daughter closed her eyes and exhaled slowly then stood up. "No. No, in fact, I feel better now. Let's see, the important thing is that everything be carried out as quickly as possible."

"Yes," Zelestina added, "can you show us something simple?"

"You wish to economize."

"Yes."

"Ah." Her directness was a little disconcerting.

"What are the prices for coffers?" Zelestina asked.

"Coffers?"

"Coffins," Yellow Bird Daughter said.

"Yes, coffins. Sometimes I mix up words," Zelestina said.

"There are many choices. A simple plank box will do. We do not sell such boxes but we can have one made for you by a carpenter. On the other hand, many people are willing to sacrifice in order to provide the best they can for the deceased. This coffin, for example, though it costs somewhat more, is both beautiful and durable and would honor anyone's memory. Between the satin and the wood exterior is a metal sheathing that keeps moisture out. The lid is fully gasketed to allow no air to enter. The brass hinges are sealed so that they will last hundreds of years even when buried underground. Nothing can get in or out so that those who were with us here on earth will remain undisturbed and unchanged. A model like this is priced at $650.00."

"That is a great deal of money."

The man moved to the child's coffin whose lid had slammed shut. He jiggled the latches.

Inside, Teague tried to move but his knees were jammed up into his chest and one of his arms was wrapped around his head. The other arm was caught behind his back and felt as if it would snap off at any moment. One foot was asleep and the tingling sensation was slowly rising from his ankle to his knee and up toward his thigh. "Goddam," he said, but his voice had grown too weak to be heard.

"Even a small model like this costs a great deal." The undertaker turned back toward the larger coffin but didn't move. "I recognize that it is a lot to spend but the price includes the metallic lining and a second outside metal seal. The viewing is also included in the price though of course with a viewing there will be the cost of appropriate clothing—a hat and gloves in addition to a formal suit. Do you plan to provide clothing?"

"We have nothing."

"We can wash and dress the deceased here."

"Yes, fine."

"I should explain that independent of the other costs there is a $6.00 fee for opening the grave. That's separate. It sometimes varies a little according to the size of the grave but I think I can promise you that it will be no more than $6.00. There's also the hearse and a carriage or automobile to the cemetery. The automobile is slightly less expensive but I consider the horse-drawn carriage more stately and dignified. Have you thought about flowers and perhaps music? The flower cost, like the coffin, is entirely dependent upon the type and quantity of flowers one chooses. Music is a flat fee of $15.00." He stopped. "Did you ask something?"

It was Teague who had marshaled his strength and interrupted, saying, "Goddam right I did. What do you think you're doing?"

The undertaker lifted his hand from the child's casket. "Yes, of course, what am I doing? I have a brochure that lists all services and fees. If you'll wait just a moment." He left the room, returning in a few moments carrying a large envelope. "Yes, here is our current pricing information." He handed this to Zelestina who because she could not read English handed the envelope to Yellow Bird Daughter who read very well, having learned English at the Lame Deer Mission

School. There was engraving plate; disinfecting rooms; transport, including wagon deliveries and city calls (coach); death notices and announcements; crape, door crape, and canopy; folding chairs; catafalque and drapery; candelabrum and candles; outlay for lot; removal or shipping charges; porters and watchers.

"Actually, we will need very few of these services."

"Of course, but you may wish to give the matter some thought. Forgive me for a certain necessary indelicacy in saying that we have modern refrigeration and so can offer the luxury of reflection."

Yellow Bird Daughter, who felt lighter by the moment, said, "We won't need to reflect. The simplest thing will be fine."

"Yes, the plain and simple thing," Zelestina agreed.

When the two women left, the undertaker followed them outside and down the steps where he nodded, bowing slightly, and said, "Good day then." When he stepped back onto the porch, he leaned on the bell which he could easily hear as it rang loud and clear from inside. He opened the door, went in, and returned to the room where the child's coffin sat locked shut. He jiggled the latches. He went for the key but when he inserted it into the lock, it did nothing. "They sent the wrong key?" He walked around the coffin and noticed that the hinges on the back were rusty as if the coffin had been stored for many years in a damp basement. He gave the box a good rap with the palm of his hand and went for a hammer with which he gently tapped at the latches. They were completely intransigent. He began to strike them harder and the room was filled with the ringing of the metal fittings. Unable to cover his ears, Teague's head vibrated with each blow.

Five days later at the graveyard, it was necessary to break the frozen earth open with a pick. It seems like it's always winter when someone dies. Well, winter lasts a long time in Wolf. As the gravedigger swung again and again, he began to sweat and the sweat froze around the edge of his hat and scarf. Even the air seemed as hard and unremitting as the earth. But the gravedigger kept at it, pulling the soil up from the earth and scattering it to one side of the hole. The misshapen chunks of dirt formed a rocky mound. The man swore at his work then crossed himself and went on.

Zelestina thought of Arnegi where, though it was only a small village, someone was always being buried—and not only those who were old or who had died in accidents and from illnesses, in fistfights, or from bad luck. A boy not yet twenty had been shot by a Spanish border patrol as he crossed the Pyrenees hauling a cartload of bracken. The Spanish and French governments called him a smuggler. There had been another boy almost exactly Zelestina's age who'd fallen on a pitchfork.

The day after the grave had been dug an undecorated pine box holding Thomas Teague's remains was lowered into the ground. The gravedigger wondered that there was no funeral and walked to the two women who stood at some distance beside a leafless cottonwood tree. When he asked them about dropping a handful of dirt into the grave, they waved him away. And when he bent over to pick up a clod of dirt himself, he realized it would be impossible to crumble the frozen earth. He stood for a moment holding the large chunk then dropped it into the hole. It landed on the coffin lid with a heavy thud. After that, he began the serious work of shoveling back into the ground the dirt he had so recently removed.

Teague, who had managed after hours of arduous work to slip between the tiny gaps in the hinges of the child's coffin, stood away leaning on the same tree Zelestina and Yellow Bird Daughter stood beside. He was close enough to touch them though of course he had no material presence with which to touch anything. Still, he could make them uncomfortable and Yellow Bird Daughter shivered. Teague stared at her for a few minutes then crossed a frozen irrigation ditch and stood next to the gravedigger who was just finishing his work. Though Yellow Bird Daughter wrapped her arms around herself and ducked her head down into the collar of her coat, she couldn't stop shivering.

"That's it," Zelestina said. "Let's go home where we can rest. My side aches and I'm tired and I don't think you are quite recovered."

Teague stood leaning on the tree where the women had stood moments before. He swore he could smell them—the stink of the living who carry their bodies like rotting fruit. He should have gone where the dead go though maybe it was better he stay on earth, a puff of unknown wind that couldn't do much harm. The gravedigger stopped and leaned on his shovel for a moment. He squinted. He'd seen something move behind a tree. It was a round dark silhouette, a badger maybe or some other animal—a skunk or a fox. He hadn't seen it well enough to be sure before it slipped away.

12

Yo Te Daré / Emango Dizut

In the spring after Zelestina's death I started studying Basque. Weird, isn't it? Why didn't I learn the language when she was alive? I went to Lazkao, a small town in Gipuzkoa where there is a *barnetegi*—a language internment camp—called Maizpide. Lazkao is in what the Spaniards call *El País Vasco profundo*—*Euskadi sakona*, the deep Basque Country. The next spring I returned and then the next. I discovered Bernardo Atxaga, author of *Obabakoak*, the mythological tale of his childhood village—spirits in the caves that underlie the hills, dark rains off the coast, whale song, river sprites, *sorginak*, bear men in the woods, priests who carry a whiff of paganism like my grandfather's Old Spice on their cassocks, in short, the ordinary Basque Country. It made me wonder how much I'd misunderstood in Zelestina's stories. Atxaga is also the author of *Gizona Bere Bakardadean*, *Zazpi Etxe Frantzian*, and *Soinujolearen Semea*—*The Accordionist's Son*.

Early in *The Accordionist's Son*, the main character David, a successful Basque immigrant rancher in California, is asked by his Uncle Juan to play a song. Juan is dying and David hasn't played the accordion for years. David's father was a Basque accordionist who played for the fascists and who expected his son to follow in his footsteps. David, as a young man, was a member of the Basque resistance group ETA. Having come to believe violence is not a legitimate means to attain Basque freedom for his country but wanted by the Spanish state, David flees Euskal Herria for California. Years later Juan asks for the song.

"Which song?" David asks.

"The one about coffee—'*Yo te daré, te daré niña hermosa, te daré una cosa, una cosa que yo sólo sé, café!*'"

I will give you, I will give you, beautiful girl, I will give you something, something only I know—coffee!

Then David remembers he'd played the song at the wedding of his Mexican ranch manager more than fifteen years ago. "Yo te daré?"

"Yes, that's the one. Of course you remember it. When I was a young man—really still a boy—herding in Wyoming, some Indians came to my sheep camp. I was afraid of them but it turned out all they wanted was a cup of coffee."

I had the chance to meet Atxaga and spend some time with him in his hometown. We walked around in the rain—into the church and by the school where he'd been a boy during the Franco dictatorship. We went to dinner in a traditional *jatetxe*—restaurant—where the food was delicious. The food is almost always delicious in the Basque Country. It's another way the place is the opposite of Wyoming.

I thought I'd learn the coffee song on the button accordion and then the next time I saw Atxaga I'd play it for him. So I looked up the song on the internet. Nowadays you can look up anything on the internet. Only you don't look things up, you Google them, the name of a corporation becoming a verb. If you haven't Googled Gernika yet, now would be a good time.

When I Googled "Yo te daré" up popped a gazillion YouTube videos and websites with information about the song known both as "Yo te daré" and "Una mañana de mayo."

The word "gazillion" reminds me of a joke that's linked to what I'm talking about. During the early months of the American invasion of Iraq, the American president George Bush (The Younger), who'd attempted to build what he called a coalition of the willing—countries who would support the US invasion—was told that there had been a firefight somewhere near the town of Tikrit and six Brazilian troops were killed. The president, nonplussed, said, "That's terrible. How many is a brazillion anyway?"

At the top of the list of web search results was Mama Lisa's World, a site devoted to poetry, stories, and music for children. There was a recording of a young woman singing "Yo te daré" in a very innocent style while accompanying herself on the guitar. It was as if Mary, Mother of God, were offering up a cup of coffee while singing a lullaby to her five-year-old son Jesus Christ. What might his nickname have been—Chris? Jesse? In Basque maybe *Irits*—something like the one who has arrived. Or the one who has overtaken us. If you look up the verb to arrive—*iritsi*—in the Morris Basque-English dictionary you'll find this example of its usage— *Betiereko bizitza lortu nahi baduzu*. It means "If you wish to attain eternal life." But that's all you'll find. There's no mention of what you must do if you want this eternal life.

My web search also turned up a YouTube video of a French group singing "Yo te daré" while lifting cups of coffee. They sang the words that Atxaga had mentioned which turned out to be the chorus but in the verse the French singers offered only la la la la la la la la la…

I changed my Google request to "Yo te daré lyrics" and found two verses:

Una mañana de mayo cogí mi caballo y me fui a pasear.
Tuve que cruzar la ría de Villagarcia que es puerto de mar.

Dicen que te vas te vas y nunca acabas de marchar de aquí
a ver a esa chica rubia que dicen que tienes en Valladolid.

One morning in May I caught my horse and went for a
    ride.
I had to cross the Villagarcia estuary which is the port.

They say you're leaving, you're leaving and from here
    you'll never finish leaving,
going to see that blond girl they say you've got in Vall-
    adolid.

I pressed on and found a website whose author began by saying that though he was certainly not a music ex-
pert, he felt that the melody and rhythm of "Yo te daré"
along with the lyrics in the form of couplets placed it as a
mid-nineteenth-century Habanera, a dance and song style
that was popular in Cuba and the Mexican state of Vera Cruz.
These are coffee growing areas so it makes sense they might
be the home of a coffee song.

According to the non-specialist, the song's composer is
unknown as is the exact place and date of composition. Some
say the song might be not from Cuba or Mexico but from Gali-
cia because the town of Villagarcia is mentioned. This ignores
the mention of the other town—Valladolid—as well as the
fact that the song shows no relationship to Galician folklore.
Whatever the song's origin, it was known throughout Spain as
a children's song by the end of the nineteenth century.

At this point in the search things took a tumble down the
lane of the surreal. Sometime in 1935 the Falange—the Spanish Fascist party—began singing this children's song as a secret expression of solidarity. It turns out the word "café" is an
acronym for *Camaradas, Arriba Falange Española*—Comrades,
up with the Spanish Fascist party. Spanish fascists sang the
café song to give warning about danger—the presence of the
police, say, or Republican sympathizers.

And so we arrive at July of 1936 when at The Yellow Plains in the Moroccan Valley of Ketama, the Spanish Popular Front Republican government was carrying out military training maneuvers. At the last supper of the training program, when the dessert arrived, officers who had decided to attempt a coup sang the old children's song ending with the word "CAFÉ!" From that point on "Yo te daré" was a rallying cry for Spanish fascism.

Why had Atxaga made his exiled anti-Franco character play this song at the Mexican ranch manager's wedding in California? And why would Uncle Juan, a staunch Basque supporter of the Spanish Republic ask for the song in the last weeks of his life? And why would I, telling the story of a Basque immigrant who arrived in Wyoming in 1902 and never saw Euskal Herria again, include all this material from the fascist nightmare that overtook Euskal Herria?

There's more—In 1968 a Spanish band called Los Stop who looked like a cross between the Everly Brothers and Jefferson Airplane recorded "Yo te daré" using the old lyrics but adding a section about going to the beach for love—"*entre murmullo de besos a mi me enseñaste lo que es el querer.*" Among the murmur of kisses you taught me what love is.

You know how on websites there's a place for you to leave comments. Everybody gets to express an opinion. In fact, we've come to conflate having an opinion and democracy. In America, the world's most perfect democracy, we're free to say anything we like and those in power, whether in government or the corporations, are free to ignore everything we say. Still, I got to give my opinion and I'm not in prison being tortured for it. I can't deny that's worth something.

There was a YouTube video of Los Stop's version of "Yo te daré" and below the video an excited listener had written, "I love love love love this song!!!!" That's how people talk on the internet. The same listener then noted that Dmitri Shostakovich had written the song for his 1938 *Second Jazz Suite*.

That's odd. How could a Spanish children's song from the mid nineteenth century that was used as a fascist anthem in 1935 have been written by Shostakovich in 1938? Shostakovich called his piece "Waltz Number 2." The *Second Jazz Suite* from which it was taken was lost during WWII. In 1999 a piano score of the suite was discovered and the three parts of the suite that were reconstructed from this score were premiered in London in 2000. But it turned out that "Waltz Number 2" was not actually part of the *Second Jazz Suite*. Rather, it was written for Shostakovich's *Suite for Variety Orchestra*. Anyway, the waltz is almost entirely plagiarized from the Spanish children's fascist song "Yo te daré."

You can spend way more time on the internet than is healthy and this day I did just that learning a little more about the evacuation of Basque children from Bilbo during the Fascist blockade of that city during the Civil War. The Basque autonomous government, struggling to keep civilians safe while fighting raged along the coast of Gipuzkoa and Bizkaia, asked for help in finding temporary homes for the area's children.

The British navy ran the fascist blockade and some 15,000 Basque children were taken on board British ships and delivered to families or orphanages in France, England, Denmark, the Netherlands, and Russia. When the children who ended up in Russia disembarked, they sang "Yo te daré" for their Soviet hosts. Shostakovich must have heard these children and later composed his waltz, forgetting where the melody had come from. He claimed to write only what was dictated to him in dreams. And in dream resides the twisted memories of our daily lives.

After the fascists defeated the Republic with the help of the Catholic Church and the Nazi army and air force, Franco settled down to run the dictatorship that would last from 1939 to 1975. One of Franco's first acts was to declare Spain neutral in World War II while making arrangements for Spanish aid to Nazi Germany. Around 50,000 Spanish fascists who all would have known the coffee song served in the Nazi Wehrmacht between 1941 and 1943. They fought mostly on the eastern front where thousands of them died in the siege of Leningrad. Leningrad was also where two to three thousand Basque children had been evacuated for protection.

When World War II ended, Franco wouldn't let the children back into Spain. It didn't matter since Stalin wouldn't let them out of the Soviet Union. They were shuttled from orphanage to orphanage, winter after winter, while the dying Spanish fascists lay whispering "*yo te daré . . . una cosa . . . te daré . . . solo yo sé . . . café,*" the ghostly words drifting across the snow back to Spain.

13

A Train Ride

It was on Friday afternoon of a long week in the hottest part of summer when God finished lining a stretch of track across the breaks of eastern Wyoming. There was no way he'd make it to Wolf. He wasn't even going to make it to Clearmont. He'd worked straight through the standard eight-hour day plus three to four hours overtime on Tuesday, Wednesday, and Thursday. With time-and-a-half for overtime it was good money but a person needs a few hours to eat and sleep and maybe do other things, too. He didn't have it in him to put in another four hours on a Friday night and it was already nearly 5:30. He'd go in on Saturday.

I've been in the same boat—sweat dripping down my forehead into my eyes and sawdust in my shirt itching like crazy and bone tired and not finished. Once late on another hot summer afternoon when I was working in a ski pole factory, I ran an electric drill bit through the fleshy part of my hand between my thumb and forefinger. I was lucky that the bit spun only through flesh—a lot of blood but no bone or nerve damage. A smarter man would have quit work an hour earlier and gone for a beer with friends. Life is, after all, more than work even when the work is the creation.

What if God relaxed? What if he didn't put so much weight on his ambition, his need to create the universe? On one page after another in the Bible God did this and that and then he looked at it and said, "That's good. That's good. That's good." Everything's so Goddamn good. Did he ever look at the design of the horse's leg? It's an injury waiting to happen. Or did he ever find himself in a high meadow when a wolf pack brought down an elk? One time hearing an elk scream in pain and he might have reconsidered that chunk of creation. Then there are intestinal parasites. God made the intestinal parasites and when he finished he looked down and said, "That's good."

We'd all be better off if we quit judging other things and especially other people and let things be. I'm aware that I've made a case for judging both God and Teague but maybe I'm wrong about both of them. What the hell is good and bad when it comes to the leaves on a cottonwood tree? A cottonwood after all doesn't ask itself if its leaves are good; a cottonwood simply makes leaves.

I don't know how God feels about this. Imagine him being interviewed for some Hollywood movie magazine and the quasi journalist asks him what he feels looking back on his oeuvre. "Any regrets?"

"*Oy gavalt*, my mother always said I was a *luftmensch*. 'Come down from the clouds,' she'd yell at me."

"Your mother would yell at you?"

What kind of a God would create Thomas Teague then have the poor bastard shoot himself accidentally? The answer is clear—a God capable of making a mistake, that is, a journeyman worker doing the best he can. And a workingman has to admit to himself that he makes mistakes. You're building a house and you've hammered in the last of a corner that isn't quite plumb or level and what do you do? You invent trim to cover your mistake.

It's like my uncle said one day when we were worming bulls, "If a man wants to get the work done, he can't be afraid to put his hands down into shit and blood." I'll repeat that every man who ever worked knows he's made mistakes. If your work is to create the universe you may make more than one or two mistakes.

Now it's late on the sixth day. God checks his watch and says, "Screw it. I've done everything I can for now. I'm going to take a day to rest." He slams his tools back into the storage locker and he walks away from the job site and the train line stops at Clearmont.

Because God quit work thirty miles east of Wolf, it was up to man to find a way between the two towns—horseback, on foot, or by stage. Public coaches had plied the rutted road for years. A person could buy a ticket and settle down for a long slow uncomfortable journey like the one Zelestina made that first February. During the course of a full day and a long evening, the battered passenger is given ample opportunity to meditate on God and his creation. If the passenger reached no conclusion regarding these things, there was the return trip.

The coach road would have served for eternity but men, filled with their own version of Godlike ambition, decided to extend the railroad without much thought of what nowadays are called unintended consequences.

An announcement appeared in the *Wolf Weekly* stating the intention of a number of investors to organize a telephone company. A list of twenty subscribers appeared with the announcement. In no time there were twenty-five more and suddenly the human voice was able to enter a single-wire grounded circuit and travel as electrical particles from one point to another. The voice then emerged and, insofar as it was connected to a living speaker, remained partly human.

Even people who had no telephones in their homes or offices could walk into the exchange at the Great Western Hotel lobby and, for a small charge, make a call to any house in town where a telephone had been installed.

Immediately after wiring up town, work started on getting telephone service to the county. Trees were skinned to make poles and the poles were hauled down the mountain. Holes were dug and the poles mounted. Wire was strung up. The ground along the creek was flat so the work was easy and went fast. Now, for another modest surcharge, subscribers could send their partly human voice thirty miles farther into the galaxy.

So much of what we do looks like a conspiracy against God's will but there can be no such conspiracy as God's will is all there is. God designed and made all things living and dead. He knows everything that is happening and will happen. God is like the United States during the presidency of Barack Obama, the first president to order the monitoring of every telephone call made in the country. When pollsters asked Americans what they thought about the fact that their government was recording and storing every phone call they made, over sixty percent said they thought that if this helped keep us safe from terrorists then it was ok. At the same time, immediately after the monitoring was revealed, there was a national spike in the sales of George Orwell's dystopian novel *1984*.

Not to go too far off the tracks but think about these haphazard pictures from Zelestina's life. It's as if someone took photos for years then threw them in a drawer. Hundreds of photos. Sometime later a great grandchild finds them and lays them out on the dining room table, trying to make sense of what happened and who the people are. A photo may capture 1/60th of a second or 1/500th. A single second holds the entirety of a life like an atom holds the energy of the universe. Bust that second open and out pour details we have forgotten, details we never noticed, details we buried to save our souls. It is like so many of the Holocaust camp survivors have claimed—it was not the best of us who survived, but the worst. We have to forget what we have done in order to survive.

The French writer Marcel Proust maintained that if nothing happened to a human being after the age of five, there would still be a lifetime of material to write about. And the Irish writer James Joyce set out in *Ulysses* to chronicle one man's thought over the course of twenty-four hours. Joyce begins with, "Stately, plump Buck Mulligan came from the stairhead, bearing a bowl of lather on which a mirror and a razor lay crossed. A yellow dressing gown, ungirdled, was sustained gently behind him by the mild morning air. He held the bowl aloft and intoned:..."

It doesn't matter so much what Buck intoned—it was something in Latin—but that he intoned. A moment later, Buck said, "For this, O dearly beloved, is the genuine Christine: body and soul and blood and ouns. Slow music, please. Shut your eyes, gents. One moment. A little trouble about those white corpuscles. Silence, all."

How many of us know what an ouns is? I didn't and I still don't. I looked it up in the Oxford English Dictionary—the old unabridged one that's printed on corpuscle thin sheets of paper and the print's so small you can't read it so the Oxford press sends a magnifying glass in a drawer built into the case that holds the two heavy volumes of the history of our language. The point is I looked up ouns and it ain't there.

How about the ungirdled dressing gown lying there on Joyce's first page? I'm still thinking about Mary's rise to Heaven in all her bodily glory and of her girdle tossed down to Thomas like a bouquet of roses. I've dreamt of having sex with Mary and I'll bet you lots of other people have too—both gay and straight.

Unlike the coach or horseback or walking, the train was fast and pleasant with cushioned seats and glass in the window frames. A person could easily and comfortably go somewhere, do something, and return without being missed.

But everything isn't a conspiracy, not by God or novelists or entrepreneurs or presidents. There's that old blues song "Jesus on the Mainline." Call him up and tell him what you want . . . the line ain't never busy . . . if you're sick and wanna git well . . . if you're feeling down and out . . . and so on. God is like a 900 chat line. It's not an 800 line—you pay to call. Still, He's sitting by the phone waiting to hear from you. Or maybe God is on break and it's Mary who will answer your call and speak sweetly to you of desire.

Then God's back from his break and settling down by the phone for eternity. Maybe now and again he's tempted to make an outgoing call. Maybe a prank call. Maybe the conspiracy was God throwing our expectations of him for a loop. If God never surprises you, what kind of God is he?

The first train to roll down the new track shuddered to a stop south of the creek near a cottonwood grove that would by the time I got to Wolf be a town park. In the light of the setting sun the dirty smoke from the engine's coal-fired boiler turned pink and gold and made the nearby station and waiting wagons appear to waver slightly. Zelestina, along with most of the town, had turned out to celebrate the inaugural run.

The whistle blew and in the moment when it was loudest, Zelestina opened her mouth and screamed. Howled. Around her, people were pointing and laughing and congratulating themselves on the progress of Wolf. Children ran forward to touch the iron wheels. Their parents pulled them back, scolding them and warning how dangerous the train was, how a train could crush you as it passed. Dogs barked and attacked one another. The engineer ran steam to the whistle again. This time Zelestina clapped her hand over her mouth and looked around, embarrassed. But everyone was shouting and laughing and throwing hats in the air. Men were pinching women who were not their wives.

Zelestina was thinking of the stationmaster. Her thoughts were so loud she feared people would overhear but there was so much noise no one could hear anything. And even if they heard, no one would care what someone else feared or desired. The stationmaster had showed up at the August 15 Celebration of the Assumption. He'd appeared several times at the dining room of the Hotel Ipar Haizea. He'd even spoken to her—casually, you know, "Hello, Miss Urza, nice night, a little cold, maybe snow later, a little hot, maybe rain if we're lucky…" Blah, blah. Once she'd seen him in the hardware store when she was buying a new ax head for the Christiansens. He was carrying a can of roofing tar and a length of rope.

When the whistle's note faded and the steam stopped billowing along the right of way and the fire took its last breath and the metal wheels no longer scraped slowly along the iron rails, the train looked bigger, the way an elephant's magnitude surprises us when we see the beast up close even if we have seen a thousand pictures. Passengers stumbled down from the cars and station employees hurriedly unloaded crates and boxes and canvas bags. A porter went through the three passenger cars picking up trash and then invited the next group of travelers on board. In a few minutes the coal boiler was fired up again, the train left, and there was silence. People looked at each other and shook their heads wondering what other new things might be on the way.

The next week another blackened engine arrived and three days after that a third train. Like the first two, it stopped briefly in Wolf then was gone. Soon the trains came twice daily—the morning train heading to Clearmont and the east, the afternoon train heading to Fetterman City and the north. These trains carried a mounting pile of culvert pipe, surveyor's tripods, rough cut planks, nails, purified water, seed Jerusalem artichokes, domestic utensils including newly designed toasters and eggbeaters, and formal evening wear for both men and women.

One day among the products and passengers, there was Zelestina Urza, who sat staring out a window as the creek flashed past. She had paid $1.15 for her round trip passage. When her ticket was punched, she carefully put the return stub into her coat pocket. Now and again she slipped her hand into the pocket to make sure the ticket was there. A week earlier, Zelestina had made a telephone call to the Clearmont stationmaster. "I have been thinking of the past," she'd said, "and studying this grammatical form you call the present perfect. Is that right?"

"Present perfect. Yes, I believe so. I'm not much of a grammar specialist though."

"No, but English is your mother tongue, *ezta*? And you studied it in school."

"Yes, but you've been here some years now and you speak about as well as I do."

"I have been working hard but you are very kind, also.

"No, it's not kindness."

"With the present perfect I think a person must have something to say about both the present and the past."

Uncertain how to respond, the stationmaster said, "I'm pleased to receive your call. The telephone is so new, I don't get many calls and the ones I do get are mostly messages concerning railroad business—items lost in shipping, or bills of lading and the like. Where are you calling from?"

"I'm in Wolf."

"Does that mean you have a telephone at home? I hear they're putting phones in everywhere, that people are crazy for phones."

"Oh, no, I'm at the exchange in the Great Western Hotel lobby. Crazy for. What is crazy for?"

"It means mad about though I bet that's a hard phrase, too. Crazy for is when you love doing something. A man likes to read in the evening after work, say. If that man really likes reading a lot, he's crazy for reading. If a young man's crazy for winter, he's probably keen on ice fishing. Though most young men are crazy for young women rather than for winter."

There was silence on the line and the stationmaster felt a little embarrassed. "Hello?" he said.

"Yes. What about this mad about and keen on?"

"Oh, they're about the same—both mean you like something quite a lot."

"I like these expressions—keen on, mad about, crazy for. A person should be crazy for something. Here in town the trains are coming and going every day. The first day I came here, that freezing day I fell down, I had to sit in the cold coach then get down and run to come to Wolf. It seems a long time ago and I wonder about time. With the train the past seems farther away. Maybe it's how fast a train can go so the time goes faster, too and the past goes away faster. I feel some days that I have been here in Wolf a thousand years."

She was talking about second chances. D. H. Lawrence wrote a novel on this that he called *The Escaped Cock*. Some of his early publishers called the book *The Man Who Died* but Lawrence never approved of that title. He told a friend, "I wrote a story of the Resurrection, where Jesus gets up and feels very sick about everything, and can't stand the old crowd any more—so cuts out—and as he heals up, he begins to find what an astonishing place the phenomenal world is, far more marvelous than any salvation or heaven—and thanks his stars he needn't have a mission any more."

Jesus staggers out of the cave. Blinking in the sunlight of a new day, he wanders away. Maybe he's had a concussion or he's weak from loss of blood or just plain woozy from being dead. Whatever. He takes off by himself and comes upon a monastery only it's not Christian but Hellenic—the last monastery for the Greek goddesses. Jesus gets a second life, for sure, but on earth rather than in Heaven and on this earth he experiences the physical union of a man and a woman along with the possibility of true love.

The stationmaster blinked and said, "I would be very pleased to see you. You could come out here on the train. We could have dinner and you could see the siding and the station. Perhaps you would like a walk along the edge of the hills. It's not as green as I've heard your Basque Country is but with the sun shining and the blue sky it's pretty in its own way. Or I could show you how we operate the signal lanterns and semaphores. These tell the engineer if it's safe to proceed." He stopped, fearing he'd gone too far.

"*Ongi*," Zelestina said.

"*Ongi?*"

"Yes, *ongi*. It means fine. I am happy to come on the train."

"*Ongi*. Perhaps you can teach me a few Basque words."

At Clearmont the train came to a stop in its usual grinding of metal parts. Already accustomed to the nerve jangling noises of modernity, no one looked up. Zelestina stepped down without slipping or falling though she made a little pretend gesture of sliding forward and the stationmaster, in the middle of taking off his hat, smiled. He held out his hand then uncertain how he should greet her let it drop. She, though, had put out her hand too so he hurriedly brought his back up and they met in the manner of two businessmen who were on friendly terms.

They walked across the street to the station restaurant where they ordered lamb, potatoes and cabbage, and matching pieces of pie made from canned cherries that had come on the train. Both uncertain what might happen after the meal, they ate slowly. When they finished the pie, they drank coffee.

Then it was time for their walk. They toured the complete and up to date Clearmont railroad facilities and Zelestina spoke of her first day in Wyoming when she stepped down, slid on the ice, and knocked herself out.

"I was very concerned," the stationmaster said. "You could have been seriously hurt. And it was very cold." He didn't mention her skirt thrown up by the wind. "Even when you came around, I had no way to talk to you, to find out how you felt. I'm sorry about that."

"Thank you but don't worry. I wasn't hurt."

They passed the coal storage sheds, the water tower, and the repair shop. "We have no roundhouse here you know. The trains come from the east, stop, and travel on to Wolf or to Fetterman City then Montana. Trains coming from the west and north also stop here then go on east, some as far as Pierre and St. Paul. But none stop here then return. It's mostly a spur for shipping. No one planned it as a passenger line. Of course, we do carry passengers, too." He paused. "Do you want to know anything in particular about trains?"

She looked around. "No, it's not for trains."

Uncertain if that was a language lapse, he said, "Trains are about all I know. My work is pretty much my entire life."

"And your family?"

"I don't have a family. Well, not here. I have a brother and two sisters in Virginia but I never married. I don't know."

Zelestina wanted to say more but didn't. She had no real plan. It would be more honest to admit that she had a plan whose nature she was reluctant to express. What about God's plan? He seemed to be encouraging her with the railroad. Maybe God was leading her where he wanted to go but couldn't go himself. Maybe God was hanging on that 900 line, filled with his own longing for Zelestina. It's too bad the closest God came to marriage was in the imagination of D. H. Lawrence. A companion could have made the work of creation easier and more satisfying. And even if he worked alone, he could have come home from those long hot days knowing that somebody would be there to buoy him up and he would be happy, too.

"I want to tell you the truth," Zelestina began. "In my homeland young people have many ways to learn to know each other. Everyone in every village knows many people— fathers, mothers, cousins, children, neighbors."

"It can be like that here, too."

"No, here I am alone. Already much time has gone by and I hope to be careful without waiting too long."

No woman had ever spoken to the stationmaster like this before. It was the mess with Teague that set Zelestina on this path. Imagine him being gone, life feeling in some ways settled and clear then he shows up and there's a nightmare of a row ending in Zelestina getting shot and Teague accidentally shooting and killing himself. You might think about the time you have in life and what you want to do with it.

"I'm trying to say that perhaps two people should know each other somewhat before they decide things that will be permanent. God, I hope, will understand this and maybe this is part of his plan."

"I understand and perhaps it's better not to speak of God's plan. Perhaps it's better not to speak."

"In only a few hours the evening train from the east will come and I must then get on it. I'm happy that you have met me here again and that we have talked and that I have been taking a walk—that is the present perfect. But when I return to Wolf, I will be alone."

"Yes, I understand. It's not necessary to always be alone but I understand and I have been and now am speaking in agreement with you." He smiled and said, "Speaking now in the present perfect tense."

He ushered Zelestina into the station office, opened a drawer in the desk, and took from it a key. He looked around the room as if he were memorizing the particular shade of off-white paint that covered the walls, the depth of brown in the molding that ran along the top of those walls, the color of Zelestina's eyes and the way her hair was folded under itself at the back of her neck. He'd long dreamt that he might find himself in this position but he'd never quite felt the magnitude of it, the atmospheric pressure against his bones and flesh. I imagine those astronauts when they first blast off and the G force grows heavier and they can feel the flesh of their face being pulled back toward the earth.

The stationmaster opened the door behind the desk and stepped aside. Zelestina passed slowly in front of him, not touching him. Then the stationmaster followed her into the second room. Inside, he closed the door and, once again, locked it.

Though the room was furnished with a cot and small chest of drawers, and though there was a sink and mirror opposite the cot, it felt no more personal than the office. It was a place where the stationmaster could sleep when he worked late and didn't feel like going home only to return in a few hours. There was a wood stove which the stationmaster now bent over to make a fire. "Need to take the chill out of the air." On the shelf below the mirror was a bar of soap and a razor. A small square of cloth hung from a nail hammered into the far end of the shelf.

"Please take this key."

"Yes?"

"You can let yourself out with it." He handed her the key. If she refused, he would accompany her back to the train. But she accepted it, put it in the pocket of her coat, took the coat off, and sat down on the end of the cot.

"Will you wait for a moment?" She nodded and the stationmaster crossed the room to the sink and toilet. Hoping it wasn't too rude, he pulled the curtain around him and stood before the mirror. He took off his shirt and looked at his face and torso. He thought of his parents and grandparents, his uncles and aunts, his brother and two sisters, his many cousins. How had he come to be alone? He was secretly pleased that Zelestina felt equally alone then was ashamed.

He wet his hands, took the hard bar of soap, and washed his face then he lathered his face again with the same soap and picked up his razor. It was quiet in the room. He was sure

Zelestina could hear the scraping of the razor across the stubble on his face.

When the train whistles blew, the prairie dogs dove into the earth, the mule deer leapt fences, and the pronghorn scattered through the sagebrush running wildly as if they'd just fallen to earth from a distant star.

Was this the way it should be? He had imagined a courtship—taking Zelestina to dinner in Wolf, bringing roses and asking the serving girl to put them on the table. The girl would go to the kitchen and come back with an empty jar she'd rinsed out. She'd set the jar on the table, put the roses into the jar, look at them for a moment to make sure they were arranged nicely, and step back into the kitchen. The other diners would applaud, lift their wine glasses, and wish the loving couple health and long life. Then everyone would sit together at a single long table like a family and eat. Now the serving girl would bring more red wine, bowls filled with potatoes and garbanzo beans, oval platters of mutton, or roast beef, soups made from garlic and onions, green beans, wheels of bleu cheese, and hard rolls. The same food he'd seen spread out on the tables at the Basque picnic.

After dinner Zelestina and the stationmaster would go upstairs to the room that was reserved for them when they came to town. They would slowly undress. Though the stationmaster loved everything about Zelestina's body, he loved best her legs and when she wrapped them around him, he lay back amazed. That's what he'd imagined.

I pictured the stationmaster rinsing the whiskers off his razor then wondered if he'd used a safety razor or a straight razor. I looked down at the page and saw that I'd typed whispers not whiskers, the P on the keyboard being up one row and one letter to the right of the K. Rinsing the whispers off his face.

It doesn't matter how he shaved—maybe aliens landed and offered him a magic gizmo that he waved around before his face and the gamma zipryonical rays removed his whiskers. I remember the first time I fell in love and had no idea if the feeling was real or some kind of delusion. And I remember how afraid I was—what if I loved someone who would never love me back. This is the terrible truth of being human—that you can be so easily hurt. Not wanting to be hurt, some people just stop being human. You don't have to go to a distant galaxy to find a planet of aliens.

Rinsing off his razor, the stationmaster meditated on what he had to offer this woman—a small house that belonged to the railroad. That was nothing since if he lost his job he lost his house, too. He had a few books, a horse and wagon, a rifle and several boxes of shells, a formal hat that had been given to him by a friend, some framed photographs of people he hadn't seen in several years, a good pair of boots, a not so good pair of boots, and a metal trunk where he stored his winter blankets. Like the house, the blankets belonged to the railroad. The trunk was his.

He set the razor on the shelf next to the bar of soap. He washed his neck and underarms. He unbuttoned his pants, pulled them and his underwear halfway down, and washed his genitalia. It embarrassed him a little to touch himself and to think of her knowing what he was doing. He again dried his hands, pulled up his underwear and pants, and put his shirt on, carefully smoothing the yoke.

He pulled the curtain open. It was the opposite of that moment in *The Wizard of Oz* when the great and powerful Oz is yelling at the four supplicants who have come to him—one looking for a heart, one a brain, one courage, and one the way home. The little dog Toto pulls the curtain aside and all that great and powerful turns out to be an overweight octogenarian in a three piece suit sweating as he manipulates a set of levers controlling the angry face in the sky, the green smoke, and the scary noises.

When the stationmaster pulled the curtain aside, Zelestina was facing away from him, her shoulders raised and rig-
id. It was as if she had been turned to stone she was so still.
The stationmaster approached her, leaned over and touched
her arm.

"You have goose bumps. You must be cold."

She put her hand up and ran it along his cheek.

Somewhat later, Zelestina closed the door behind her
and, in the outer room, placed the key in the center of the
desk. She stared at it for slightly longer than it took the first
interplanetary probes to go from Florida to Mars, seeking to
learn what strange liquid might run in the mysterious canals
of the Red Planet. I mean that she stared at the key for a long
time then picked it up and put it again in her coat pocket. She
left the building, walked to the platform, and stood waiting
for her train, her arms wrapped around her, shivering though
the air was warmer than when she'd arrived. In front of her,
there was a hill and above it another and above it. All this was
blotted out as the train appeared. The whistle screamed, the
brakes screeched, the engine came to a stop, and Zelestina
got on board.

In the room behind the office, the stationmaster lay on
the cot watching the paint on the walls. It was old paint—dirty
and streaked. Aging, it had come to resemble nothing so
much as an overcast sky on a dark day. Then a wind came up
from the south, the clouds blew away, and sunlight flooded
the sky. Closing his eyes, the stationmaster momentarily forgot the walls.

Part Three

14

Curved Dash

When I met Dr. Arthur Jameson, he was a hundred and two years old. Even at that age, Jameson was excited by progress. He was the first resident of the Cottonwood Care Center who owned a cd player and he lived long enough to be the first one to own an iPad.

Dr. Jameson was also Wolf's first dentist and the first person in town to own an automobile. I knew about him because of this love of cars that he shared with Zelestina. They both put their faith in the automobile. Jameson ordered his first internal combustion powered vehicle from the Ransom Eli Olds Company. When he told me about that long ago car, he called it a light locomotive.

"It was like a little train engine, you see. Only you didn't need a track. You could go just about anywhere. Well, in theory." He grinned and his 102-year-old face became a mask reminiscent of the devil at a cocktail party celebrating the discovery of the speed of light.

In Quebec people sometimes say, *"Je vas met' d'gaz dans mon char."* Then the high school French teacher says,

"Remember, students, in French the correct word for automobile is *voiture—ça c'est ma voiture. Char* is a loan word from the English car used by poorly educated French speakers who don't know any better."

But char is as French as soufflé or camembert and much older. It comes from the Latin *carrus*. French is, after all, degenerate pigeon Latin. In the *Nouveau Petit Larousse* char is defined as, "among the ancient peoples a two-wheeled vehicle used for combat." A chariot. In standard French, char is used as in *char de combat* or *char d'assaut*. In English that's a tank. In both languages the definition is a caterpillar tracked armored vehicle mounted with machine guns, cannons, flamethrowers, rockets, etc. My favorite part of the definition is etc. I was hoping that meant paintball. According to *Larousse*, the British in World War I manufactured and used the first tanks so maybe char really is to some degree a loan word from English.

For Dr. Jameson the car was exciting, symbolic, practical, liberating, etc. It marked him as modern and would not for many years devolve into what it is now—a chain around our neck disguised as a noisome bad habit. It is not lost on me that Zelestina was born before automobiles existed. Maybe there were some early prototypes, I'm not sure but I know that for her entire childhood in Arnegi people walked or they sat in wooden wagons whose ride was so rough that it would break the bones of the fragile old.

The Algerian French writer Albert Camus in his 1957 Nobel Prize acceptance speech first expressed his gratitude and his sense of shock then said, ". . . the writer's role is not free from difficult duties. By definition he cannot put himself today in the service of those who make history; he is at the service of those who suffer it. Otherwise, he will be alone and deprived of his art. Not all the armies of tyranny with their millions of men will free him from his isolation, even and particularly if he falls into step with them. But the silence of an unknown prisoner, abandoned to humiliations at the other end of the world, is enough to draw the writer out of his exile, at least whenever, in the midst of the privileges of freedom, he manages not to forget that silence, and to transmit it in order to make it resound by means of his art."

I know Camus wasn't talking about things like the invention of the car but I feel that so much of modernity oppresses in ways that are even more devastating than political tyranny and torture. That sounds implausible and may only be the words of someone who hasn't experienced real political oppression. What I mean is that the human world we've made often ends up diminishing our humanity. We become as machinelike as the machines we surround ourselves with.

My wife said something that, though framed in a more lighthearted way, is similar to what Camus expressed before the Swedish Royal Academy of Sciences at dinner that night in Stockholm. It was years later and she was sitting at her desk sifting through the mounds of paper, Kleenex, plastic bags, socks, pens that are out of ink, coins, unopened mail, and lists of things to do that she'd made then lost when I heard her say, "Damn... Shit."

"What is it?"

"I lost an email I've got to answer. I don't have the address written down anywhere and I don't know the name of the person who wrote to me. I really have to answer this note and I've somehow deleted the file. I hate computers." She was quiet for a few seconds then went on, "You know how we learned that the Obama administration has been secretly storing the records of all phone calls and emails sent and received in this country and around the world, too?"

"Yes, of course, I even mentioned it in the book I'm writing. It's unbelievable."

"Your book?"

"I meant the Obama administration."

"Since they've finally admitted they can and are keeping digital records of every phone call and email message, I wonder if I could call the White House switchboard and ask them to retrieve my lost email."

"Good idea," I said. "I bet a lot of people could use that help."

Ransom Eli Olds is the man who first made automobiles widely available. In 1901 he designed the Curved Dash and, using manufacturing methods like those Henry Ford would later use to build the Model T, Olds built a vehicle he could make a profit from with a selling price of only $650.00. With the slogan "Nothing to watch but the road," he hired Roy Chapin to drive from Detroit to the New York Auto Show. The two men shook hands, Olds pointed out the box of spare parts in the back of the car, and Chapin set off. A week later he arrived in New York where he took orders for the new Curved Dash. By 1904 over five thousand had been sold.

Dr. Jameson was sure that he could make less burdensome the exigencies of dentistry through the pleasures of the open road. He would treat his patients in their homes rather than in his office—an uninspiring windowless room behind the barbershop. He placed ads in the Wolf paper that read, "If you have a pain in your teeth or your gums, I can cure it right away. And I can be there in minutes both alert and rested as with a simple press of the foot I can travel more quickly and more comfortably than in any horse-drawn conveyance."

Dr. Jameson had been bogged down in mud, blinded by ground blizzards, stopped by swollen creeks or ravines, lost. His tires had been punctured by prickly pear cactus and twice a rock had knocked a hole in his gas tank so he ran out of gas and had to walk miles to town. He liked to walk. It reminded him that the old and new must travel together. In the heat of summer, he carried canvas bags of water tied to the front of the Olds. When the radiator boiled over, he happily waited for it to cool before he added more water. There he sat on the running board watching the sky. He was a man who wanted to go as fast as he could but was never impatient or in a hurry.

"I never saw such a blue sky," Jameson told me when I visited him in the care center. "It must be the altitude."

Zelestina too had been struck by the sky. "I was so lonely when I first came to Wyoming. In Euskal Herria everything is green. The rivers and streams rush down from the hills and the ocean is never far away. It rains and rains. Here it is dry and brown and the prairies are a great emptiness. It was the sky that helped me most—that blue."

"A wonderful thing, the automobile," Dr. Jameson told Zelestina. "And what with the discovery of oil in Texas, the price of gasoline is sure to come down dramatically. I plan to drive everywhere."

"Yes, I agree. You can go anywhere."

Dr. Jameson, who was a member of the Populist Party and who was proud that Wyoming had granted women the right to vote, said, "Yes, and a woman, too, with a car, can go anywhere. She can be as free as a man."

"You think a man is free, then?"

He looked at her thinking that she had awfully nice teeth but said only, "Surely you can see that a woman could learn to drive as quickly and as well as a man."

"I'm sure it's true," she said, for her part noticing that, for a dentist, he had remarkably unattractive teeth. "Yes, I agree that for driving a motor car a woman is no worse than a dentist."

"What on earth do you mean? Being a dentist has nothing to do with driving."

Dr. Jameson, who drove his Olds as fast as he could, had been cautioned by the county sheriff not to hit someone's sheep or cow. "Slow down," the sheriff said. "Yer gonna git where yer goin' soon enuff." The warnings did no good. In summer there was a perpetual plume of dust on the county roads. And in winter, any number of local men had found themselves trudging through the snow with a shovel to where Jameson was stuck in a snow bank.

When I look back, I wonder at the freedom these people had with their cars. There were no drivers' licenses, no speeding tickets, no no-parking zones, no seat belts or airbags, no multiple car interstate pile-ups leaving entire families dead. Or worse—leaving all but one member of a family dead. And there were no in-car GPS computers that the government and advertisers can use to find out where any car has been at any time.

The Bluebird Grocery owner, Skip Brandon, bought the second car in Wolf—a Ford van he used to make deliveries. Skip himself tossed the groceries into the Ford and rushed them to their new owners. As the dentist had been, so the grocer was warned by the sheriff about the dangers of doing his work too rapidly. But, imagine, the two men thought, speeding down the road at thirty miles per hour!

It was possible to drive anywhere as long as the land was flat and without rocks, cactus, rabbit brush, or sage. In Wyoming that meant that in reality a person could drive just about nowhere. In response to this lack of natural driving surfaces the state legislature in Cheyenne appropriated $15,000 for road building equipment including a mule, a scraper the mule would pull, and a large number of picks and shovels. The legislature also authorized the use of convict labor in road gangs. Still, the work was slow and automobiles spent as much time stuck as they did moving. People in Wolf joked that there were now only two seasons in the year—ten months of winter and two months of furious road construction. The old joke was that there had been the same two seasons but that they'd been labeled ten months of winter and two months of bad skating.

We were sitting on Zelestina's porch watching a late summer late afternoon thunderstorm coming toward us. The sky went from bright blue to nearly black and the automatic yard lights started blinking on. The wind whipped up and the rain came down in pellets large enough to splash. Then it hailed and the tomato plants in the garden were beaten to the ground.

"*Beltza zen,*" she said.

"*Beltza.*"

"Black. That first car of mine was black like this sky."

"I think cars were only black in those days."

"Yes, but I didn't know that when I bought the car. I didn't think about it. I didn't want a black car. Black is for dying. I had saved a long time to be able to buy a car and I wanted what I wanted—a real color that would be exciting and people would admire it. I think that Arthur Jameson had bought and sold four or five cars by the time I got my first one. I didn't know who could repaint a car but I took it to the blacksmith because I knew he had painted iron. Aitzol Goikoetxea. That's his name. He's an old man now but he still does good work. Have you met him?"

"No."

"You should. You should meet everyone. We should all meet everyone but there's so little time. You don't feel this yet."

For Dr. Jameson, for Skip Brandon, and for Zelestina the car would change their lives. But the edge of the new wears dull pretty quickly. We see this in Jim Hall's poem "Maybe Dat's Your Pwoblem, Too." The poem's narrator is Spiderman who tells us that all his pwoblems, maybe evwybody's pwoblems are due to da fact, due to da awful twuth dat he is Spiderman. He is called upon to do the same thing day after day and often it is no more inspired than catching a couple of bozos who've stolen a color TV set. Spiderman could care less about color TV sets but he pulls on his suit, his "stinking suit wit da sucker cups on da fingers," and heads out hunting for criminals. He gwabs his wittle bundle of wopes and equipment and goes fwying like cwazy acwoss da town fwom woof top to woof top. When he finds the criminals, they westle awound a wittle bit until he gits 'em all wapped up. He takes them to the powice and then the gubbenuh calls and he does it all over again—the same bozos in different outfits, the same color TVs or maybe microwave ovens, the same embarrassing speech defect or mock Atlantic City Mafioso accent.

So Spider man suffers angst. And this is long before Hollywood taught us that superheroes are as confused and muddled as the rest of us. They're often in worse shape than the rest of us as your stock superhero has the strength of a particle accelerator coupled with the emotional maturity of an enraged thirteen-year-old. Spiderman thinks that his suffering will be relieved if only he can do something different, something exciting "like wacing caws."

"I took the car to Mr. Goikoetxea and asked if he could paint it. He said, 'Of course I can do that—metal's metal.' I can see him looking at me and saying again, 'Of course I can do that' in the tone of a man who believed he could do anything he set his mind to. I've always admired that in men, that way they believe in themselves. Sometimes no matter how much evidence there is to the contrary."

My wife told me about a study on self-esteem—hundreds of people of different ages and stations in life were interviewed and the researchers found that the men with the worst self-esteem felt better about themselves than the women with the best self-esteem.

"Then he said he'd have to take the black paint off before he could repaint the car and how it seemed a shame to remove brand new paint for no better reason than personal whim. He put an awful emphasis on the word 'whim.' Like my level of seriousness was about on a par with a Miss America candidate. Well, let him think what he wants. Anyway, in those days I didn't know about Miss America."

"I don't know if they had Miss America back then," I told her.

"After that he said, 'It'll take a grinder,' and by now I'd had it so I said, 'Fine. Grind away.' Then we got down to business. He would have to give me an estimate and see how he could fit it into his schedule. And what color was I thinking of?

"Something creamy, ivory but with a little more yellow or a little more of hay fields in late summer. Butter and sugar creamed together. That was it—exactly the color I wanted—butter and sugar creamed together. I bet there wasn't another car in the world that color. That was a beautiful car."

I hope Zelestina drove to Clearmont to meet the stationmaster again and again. I never asked her and after telling me about her one trip there on the train, she said no more. I've said a secret is something we agree to pretend we don't know but maybe she and the stationmaster really had a secret. Or maybe not—she told me she kept the key.

I feel a longing for an inner life that is mine alone, that is not to be told to others. When I think I have that, I feel happy. But I don't know what other people feel. I've lived long enough to enter the age of Facebook. People sit down at their computers and tell the world things like, "I'm eating a piece of toast" or "The Lord blesses me everyday" or "I hate stinky animals." We blab our lives away and they disappear like horse farts in the wind.

15

The Pioneers' and Founders' Day Parade

Two-thirds of the people in Wolf were watching the parade while the other half were in it. Two-thirds of one and a half of the other. That's how the great baseball player and ethnolinguist Yogi Berra talked. Berra, a catcher who always managed to be in the right place at the right time, was the American League's most valuable player of the year for 1951, 1954, and 1955.

Apropos of the parade, Berra said, "You can observe a lot just by watching." And apropos of the lives of Zelestina and Yellow Bird Daughter, "When you come to a fork in the road, take it." Apropos of Thomas Teague's death was, "You should always go to other people's funerals; otherwise they won't go to yours." Like all of Berra's sayings, this one was sort of upside down since you didn't want Teague at your funeral so you'd be damned sure not to go to his. Only thing is Teague tended to show up just where and when you least wanted to see him. It's like Yogi said—"If people don't want to come out to the ball park, you can't stop 'em." The most famous Berra quote of all is "It's déjà vu all over again." That's just life whoever's living it. My favorite Yogi-ism was coined not by Yogi but by his son Dale who when asked how he'd compare himself to his father, said, "You can't compare me to my father. Our similarities are different."

This is how I was thinking while sitting in an aluminum lawn chair waiting for the parade to start. Zelestina sat next to me in a similar chair, a slight frown on her face.

"What?"

She shrugged.

"What?"

"I'm an old woman."

"Apropos of nothing, I'd say. Anyway, you don't seem so old."

She snorted. The parade always starts late so we sat watching the clouds in the sky.

"Did you bring a camera?" Zelestina asked me.

"No."

"You don't like pictures?"

"I like pictures, sure, but I feel funny going around with a camera, like a vampire of my own experience watching life but not living it."

"Maybe." She waited a minute then went on. "I've never liked this parade. Not since the first one. I'm glad I didn't have a camera then. I'd have to look at the photos."

"The first Fair and Rodeo Parade?"

"I don't know what they thought they were celebrating. They called it Pioneers' and Founders' Day. That's backwards. The founders come first then the pioneers. Maybe they're the same people."

"Tweedle Dum and Tweedle Dee."

"What?'

"Never mind. What happened?"

"I was standing next to Yellow Bird Daughter. She kept talking about the night Teague broke in and accidentally shot himself.

"'I can't get that porcupine out of my mind,' she said. 'It saved our lives, I think.'

"And I said, 'Yes, it helped us, even if accidentally.'

"'I don't think it was an accident. Many animals help us and we all have an animal part of ourselves. My father's animal helper was Wolverine, the Little Bear. And I think my father wanted to help us but he couldn't be there and he couldn't send Little Bear either because the two were together. The person and the animal have to stay together after death.'"

In Philip Pullman's *His Dark Materials*, human beings are accompanied by a visible animal presence that is always with them. Called the daemon, it's not a pet or a helper or a totem. It's outside the person but it and the person are one being. The animal part of a child can change at will—be a monkey one moment and a moth the next or rise up like a lion to defend itself. When the child reaches puberty the animal settles into one form. The main character in Pullman's novel, a girl named Lyra, is inexpressibly saddened when she thinks of humans who have no daemon and so are alone.

Born about 450 years before Christ, the Greek writer Aristophanes believed that in the beginning humans were both male and female in one body. Each person had four arms and four legs and a face on both sides of the head. Or maybe each person had two heads. Aristophanes was uncertain. These early human beings were psychologically and physically stronger than we are. The gods were afraid of being overthrown so Zeus split the humans in two. Since then we have passed our lives looking for our missing halves. I don't know how Aristophanes thought gay people were configured. I guess we'd be the same only the four legs and four arms and two heads and of course the two sets of genitalia—don't forget the genitalia—would be all female or all male.

Anyway, I feel about humans and animals the way Aristophanes did about male and female. I've spent my life looking for my animal being. But the animals flee. To them I am at best a clumsy intruder and at worst a genocidal psychopath. The Lord claimed that humans were to have dominion over the animals. It's another good reason that no animal with half a brain would want to cozy up to a human being.

As a child I wanted to be an otter. I would go to water—a lake, pond, irrigation ditch, a municipal swimming pool—and lie on my back, paddling about. I'd take a little food—a piece of bread or fruit—and I'd put it on my stomach and eat the way an otter would. Then I'd turn and roll in the water. I didn't do this at the public pool because people would think I was crazy but when I was alone I was half otter.

"Are you listening?" Zelestina said.

"What, oh, yes, well, now yes. Go on."

"I said to Yellow Bird Daughter, 'Do you think your father wanted to help us but couldn't and wanted to send his spirit helper Wolverine but couldn't do that either so he sent a porcupine that lived nearby?'

'I don't know if he sent it. Maybe the power of his wanting to help caused someone else to send it. Someone we don't know. It is often strangers who help us.'"

Zelestina looked at me and said, "What she was saying is that our best option is to recognize the good in strangers. You can cry about life but it won't change anything. So why cry even if you feel like it?"

"I know the feeling. Sometimes things are so painful you have to accept them as funny, ridiculous. It's the absurdity of life."

"I don't know this word 'absurdity.'"

The parade still hadn't started. We sat in silence for a few minutes then she said, "What do you think about what happened to Abraham and Isaac?"

That made me think she was lying about her vocabulary. "I wasn't raised Christian," I said.

"But you know what happened."

"Yes, I know the story."

"Alright, we can call it a story."

"Abraham and Isaac."

"That's right, Abraham and Isaac." She cocked her head.

"You really want to know what I think?"

"Yes. I really want to know what you think."

"Well, it seems like a model of mental illness, something only people out of touch with themselves and the earth would consider."

I was not unaware of the fact that there are over a billion Christians on earth, maybe two billion. I'm sure someone is counting. A billion or two, either way, it's a lot of people who believe something I just called a mental illness.

"The Lord must have had some kind of attack of hubris or maybe he suffered from an overwhelming insecurity complex. He needed validation from somewhere—proof that he was all powerful and all good at the same time. He needed loyalty no matter what or he couldn't believe humans really loved him."

Like my father and me but in reverse. Only I didn't tell Zelestina that. I never talked much about my father. With him I was always wondering if anything I did would ever be good enough and so spent my childhood trying to prove that I was worthy. In the Abraham story God needs to believe he is worthy and can get this feeling only from outside himself— from his creation. God the Father wondered if he were good enough but he had no father or mother to turn to as he'd invented himself then invented the world.

Zelestina waited for me to go on. But I was still thinking—long after his Abraham and Isaac encounter God came to earth as Jesus and announced that he was both his own father and son. Talk about making up for what you're missing. And Mary, who was born thousands of years after God created himself would be his mother from genes magically implanted in her by her own son before he was born.

"A model of mental illness?" Zelestina asked.

I still said nothing, thinking now of the Mark Graham song "Oedipus Rex"—"Oedipus Rex, Oedipus Rex, another sad story of death and sex. Well, you killed your Pa and you married your Ma. They don't even do that in Arkansas."

"It's absurd. I mean if you want to know what absurdity means, the story of Abraham, the Lord, and Isaac is a good example."

"Go on."

"God needed proof that human beings were grateful. And obedient. So God tells his best servant Abraham to take his son and climb up a mountain where at the top Abraham the father will start a fire and burn his son to death as an offering to God. To top it all off, Abraham's son is to carry the bundle of wood that will be the fuel for his personal holocaust. To prove he's a good man, Abraham is to murder his son."

"But it doesn't happen, does it. God stops him. Is that part of absurdity? The stopping?"

"You're pretty shrewd for an old woman."

"I only mean when does absurdity start and stop? I'm a little uncertain about the meaning of shrewd, too."

"If the story reflects life's absurdity, maybe Abraham is shrewd. He goes along, gathers up the wood, gets kindling, loads it on his son's back, lies to his son about what's up, and they head off up Mt. Moriah. Abraham binds his son and is about to douse the kindling with lighter fluid when an angel of the Lord appears and says, 'That's enough. There's no need to actually do it.'"

It's like that moment in the movie *Galaxy Quest* when the universe is about to come to an end and the film's romantic leads played by Tim Allen and Sigourney Weaver, who by the way has had her intergalactic officer's uniform torn to reveal a quite stunning burgundy colored satin bra that was apparently star fleet standard, are poised by the button they're to push to stave off the destruction of the universe. They push it but the timer keeps clicking down the seconds toward the end of the universe and then like a nanosecond before the dial reaches zero and ka-blam it's all over, the machinery whirs to a stop. The hero and heroine are clinging to each other for dear life and when there's no explosion, Sigourney looks around a little dazed, wipes her hair away in a delicate and comely manner and says, "Oh my God, that's how it always happens on the show, it goes right down to the last moment before we're saved."

Zelestina said, "Abraham's experience tells us that if we have absolute unwavering faith we can trust that he will never lead us astray. A faith like that is worth a lot. And a God we can trust that much."

"That wouldn't inspire me to trust. And why is it an angel of the Lord who tells Abraham he doesn't have to kill his son? Why wouldn't the Lord himself bring the good news? Did the Lord even know the angel had shown up? Angels created the first rebellion. Maybe some angel took it upon himself to stop the craziness."

"Herself. Could be herself."

"Of course, I know that. Herself, fine."

"You know there's no gender in Basque. No he or she, her or him. Just this and that. If a person is close to you that person is *hau*—this one—and farther away the person is *hori*—that one. Really far away it's *hura*—that one over there. At that distance you can't tell if a person is male or female anyway. Or an angel."

"Wait, you're saying that because the Lord didn't actually carry out his threat, it was ok. Just a test we had to pass. The Lord would never actually make Abraham kill his son. I've heard this before. But it's no test if there's no carry-through on the consequences of failing the test. That's the case in which Abraham is being shrewd. Or the Lord is being shrewd knowing Abraham knows but says nothing, the two of them trying to outshrewd one another."

Abraham's God was like Richard Nixon during the Vietnam War threatening to use nuclear weapons on the Viet Cong and North Vietnamese. Even his advisors said it was crazy. Nixon said the enemy had to believe he was crazy, had to believe that he was capable of using nuclear weapons and maybe destroying all life on earth in order to defeat the communists in Southeast Asia. If they didn't believe he could do that, then his threats were empty and we'd lose the war.

"If the Lord tells you to burn your son in a holocaust, you have to believe he's willing to see it happen. Otherwise, you just fiddle faddle up the mountain chewing coca leaves or *chicle* and smelling the flowers knowing full well there'll be no pyre up top. If the Lord isn't crazy this way, then the story is pointless. If he is crazy this way, he may be the Lord but he's a madman, too. Either way, when he said, 'take your son and burn him as an offering to me,' Abraham should have said, 'With all due respect sir, I can't do that.' A human being has to grow up, think independently, and use his conscience. Henry David Thoreau suggested that God wouldn't have given us a conscience if he didn't mean us to use it."

"Who's Henry David Thoreau?" Then she paused and waved her hands as if to say, *it's not important.* When she went on, it was to ask, "What about the Lord allowing his son to be killed to redeem humanity? What do you make of that?"

"I don't know why you want me to answer these questions. You've answered them I'm sure."

"Things are strange, I grant you that. Maybe faith is all we've got to face the strangeness. I want to know how other people make sense of things."

"Ok, you asked for it. The church teaches that Jesus is the Lord—one Lord indivisible—The Father, the Son, and the Holy Ghost. This means that sending his son to his death was suicide not murder. But the church condemns suicide, too. Double but—then the Lord used magic to resurrect his dead son who was himself. What died was only the body and apparently the body is not the person. For someone not raised in the Church, this stuff might have been dreamed up by the inmates of an eighteenth-century French insane asylum."

"I agree it would be French," Zelestina said, and smiling, added, "I think I can see the beginning of the parade."

The long ago first parade was to honor the heroism of General George Armstrong Custer and the importance of the sheep and cattle industries. The County Ranchers' Association hoped to celebrate Wolf's growth and put the past to rest. It was time to turn Custer's Last Stand from a sad page in American history into a tourist attraction.

To advertise the parade, Sam Cotter of the Lazy Moon Guest Ranch hired several boys to walk around town putting fliers in doors. "Help your town grow! Come out to watch our first town parade and honor those who made Wolf what it is today." That was ambiguous enough. What Sam Cotter meant was come out and help my business. Sheep and cows had done fine but Sam had been one of the first to see that it couldn't go on forever.

"Only so much grass," he'd said to his neighbors. "Once it's all eaten, it's all eaten. On the other hand, never going to run out of people wanting to visit God's Country and experience again the glorious events of the past."

Starting the Lazy Moon had been a smart move and now other ranchers were switching from cows to people. Even in the early days when the myth of the west was not yet solidified, there were plenty of dudes to go around. They lounged under the pines at Middle Mount on Long Ridge, the Garden of Eden on Lost Creek, and the Circle P on North Fork. These well watered guest ranches attracted the Eastern elite who came out by train stopping in the Black Hills then coming on to spend several weeks in the Bighorns. In addition to the big outfits, there were Mom and Pop operations like The Aspens, The Eagle's Nest, The Teepee Inn, and The Broken Arrow. It

wasn't so much the wealthy who populated these latter re-
sorts as the new middle class, motor tourists driving with
their families from Illinois, Indiana, and Minnesota.

"These dudes drive out here through rain and mud or
heat and dust. Some years it even snows on 'em and they like
it—snow in June, it's exotic. By the time they get here, they're
tired and about plumb wore out and they want good food, a
nice soft bed, the wind whispering in the pines, of course, and
some kind of event, something to do, or see. Like the parade—
cowboys on horseback, sidearms blazing. Look how Bill Cody
took Europe by storm with his Wild West Show. We've got the
Real Wild West. They'll come from the whole world to see it
and they'll tell their friends who'll come next year."

It was Sam Cotter who wrote the proclamation announc-
ing the first parade's theme. "Whereas this being the anniversary of Custer's Last Stand…" and "Whereas we honor the
memory of those who died bravely such that this land might
be opened to civilization and progress…" and several more
such clauses.

The mayor read the proclamation at an evening meeting
in the Wolf Town Hall. In the low ceilinged room, the newly
installed electric lights made the dust motes shine like stars.
The dry leather of the chairs creaked as council members
and guests shifted in their seats. In the few paragraphs of the
proclamation, the infant tourist industry was verified and the
parade was implicitly identified as a vehicle for private profit.
Recent history was to be recreated in a way that made it nearly
unrecognizable to the victims of that history.

"This will be a boon to Wolf," the mayor promised and
the meeting was over.

That night grown men—fathers and uncles and brothers
and grandfathers who'd lived through the last quarter of the
nineteenth century—were overcome by a kind of double af-
fliction. They suffered simultaneously from amnesia and a
never before diagnosed illness we'll call Sudden Enhanced

Memory Syndrome (SEMS). Every man jack over seventy-five—and you'd be surprised how many there were—recalled that he had known George Armstrong Custer personally, and had a story to tell about the great and flamboyant General.

Zelestina had been nervous about mentioning the parade to Yellow Bird Daughter who you recall was half Cheyenne and half Arapaho. These weren't folks who had much to celebrate concerning recent events on the northern plains. Then too Yellow Bird Daughter was born on the day of the Wounded Knee Massacre. You'd think about it.

But Yellow Bird Daughter, who was already known to many as our local Indian said only, "The past is the past." That's about as good as Yogi Berra's quip that "The game isn't over until it's over."

Maybe this is making too much of it. It was a parade after all—the paper floats, the high school marching band, the politicians and local dignitaries, the horses with silver tack, the riders with gleaming boots.

A group of high school girls who had managed to get lipstick on and then get out of their houses wearing it appeared at the double doors leading into the Great West Hotel lobby. When they stepped in, a group of high school boys rose from the lumpy couches that littered the room. The boys loudly negotiated with one another over the right to buy a particular girl a sundae or malt or perhaps a three-scoop banana split.

Afterward, both boys and girls left the lobby and strolled up and down the street looking in the shop windows as if they'd never before seen the products on display. The girls lifted their hands to cover their mouths and so make more discreet their small exclamations of pleasure. When they ran their fingertips along the skin of their arms, the boys' eyes followed.

Looking up the street, a person could see beyond the edge of Wolf to the expanse of prairie flowing away toward

Minnesota. It was hot and though Yellow Bird Daughter wanted to remove her hat and wipe her brow, she didn't. She planned to remain motionless and so, for the duration of the parade, invisible.

"I'm sorry," Zelestina said. "For being so stupid. I don't know what I was thinking."

"No. It's alright. It's only a parade."

"It's not too hot?"

"I like the heat. Anyway, it doesn't look like the buffalo are going to be rising out of the earth any day soon."

"What?"

"It's the Ghost Dance prophecy. Just before I was born there were some who said that if we did the Ghost Dance, then in one year the white people would disappear and the buffalo would rise from the earth to fill the plains once again. My parents were Ghost Dancers."

They could finally see the parade coming up the street—the mayor and town council members waving as they walked along. Behind them came James Hopp driving a horse-drawn buggy. While other people had switched to the faster more efficient automobile, Hopp had remained attached to his horses and wagon. He went everywhere in it hauling seed, hay, wood, and groceries. A week before the parade, he disappeared, locking himself into his "warehouse"—a sixteen by thirty-two foot post and beam structure whose walls were stone mortared with mud. In winter, it was a terrible place to work. Periodically a chunk of mud would freeze and crack then tumble out of the wall leaving a hole through which the wind would come whistling. But in summer it was cool and a few holes in the wall only made it seem airy and light.

The warehouse had a long workbench upon which were scattered a mass of greasy tools. Beneath the workbench were pails filled with nails, rags, wood and coal chips, old newspapers, apple cores, and banana peels. Hopp loved bananas and was willing to pay top dollar for them. He kept a bowl of the fruit on the workbench. At the end of the bench, there was a table vice that Hopp's father Christopher had brought from New York when the family had come to Wyoming. There was also a photograph of Hopp's mother Louise who had died on the journey west.

Hopp had always loved tinkering and though he would turn apoplectic if someone said it, his was the kind of mind that might have invented the automobile. First, he removed the wagon's sideboards and repainted them red, white, and blue. He also removed as much of the metal hardware as he could and polished it with steel wool. To the hub of each wheel he attached four steam bent pieces of willow and, using upholstery tacks, he attached folded paper blossoms to these willow rods. When the wheels turned the effect was of horizontal bouquets whirling down the street. At each corner of the wagon, Hopp mounted a one-inch diameter piece of turned wood that served as both a flagpole and support for a line running around the perimeter of the wagon six feet above it. On these lines hung Hopp's personal manifesto against the invention of the automobile and more generally against progress.

When asked about his atavistic opinions, Hopp said, "There are ghosts everywhere. They walk among us. But some people don't believe in ghosts. No, they believe in time."

Besides the manifesto and the whirling paper flowers, there was a carved bear, its head uplifted, sniffing the air. There was a mountain lion poised to leap and an eagle trying to carry away a lamb. Salmon swam upstream through strips of undulating sheet metal. The spawning fish were mounted on steel rods which ran on a chain attached to two flywheels. These were attached to a third flywheel set at a ninety-degree angle to the first two. The wheels turned a gear that by its attachment to another gear turned a chain so that the fish quivered and leaped, swimming upstream as Hopp's wagon rolled up the soon to be paved main street of Wolf. Just ignore the fact that salmon never got to the streams around here.

Behind Hopp's wagon were two high school girls, their hair tied up in braids and adorned with wildflowers. Wearing white dresses as a representation of purity, the girls carried a banner proclaiming in large red letters, "Wolf Honors the Memory of those Brave Men who Died at Custer's Last Stand." Below this in smaller black letters were the words, "The Order of Job's Daughters, Bethel 3."

The high school marching band played "The Battle Hymn of the Republic" and the high school fight song "Hail Wolf." After the band there was a group of children with their cats and dogs and rabbits and even a deer led by a girl half the size of her pet. The minister of the Danish Evangelical Lutheran Church led a collection of lambs that though tied together clattered and banged in every direction. Now and again a lamb fell and was dragged along the street until the minister helped it up. Following this was nearly every automobile in Wolf and the two town policemen in starched uniforms riding what appeared to be sedated horses. The volunteer fire department members walked next to the new motorized fire engine. The ladies of the Wolf beautification committee pulled carts carrying small fir trees that, after the parade, would be planted along the creek in the town park. Following the planting there would be a speech by the mayor and the grounds would be renamed Custer Memorial Park.

The last entry in the parade was the town band dressed as Custer's Seventh Cavalry. The band had learned to play the two songs General Custer always asked for before his troops went off to battle—"Garryowen" and "The Girl I Left Behind Me." Custer chose "The Girl I Left Behind Me" for its romantic and sentimental allure. "Garryowen" was a more strident piece, one Custer may have imagined played on highland pipes though it was an Irish drinking song that had no military significance:

Let Bacchus' sons be not dismayed
we'll break windows, we'll break doors,
but join with me each jovial blade,
the watch knock down by threes and fours.
Come booze and sing, and lend your aid
then let the doctors work their cures
to help me with the chorus
and tinker up our bruises.

Instead of spa we'll drink down ale,
we'll beat the bailiffs out of fun
and pay the reck'ning on the nail.
We'll make the mayors and sheriffs run,
no man for debt shall go to jail
and are the boys no man dares run
from Garryowen in glory
if he regards a whole skin.

We are boys that take delight in
smashing the Limerick lights when lighting.
Our hearts so stout have got us fame
through the streets like sporters fighting
for soon 'tis known whence we came
and tearing all before us
where're we go they dread the name
of Garryowen in glory.

Behind the band rode local men playing the role of the
7th Cavalry. In dress blues atop sleek horses, the mock cavalrymen waved and smiled. As the horses trotted nervously
left and right, the dust rose and the troopers were enveloped
in a haze. At the head of the troops and in front of most of
the dust rode Sam Cotter playing the role of Custer. Cotter
wore a blond wig that remained crisp and lifelike in the rising heat. His uniform was modeled on Custer's favorite, the

one he wore on the day of his meeting at the Little Bighorn—a fringed buckskin suit with a double breasted blouse, polished buttons, and a light gray low crowned hat with a broad brim.

In the space between Cotter and the pretend troopers, two high school boys each led a horse. One horse wore a hand-lettered sign around its neck reading "Vic." The other wore a similar sign reading "Comanche." Vic, who was Custer's favorite mount and who died at the Little Bighorn, was draped in black crepe. Comanche, who was the sole American survivor of the battle, was also draped in crepe but red, white, and blue.

Sam Cotter as Custer sat loosely in his saddle, a man at his ease. It was as if the gallant, reckless officer was once again preparing to set off for his doom. As the dust thickened, the troops became more subdued. Many of the men pulled their neckerchiefs up to keep the dust out of their noses and mouths.

Custer's defeat at the Little Bighorn marked the last great victory of the Northern Plains people over the United States. In response, the government redoubled its efforts to destroy Indian resistance. It's too bad there weren't two countries competing to steal the Indian homelands. Like in the Basque Country where for hundreds of years both Christian and Islamic armies invaded. The Basques would align themselves first with one faction then with the other, always keeping each group a little uncertain. Busy fighting each other, the Christians and Muslims had been unable to completely subdue the Basques.

In the thickening dust, Yellow Bird Daughter could barely breathe. She coughed and rubbed her eyes. There amongst the soldiers in the street were her parents sliding over the cliff. They hung suspended while she held her breath, the dust turning to snow. She leaned forward straining to hear her parents' voices but all that came to her was a slight whoosh, the sound of the air being stirred by arms and legs waving in flight.

Then it was silent—no music, no man in a blond wig, no girls with banners, and no falling. Of course, that's impossible. If two people go over a cliff, they fall and they do so at the speed that all things fall no matter their weight. An American astronaut, standing on the surface of the moon, proved this when he dropped a feather and a stone from the same height at the same moment. As there is no atmosphere on the moon, there is no frictional drag on falling objects, and the feather and stone hit the ground together.

When they landed, Feather and Coffee Woman stood and brushed the snow from their clothes. They shook their heads and blinked their eyes. They threw their arms around one another and felt the heat of their bodies, the steam rising into the cold air. For a moment their bones felt as fragile and flexible as green saplings. They were afraid they were dead and laughed nervously then felt relief. The dead have no fear and they do not laugh.

"So we must be alive," Feather said.

"Are you sure?" Coffee Woman asked.

"Yes, I think so."

They laughed again and called up to Yellow Bird Daughter, "We're alive. Jump. You'll be fine." They waited a few moments but no daughter came hurtling through space. "Jump!"

"She can't hear us," Coffee Woman said.

"Louder, we have to call louder."

"Ju-um-m-mp!" they shouted. "Ju-um-m-mp!"

It was like a science fiction movie where they put the person in a gelatinous plastic bubble. You can push on it all you want and it just changes shape and you can see what's going on outside the bubble but you can't hear much. The world is muffled and thick.

"It's no use, she can't hear us." Tears rolled down Coffee

Woman's cheeks and began to freeze. The sun rose, the air warmed, and the tears melted. The snow grew wetter and heavier until it was slushy rain, pounding them. Water ran down from their hair and across their faces. Soon they were soaked and shivering.

"We can't stay here," Feather shouted. "We've got to get out of this rain and find a way back up the slope to her. Come on." Coffee Woman held up her hands in a hopeless gesture then ran. She and Feather stumbled through a stand of bare willow and aspen toward a hillside covered by spruce and fir.

Yellow Bird Daughter had heard nothing but she knew that she must follow her parents. Throwing one foot in front of the other, she reached the same stand of willow and aspen. The branches tore at her clothes so that the skin on her arms and face began to bleed. When she reached the spruce and fir trees on the hillside, she called out, "Here I am. Can you hear me? Are you there?" She ran furiously in circles, grabbing at the trunks of the trees, pulling the branches away to see where her parents had gone.

The high school boys guiding Vic and Comanche were unable to hold the halter leads when the two horses reared up. "Whoa, there. Take it easy." But it was no good. The horses battered the air with their hooves. Then they took off up the street, tearing through the commemorative banner and knocking down one of the girls who carried it.

Sam Cotter turned and rose in his saddle. "What the...?"

Yellow Bird Daughter was now in the middle of the troopers. She ran around one mounted soldier then another, grabbing at the first man's pant leg then pivoting around him and grabbing another rider's sleeve. She might have pulled the man to the ground but the horse jerked up and she stood holding the empty space. The cavalryman's hat flew into the air.

Zelestina called for help but no one moved. She called again and then she ran into the street dodging the horses until she came to Yellow Bird Daughter now standing motionless in the center of a circle of blue uniforms. She stopped.

When a battle ends, there is an extraordinary quiet. If you've been there, you know what I'm talking about. The parade goers stood with their mouths open, staring. A few stepped forward to get a better view. On tiptoe, Zelestina took a last step forward and grabbed Yellow Bird Daughter. Hugging her, she could smell the other woman's hair and the sweat under her arms. The dust, following the same immutable laws of nature that were illustrated on the moon, fell to the ground.

Sam Cotter approached the two women. Ten feet away he inadvertently stepped in a mound of horse manure. His smooth soled riding boot slid forward and he went down on his back with a whoomph of air being pressed from his chest. His blond Custer wig flew off and landed in the same manure he'd slid on. There was a burning in the palm of his right hand. He'd scraped it as he fell and it now began to bleed. He wiped it on his thigh but that only made it burn hotter. When he looked up he saw Yellow Bird Daughter leaning over him. She reached down and he took her hand and stood. The cavalrymen were busy calming their horses.

Sam had meant to say something on the order of "What the hell is going on?" Instead he looked at Yellow Bird Daughter's hand and, while thinking she was quite pretty, said only, "Thank you." Sam was neither cruel nor ignorant. He was aware that General Custer had famously said the best way to defeat the Indians was to go after the women and children first. Hold them hostage and threaten to kill them if the warriors didn't surrender. The savages will put down their weapons to save the women and children.

"Thank you," he repeated as he stood.

"I'm sorry," she said. Then Zelestina pulled her to the edge of the street, the parade goers backing up before the two women. Soon everything and everyone was back in their assigned places including the sun and the dust, the nervous horses, the seventh cavalry, the slightly soiled wig, and the dead parents. As Zelestina and Yellow Bird Daughter walked away, the parade started again. When Sam Cotter waved to the crowd, people could see the dried blood on his hand.

16

Lame Deer

The saturation bombing of Dresden in 1944 created a firestorm that incinerated 25,000 people. There might have been more but that sixty of the American B-17 bombers sent on the raid missed the city entirely and bombed Prague. Imagine this—the war nearly over so that a feeling of relief spreads across Europe and one night a Czech husband and wife are having a cup of tea and reading aloud to one another when they are blown to bits by a bomb meant for a German husband and wife who are having a cup of tea and reading aloud to one another.

Novelist Kurt Vonnegut, who was a prisoner of war in Dresden when the bombing occurred, remembers being sent out with other POWs to gather bodies for mass burial. But there were too many and German soldiers were ordered to incinerate what was left of those who hadn't been incinerated in the fires.

Vonnegut described the Dresden firebombing as an "atrocity" which was "tremendously expensive and meticulously planned." It did nothing to bring the war to a close

more quickly. Its purpose was to terrorize both the city's res-
idents and the 300,000 refugees who had fled to Dresden
from fighting in the east. Of the bombing's results, Vonnegut
wrote, "…only one person on the entire planet got any bene-
fit from it. I am that person. I wrote this book, which earned
a lot of money for me and made my reputation, such as it is.
One way or another, I got two or three dollars for every person killed. Some business I'm in."

A few months after the bombing of Dresden, Germany
surrendered to the Allies and the war in Europe ended. The
Japanese fought on and the American president Harry Truman, in what he implied was a humanitarian gesture, ordered
that the newly created atomic bomb be dropped on the Japanese city of Hiroshima. Well, I don't actually know if Truman
picked that particular city where 150,000 people would die.
First there was the firestorm and the blast wave then radia-
tion sickness. Very few of the people who died were soldiers.
I don't mean that soldiers aren't people only that in war soldiers are meant to die. For most of our history we reserved
death in war for soldiers. But not anymore. In World War I
five percent of those killed were civilians. In World War II,
seventy-five percent were civilians and in the wars going on
around the world in the 1990s ninety percent of the dead
were civilians. Those figures come from Philip Metre's book
Behind the Lines.

After the bomb fell on Hiroshima, the Japanese didn't
immediately surrender so the United States dropped a second bomb, that one on the city of Nagasaki. With this second
demonstration of American destructive capability, the Japanese surrendered, WWII ended, and we imagined we might
be happy once again.

Why do I tell you this? I have a friend I show my writing
to each week. I ask my friend if it's any good or if anyone will
want to read it or, more to the point, if anyone will want to
publish it as it's not so important what a reader thinks but

what a marketing analyst at a publishing house thinks. That's another topic. My friend says I should stick to the subject.

"But what is it?" I ask.

"It's Zelestina's life here in Wolf. Don't be disingenuous."

"But I'm not," I tell my friend. "When I think of Zelestina, I think of the times she lived in, the things she lived through. I think of her friendship with Yellow Bird Daughter—the Indian and the Basque. Imagine—Yellow Bird Daughter was born while the US army was murdering Indians at Wounded Knee and she and Zelestina lived to see the moon landing. Those two women were as much astronauts as the American NASA trained ones except that, unlike the Americans, Zelestina and Yellow Bird Daughter had gotten into a rocket that had no way to return home.

As a writer, I feel like Kurt Vonnegut who made two or three dollars for every person killed. Only in my case, being a much less successful writer, I've made two or three pennies. Still, it's money from the pain of others. It's too bad we don't have spaceships waiting to take us to planets where people aren't so cruel. On the other hand, if such planets exist, maybe it's better we don't have the ability to reach them.

When apartheid fell in South Africa, the newly formed government set up a truth and reconciliation commission. People were given a way to apologize for the crimes of the past, to ask for and offer forgiveness, and to imagine a future free of racial hatred.

When the Proceso ended in Argentina, the government set up a commission to find out what happened and suggest what might be done to heal the nation's wounds. No political figure was untainted and so the new government named as chair of the commission the novelist Ernesto Sábato. Sábato and the commissioners traveled throughout the country interviewing thousands of Argentines. They charted the locations of secret torture chambers, police holding tanks, prisons, and airstrips where the Disappeared were beaten, stabbed, shot, where their fingers were bent back until they snapped, where the women were raped while their husbands were forced to watch, where, finally, they were drugged and loaded into small planes to be flown out past the coast line and dumped into the sea.

I put all this in the passive voice as it's still unclear who committed these crimes. We know who the generals were, that is, who ordered these murders but thousands of people helped—local policemen, neighbors denouncing their neighbors, ambitious journalists.

The Argentine commissioners photographed the dried blood on the walls and floors, the rusting drains in the middle of concrete rooms. They found the fragments of records the torturers had not fully destroyed, the lists of names and dates. When they issued their report, it was called *Nunca Más*. Never Again.

In the US we have never had a reconciliation based on confronting the truth of our past—the fact that our country was founded on genocide. This shadow lurks behind everything we do. For want of a public apology we pretend no apology is needed. The same is true in the Basque Country. In 1999, the German government officially apologized to the Basque people for the Nazi bombing of Gernika—have you Googled this yet?—but the Spanish government has never apologized.

Zelestina stood behind the house smoking a cigarette—a habit she'd taken up during World War II. She looked down into the empty water tank, finished the cigarette, crushed the charred end between her fingers, and put it in her apron pocket. The weather had been warm and dry. The windmill fan turned, the fantail jiggered around with the wind, the rods moved up and down, the check valve rattled, seating solidly in the working barrel. Everything seemed to be in order but no water came to the surface.

That night Zelestina had a dream. She was waiting for a bus. In waking life, the bus stop in Wolf was just that—a stop, a sign by the road in front of the Great West Hotel. In the dream it was a depot with a café, with lockers where people left their bags, and with a claims office. Hundreds of buses came and went twenty-four hours a day seven days a week. It was snowing even though it was summer and hot. The buses had chains on their tires but the road was dry and bare so when the buses moved there was a loud rattling noise. Zelestina was dressed in shorts and a blouse, no hat, no gloves. And no bra so her breasts bounced around like pieces of fruit hanging from a tree branch being blown about in the wind. Embarrassed, she crossed her arms in front of her chest.

There was the screeching of brakes and the blast of a horn and a bus skidded to a halt in front of her. The driver leaned out the window and screamed, "Hey, Lady, get outta the road. Ya wanna git hit?"

Zelestina looked around and thought she must have been sleepwalking but can you sleepwalk in a dream? Then she was asleep again and there were buses parked at the head and foot of her bed.

When she woke up, she dressed, and without eating, walked to the Great West Hotel to buy a bus ticket to Lame Deer, Montana. Lame Deer was the capital of the federally recognized Northern Cheyenne Nation and Yellow Bird Daughter had gone there to enroll in the tribe she was half born of.

As Zelestina walked to the hotel, she kept hearing the bus driver in the dream yelling "Get outta the road. Ya wanna git hit." It was the dream that made her decide to take the bus rather than drive.

Then she remembered Otxanda Elordi's husband Arkaitz who'd been killed right at the end of the war when Allied troops entered Berlin. A German tank was blocking the street.

Arkaitz and nine other GIs waited while American artillery shells rained down in front of them to clear their way. Finally, a shell hit the tank. Smoke rose from the battered German vehicle but the cautious GIs didn't move. When Arkaitz finally stood up and stepped forward, a German soldier rose from the now burning tank and fired a pistol hitting Arkaitz and killing him. The other GIs shot and killed the German who turned out to be a boy of fourteen or fifteen, a child apparently drafted by the Reich in its last days.

Now Zelestina remembered something else. In the dream she woke up and saw that her bed was made of airplane parts and windmill blades and her sheets were made from torn up parachutes. She stood and there on the floor was Thomas Teague. He was missing his arms and legs and the bones were strewn around the floor.

"What happened?" Zelestina asked.

"Nothing," Teague answered. "These are animal bones. Just sheep and cows. The little ones might be squirrel."

"They're not your arms and legs?"

"No, I'm fine." Teague waved the bloody stumps of his missing appendages.

"Alright then, I'll just step over you."

In Lame Deer, Zelestina walked up and down the street for a few minutes then stepped into a café and ordered lunch. Feeling sick, she couldn't finish and went into the café's bathroom to rinse her mouth with cold water. She leaned on the sink and thought how quiet it was. When she came out, she went to the counter to pay.

"Are you alright? You look a little pale."

Was this a joke? No matter. Zelestina said only, "Yes," and left.

She walked three blocks from the café to the Tribal Headquarters of the Northern Cheyenne nation. Two trees had been planted in front of the building but no grass. When the wind gusted, dust swirled up in clouds, leaving a reddish brown film on the walls and windows. Inside, there was no receptionist. A piece of paper was propped up on a desk with the hand-lettered word "Information" and an arrow pointing to the left. Zelestina followed the arrow but none of the doors in the hall was marked. She stopped at one, turned the knob, and walked in. A middle-aged woman who was typing a letter looked up. The wrinkles at the corners of her eyes and over her upper lip were shaped by years of smiling.

"Just a minute," she said. "I'm almost finished. Let me get this." The typewriter clacked away. "There." She pulled the paper out of the carriage, stood, and walked to another desk where she set the letter down. She was a big woman wearing a bright red dress and white stockings. The red made her look bigger. The stockings over the brown of her skin made her legs look dusty. Her long hair, starting to gray, was fixed in a single braid wound tightly and piled on top of her head. "You need some help."

"Yes, I do."

"About enrollment? First, this is Northern Cheyenne only. Other tribes, God forbid Crow, for example, can't be done here. Excuse me, but I have to make sure and you kind of look a little Crow to me."

"No, I'm Basque."

"I never heard of them. Is that an eastern tribe?"

Was this joking, too? Zelestina had heard that Indians were funny but Yellow Bird Daughter had always been so serious. The woman went on, "Basque is ok. I mean one Indian's as good as another if you know what I mean. But like I said, this is the Northern Cheyenne Nation. No Crow, no Lakota, no Blackfeet, no Arapaho or Shoshone, no Mohawk or Iroquois or Pawtuckarapagansett or whatever those Rhode Island Indians call themselves. Let me think. Basque. Maybe from Maine or New Brunswick—Micmac, Abnaki, that sounds kind of like Basque. You know the three people that Sebastian Cabot kidnapped in 1497 and took to Europe were Micmac.

Why do I know that?" She stopped. "I repeat—no Basque enrollment here. Northern Cheyenne only. You need proof of
some kind—agency records, baptism, something that shows
tribal affiliation. There are forms I can give you—the blank
forms—from the BIA. You can also use a regular birth certif-
icate or state birth registration records. Copies in Helena if
you have to order those."

"I'm not from Montana."

"Where are you from?"

"Wyoming. Wolf."

"Wyoming. It's the same as Helena only you have to write
to Cheyenne. Were you born in Montana or Wyoming?"

"I was born in Arnegi, in Euskal Herria."

"Whoa, that really is a tribal homeland even I have never
heard of. Maybe Alberta?"

And maybe Indians were funny. Zelestina said, "No, not
Rhode Island or Maine or Alberta but Arnegi is a village that
goes back a thousand years—oldest tribe in the land."

"You don't say."

"Yes, and I'm not here to enroll."

"Well, I knew that. I was just wondering how long it'd take
you to tell me."

"I'm trying to find a friend of mine who lives here. Her
parents lived here too but they died a long time ago. Her
name is Yellow Bird Daughter. She was born in 1890 so she'd
be nearly sixty now. Almost as old as I am."

"Yes, of course I know her. I pulled her records when she
came home—church records. She was born on the day of the
Wounded Knee Massacre."

"Yes, she told me about her birth and about the Ghost
Dance that ended with that..." Zelestina stopped, unsure
what to call the event.

"The Ghost Dance—that was before my time but when we
were little we would play Ghost Dance. We didn't know what
it meant."

The woman went to a filing cabinet and rifled through the folders. "Yellow Bird Daughter—father Broken Nose called Feather when he was born. Maybe he fell out of a tree one time too many."

"I don't know."

"Mother was Coffee Woman. But that wasn't her original name either. She was born Falcon Walking. These are unusual names. But I don't know. Take my name—Betty. It's ordinary but it sounds strange when I look in the mirror and say it. 'Betty,' I say, and think, who's that? But it might just be getting old I don't recognize myself. Would you believe I was pretty?"

"Yes, of course I would."

"Well, I wasn't."

They both laughed.

"Excuse me," Betty said. She stood, went to the door, and shouted toward another office, "Burton." She waited and called again, "Burton?"

"Huh?"

"You remember when that woman Yellow Bird Daughter came in?"

"No."

"You remember her parents Broken Nose and Coffee Woman?"

"No."

"How about Feather and Falcon Walking. You remember them?"

"No."

Betty turned to Zelestina and said, "Who knows if he's telling the truth."

Burton ambled in from his office and said, "Those are real pretty names—real old timey."

I love the idea of a person who ambles. Makes me think of a bear in a good mood. There's a creek near a town in Alaska I once worked in where the bears would come to feed in late June and July. They'd wade out into the stream and wait then suddenly slam their big fists into the water and often as not come up with a fish. They'd eat, belch, sniff the air with a happy look on their faces, and amble off.

Burton was beefy but not fat. He wore a crisp white shirt and though he looked to be in his late fifties, his hair was jet black. He stared around the room for a moment then let his eyes settle on Zelestina whom he approached, right hand held out before him. The two shook hands. "I'm pleased to meet you, ma'am. Of course we know where Yellow Bird Daughter is. Betty here is fooling around with you a little. The person you're looking for lives with Simeon Standing Dog Chief. That's a good old name, too."

Betty put the back of her right hand up to her mouth, rolled her eyes, and looked as though she was trying to concentrate on a fly crossing her desk.

"Betty, could you get Simeon's phone number, please?"

"Burton, you know Simeon hasn't got a phone."

"Well, his kids then, don't they have a phone?"

Betty was hunched over her desk scrawling something on a piece of paper. She handed it to Zelestina and said, "You take this map. It'll get you to the house. I'll bet you if anyone knew your friend's parents, it'll be Simeon Standing Dog Chief. He's nearly ninety but he's still a firecracker."

Burton put out his hand again, shook Zelestina's a second time, and said, "Good luck." Then he ambled back into his office.

"Do you have a car?" Betty asked.

"Yes, but I didn't drive. I came on the bus."

"That's alright. It's just over four miles walk. Let me see that map again a minute. First thing is the main road out of town east then the second dirt road to the left, it's not marked. Second dirt road to the left. Follow that up to the new wood frame house. It's the only one like it. It's got paint. Tell them you came to see Mr. Standing Dog Chief. There'll be a lot of kids around. The grandkids. Simeon's some kind of cousin of mine so those kids are some kind of nieces and nephews of mine I guess. They're wild, I tell you. Sometimes I think they're part Crow. Of course that would make me part Crow." She winced.

"Ask the kids to show you the way up to their granddad's." She handed the map back to Zelestina.

The walk took a little under an hour and a half—sky overhead, earth below, one foot after another, the small slap of her shoes, the rising dust. At the new house, she could hear a hum, a refrigerator motor maybe. The wind blew through the cheat grass at the edge of the rutted road. A magpie came careening down and landed not far away. It turned and hopped two steps forward, pecked at a chunk of bentonite gumbo stuck to a piece of mica, then cocked its head as if it were looking at its reflection in a mirror. Satisfied with its good looks, the bird cocked its head again, this time toward the sky, and flew off.

The new house was painted blue. There was no porch, just a little stoop that had pulled away from the building so that there was a six-inch wide gap between the edge of the top step and the doorway. The door itself was painted yellow but it needed another coat. There were several bicycles lying on their sides in the dirt.

A few hundred yards up a wash from this house was a smaller log cabin. The logs were hand notched and uneven. The chinking was gray and, in a few places, it had fallen out. Zelestina stepped toward the cabin then remembered that she was to check at the new house first. She stopped but before she could turn and move away, the cabin door opened and a man motioned to her.

"It's alright. They told me you was coming." The man might have been sixty-five or seventy-five. He certainly didn't look nearly ninety. The wrinkles in his face were deep but he stood straight and his eyes were clear so he seemed both ancient and ageless.

Zelestina turned as if the man might be speaking to someone behind her.

"No, I'm talking to you. Yes, that's right. I don't mean to be impolite. I spend a lot of time alone these days and maybe I forget how to talk to people. You come in if you like."

The man lifted his hands up before him and waved, palms out. The hands, though large, ended in narrow fingers. They would have been delicate but that the knuckles were swollen and twisted. The thumbnail on the man's right hand had been left to grow long and then been filed to a sharp point.

"Mr. Standing Dog Chief?"

"Nobody but," the old man said. "And you are the lady who stopped in town. My kids across the way there gave me the message from Betty. They got a phone so they can take messages. They're real good about passing messages along to me. Betty didn't tell the kids your name."

Without thinking, Zelestina asked, "Why didn't Betty call when I was in the office? She could have checked to see if you were here."

"I'm always here. Besides Betty don't know the kids got a phone."

Again without thinking, Zelestina asked, "She called a phone she didn't know they had?"

"I might be mixed up. Maybe it was somebody else who called them, somebody Betty had talked to, and that other person knew about the new phone and told Betty and then she called. I expect it won't be long before most everyone's got a phone. I got the message you was coming anyway.

"I knew those people you was asking about—Yellow Bird Daughter and her parents Feather and Falcon Walking who later were called Broken Nose and Coffee Woman. How could you forget names like that? I know their daughter, too. She's getting up there to be near as old as me though you never can catch up. She'll be here soon. I sent one of the kids to tell her. She come to me wanting to know about the ghost dancing."

He shook his head. "What an idea that was. You wear a magic shirt and do a magic dance and the white people will disappear and the dead buffalo spring back alive out of the earth and the dead people spring back with the buffalo." He looked away. "Desperate." Then he stopped.

Zelestina said, "Where I came from the people have always danced—fandangos and arins, for pleasure but to reach toward Heaven, too."

"Well, I guess getting to Heaven's more reasonable and modest than what we come up with—having the dead come back and the whites gone. Excuse me." He went on, "So you dance?"

"Yes, well not so much anymore."

"I danced all my life—no Ghost Dance. Just dancing. At ceremonies and parties, then later at rodeos and pow-wows. I don't dance so much anymore either but I keep at it. Won't do no good to stop. And I make dance regalia." He pointed to the corner. "Been repairing this willow backrest and sewing jingles onto a dance shirt." He lifted the shirt from the back of a chair and held it in front of himself. "Never had much of this jingle stuff when I was young but people now like it. Pretty in a kind of brassy way. I admit I like it too and I make jingle shirts my granddaughters and nieces and other young people been using. They always go over to Crow Fair. Nowadays people aren't so fussy as they used to be about which tribe you are and who did what seventy eighty years ago. Far as I know weren't no great warriors in my family so I'm not too hard on somebody whose granddad was a scout with Custer. Let's see, I been to Cheyenne Fair and Spring Creek, down to Ethete, too. Once I even went out to the Yakama pow-wow. Lots of Mexican people living in that Valley. Mexicans are part Indian, they say. You go to a pow-wow you get away from ordinary life for a while."

Standing Dog Chief picked up the shirt he'd mentioned

and shook it so the jingles rattled. "I could show you about these."

"I'd like that."

"Anybody who's interested, I'm happy to tell 'em." Standing Dog Chief stared at the shirt, turned it over and stared a little longer. "It wasn't always like this but this is how we do it now, we take these pieces of metal, they're cut out of pieces of tin cans like sardine cans or Campbell's soup—chicken noodle or tomato or cream of mushroom. That's the one I like, the mushroom. I like sardines, too. You like sardines? I'm not much of a cook. You'd think a man living alone would get to cook a little better than me but no, I open cans." Standing Dog Chief smiled. "The soup cans are hard to work with but they make a nice sound—better than sardine cans. Course it's a little easier to cut the sardine cans cause they're not circles. Sardine cans got a different sound than soup. Some people use chewing tobacco lids but I don't chew so I can't see buying chew and throwing it away to get the can. Same with rolling tobacco cans. Somebody could make a little money if he started a business selling tin jingles cut to the right shape and size. I 'magine somebody'll think of it soon enough. Then we'll go on down to the store and buy tin that's a genuine copy of Copenhagen chewing tobacco lids to make genuine copies of old time Indian jingles."

"Sounds like you don't like it."

"No, I'm just poking fun. Things change and if it bothered me all that much I wouldn't still be alive cause there's been a lot of change these past hundred years."

It's like Standing Dog Chief was talking about that Brave Combo song "Nothing is Permanent."

"Nothing is permanent. Nothing will last forever.
     Nothing is permanent.
You know all things always change and change is fast if
     it's not slow.

Where was the neighborhood before they marked off
all the streets and roads?
Who came to live here first and does it really matter? I
don't think so."

I've left out a lot of the words and I'm pretty certain Brave
Combo is wrong about how it doesn't matter who lived here
first but I think I understand the need to believe this. After
all, we're stuck with each other and we can't undo the past.
Maybe even that is wrong, maybe we can undo the past at least
a little.

Standing Dog Chief said, "I'm sure it wouldn't matter if
they made jingles in factories. Not like the Great Spirit give us
jingles thousands of years ago." He smiled again and waited
to see if Zelestina thought this remark was funny. "Ok, here's
how you do it." He went to a cabinet, took out a leather bag,
and opened it on a low table. Then he sat on the floor by the
table and spread out his tools and tin. "You cut the metal into
a shape like a teepee with the top torn off. Like this. Couple
a inches long, maybe a inch and a half wide at one end and a
inch at the other. Then you take a strip of rawhide maybe four
or five inches long. Tie a knot in it like that then wrap the tin
around the rawhide. Roll the tin around this stick I made—
It's shaped like a cone see so the tin ends up in the shape of
a cone, too. The leather will end up going through the little
hole left in the top but you got to make sure the hole's small
enough so the leather can't slip."

He handed Zelestina the cone shaped stick and she sat
down on the floor, took the metal, wrapped it around the
rawhide, tied the knot.

"That's right, that's good. So you make a lot of these,
you're gonna need a whole lot for a blouse or skirt. I forgot
to say it's mostly only women do this jingle dancing. Kind of
too bad, if you ask me. But it's a fine sound the rattling of the
jingles like maybe it'd wake up some good but tired spirit we

could do with a little more of."

"At home we have this."

"Jingle dancing?"

"In a way. The *Joaldunak*."

"*Joaldunak*."

"It means big noisemakers. Not big in size but a lot of noise. Some people call them *zaratalariak*. The people who make *zarata*—a real racket."

"Racket."

"Yes, *zarata*. The *joaldunak* wear two bells as big as watermelons tied to their backs. They have to be tied on so tight sometimes it hurts. And they walk in two lines through the streets with a bouncing movement up and down on their heels so the bells go up and down, all of them at the same time clanking and banging. They have tall hats with chicken feathers on the top and they wear a sheepskin around their shoulders and carry a switch made from a horse's tail."

"Chicken, sheep, horse—three animals that have served humans."

"Yes, and the *joaldunak* walk out and meet the *joaldunak* of another village then they all go through the countryside clanking and banging in rhythm. They are waking up the earth from the death of winter. It's a resurrection."

"Are you a Christian then?"

"I don't know. Once I was. Some people say the *joaldunak* are not so much waking up the earth as driving away the bad spirits that sleep in the soil, or sicknesses that lie in wait, or even pests that eat the crops."

"Well, that's pretty interesting. Look, you've about finished with all that tin. I'll get you some more." He went into another room for the tin and when he returned asked, "You ever been to a pow-wow?"

"No. I'm sorry."

"No need to be sorry. You can always go. Usually with the dancing there'd be singing, too. You ever hear of the song

'One-eyed Ford' or any of the honor songs—'Chief's Honoring Song' maybe?"

Zelestina said no again and kept working on the jingles, sewing each finished one on the shirt.

"Those are good songs for anybody to know. Take 'One-eyed Ford.' When the dance is over sweetheart, I'll take you home in my one-eyed Ford. That's how it always starts. Then the singer makes up other lines. Used to be a singer might mention a Model T Ford and before that a wagon that's got some kind of a problem, broken axle or spring, and before wagons it might be a half blind horse. Whatever it was, it was a Indian Cadillac."

"Indian Cadillac?"

"That's a big deal fancy car only maybe it don't work so good, like it's not firing on all eight cylinders or like in the case of this song it's got a headlight out."

"One-eyed Ford."

"Yup." Standing Dog Chief laughed. "The dance that goes with that song's a good one—easy and you can add steps to make it personal. Honoring songs are easy too and can be to honor anyone. The same song you can change the name of the person being honored. Lots of times that's how people do it—just change the name, make it about somebody everybody knows. Might make up one like this say—Yellow Bird Daughter, you been away a long time, now you're home. Tell me what you saw."

Zelestina looked at Standing Dog Chief. "It's been many years I've been away from home."

"Is that why you come to see your friend? See what she found out going home?"

"No, my home has been here for a long time. I'll never go back to Arnegi."

"That's your village?"

"Yes."

Then they worked in silence until Standing Dog Chief

said again, "I'm sure she'll be along pretty quick. I don't mean to be rude but what does your name mean?"

"From the sky."

"A good name. So are you from the sky?"

"I guess we all are from the sky somehow."

"Betty said you come on the bus. Betty, that's a odd name for a Cheyenne woman but you know lotsa us Indians go to the Christian church now and give our kids names like Thomas and Sarah and Betty. I don't know what those names mean. Yellow Bird Daughter means something and your name too means something. But I should tell you that in a honoring song the second verse is the reverse of the first so if I sang you been gone a long time I might later sing, 'Are you going away.'"

"Maybe I am, I don't know."

Standing Dog Chief turned away. "I'm sorry. I have been too forward and that is rude."

"No, no, it is right for you to speak. I thought I just came up here to see Yellow Bird Daughter but maybe you're right and it's something else."

"Betty sent your friend to me when she got here. She wanted to know about her parents. But I didn't know them. She was born in the year of the Wounded Knee massacre."

"Yes, she told me many times—1890."

"Yellow Bird Daughter's mother coulda been real young when her child was born. That wasn't uncommon. Say sixteen or even younger. Fourteen maybe. But she mighta been as old as thirty or even older. That's possible, too. It's strange I never hearda them. With those names—Feather, Broken Nose, Falcon Walking, Coffee Woman." He snorted. "I been trying to remember since Betty first told me but I don't remember nothing. They disappeared and you'da thought people would talk but they mighta told people where they was going and everybody figured they got there and that was that. Not like anyone had a phone in those days or knew how to write. Even if you went to mission school, they taught you to write English not Cheyenne. The kids couldn't write home to their parents so no letters."

Standing Dog Chief looked at the jingle shirt. "Let me see that." He took the shirt from Zelestina. "These are sewed on real good and you rolled 'em real even. They'll make a fine sound."

They rolled and sewed jingles for a time longer, again without speaking. Then Standing Dog Chief said, "Did you know that one of the only kids who survived at Wounded Knee was named Lost Bird?"

"No. Lost Bird. A little bit like Yellow Bird Daughter."

"And her mother was originally Falcon Walking. All bird people. And they all flew away. Then your name that means from the sky and here you are with the bird people. I was never connected to bird people but in those days I think everyone had to be part bird person—Northern Plains people going this way and that running trying to stay alive. Flying in front of what turned out to be the future. Still flying, if you ask me. Maybe your people been flying, too."

"I never thought of it that way but yes maybe."

"You think flying like a bird would be freeing, but if a person never has a place to land, flying can be pretty tiring. Even the birds that cross the ocean stop to rest sometimes."

Zelestina put down the jingle shirt and pressed her hands to the side of her head.

"You want to stop for a while?"

"No, no." She paused and looked at Standing Dog Chief. "It's true about the flying, I think. Only very strange for us Basques since we have lived in the same tiny country for thousands of years."

"That's good having your own land all those years. Look, we got enough jingles here for two maybe three shirts. My eyes not so good as they used to be. Can you thread this needle for me?" He held out his hand and Zelestina took the needle.

As she did, her hand touched his and he looked at her. "Just a minute," he said and left the room. When he returned, he carried a finished jingle shirt, a yellow satin one that shone like the sun. It had a round collar and the sleeves were long and loose with narrow cuffs. He laid it over the back of a chair.

"Once I was down in Gallup and saw a basket dance the Pueblo people did. It was a beautiful dance. There was four dancers each one standing at a point of the compass. Young women. Not girls at all, but young women. These young women are supposed to be virgins. They stand for the future of the tribe. The four each got a basket filled with beans or corn. They shake the baskets and the beans and corn fly up. All the trash stuff—the dust and sticks and husks—falls out of the baskets. Pueblo people say it's a Thanksgiving dance for the harvest."

"There's a Basque dance almost like that. And women do that one, too. Most dances are done by men so you notice this one."

"Tell me about it."

"The dancers carry fish in the baskets. Most Basque people live near the ocean so we eat a lot of fish."

"Fish eaters, I don't know."

But he was smiling again and Zelestina was getting used to him. Like Betty, he was an awfully lighthearted person.

It was late afternoon and the light was growing sharper. Standing Dog Chief looked at the yellow shirt he'd laid over the back of the chair. "I been thinking on who this shirt might be for and here you come along. It'll be dark soon. With my old man eyes I'm done sewing. You put that shirt on. I'll go outside so you can have some privacy. Anyway, I want to see the sunset."

In a minute Zelestina came out wearing the sun colored satin jingle shirt.

"When a Cheyenne person dances, he presses his feet down flat to let the earth know he's there. With both feet. See, your feet lay flat like this." Standing Dog Chief lifted one foot and thumped it on the ground. "Go ahead," he said.

Zelestina lifted her foot and brought it down hard.

The sun dropped behind a hill and it was suddenly dark.

"Guess we're really done now."

They went back into the house and Standing Dog Chief took candles from a counter and lit a kerosene lamp. "They wired the house all up for electricity—got switches and switch plates and light fixtures but there's no electric pole runs out here so I use kerosene."

In the morning, Zelestina awoke lying in a circle of sunlight coming in through a small east facing window. She sat up and the blanket that covered her fell to the floor. She picked it up, wrapped it around her shoulders, stood, and walked up and down the room a few times, working the tightness out of her legs. She was too old to sleep all night on a couch, her legs bent under her.

Before going to sleep, she'd folded the yellow shirt and left it on a small table that stood against the wall. There was a note on top of the shirt: "I don't know what coulda happened so's Yellow Bird Daughter never got here. Could be some kid never took the message but maybe something else so I'm gone to check." Under his name was a PS: "Don't forget to take the yellow jingle shirt. Maybe you can use it for that fish eater dance."

Zelestina took off the blouse she'd been wearing and pulled the jingle shirt over her head again. She went outside and took a few tentative steps. The jingles sounded different than they had the day before. She was facing the sun and, turning, she couldn't see anything in the glare. She looked away from the sun. No clouds in the sky.

She lifted her shoulders three or four times and listened to the jingles then stood still and listened to the silence coming from the house wired for electricity but with no power.

"You could make these jingles outta just about any metal," Standing Dog Chief had said. "Really it don't matter."

Zelestina looked up at the sky and jumped as high as she could coming down with a thud that about wiped out her old lady knees.

"Not just any metal but about anything that'd make a rat-tle noise. You could drill tiny holes in birds' beaks and string them together. Or little bones. Or rattlesnake rattles. Could be factory-made stuff, too—nuts and bolts and washers. Or pennies. You could drill a hole in a bunch of pennies and string them together like the birds' beaks. Belly dancers make jingles outta money, you know. Really, could be anything."

17

Adam and Eve

At the beginning of the Torah God separates the light from the darkness—"He called the light Day and the darkness He called Night. And there was evening and there was morning, a first day."

That is beautiful not least because like every utterance made it reveals more than it says. What would it be like to start anew, not only for yourself but for all of being? There was nothing and then there was something—the dawn of all dawns, the world never before seen, the moment untouched. It would make of creation a haiku—that brief Japanese poetic form in which the intangible becomes flesh and is held for infinity outside time.

I wonder if this is why we go traveling, seeking what more often than not makes us uncomfortable. Maybe it's why we spend millions and billions and trillions of dollars building machines to go to the moon when we know we can't live there. There's no atmosphere, for chrissake. Or go to Mars, an equally unlivable place that will take us years to get to and where we'll find dust and, maybe, ice locked up since God first

made it. Imagine God on day three or four and it suddenly occurs to him he created Mars and maybe he should put some
ice there. But Mars will be a change for us and some charmed
astronaut will step down on a new planet for the first time.
It is as if a man sought to give birth to himself without the
intervention of woman. You notice that it is mostly men who
fantasize about going where no man has gone before, as they
say on *Star Trek*.

But there are women astronauts too and it could be one of
them—Zelestina stepping down and slipping on the Wyoming
ice. When the Viking I landed on Mars and sent back the first
photo taken of the surface, I remember a newscaster gasping
and saying, "My God, it's northeastern Wyoming."

When Zelestina got to Wolf everything that had come before in her life was gone forever. She never saw her brothers
or parents again and she never told me what happened. Could
be that Iñaki and Andoni died as partisans in WWII smug-
gling downed Allied fliers over the Pyrenees and across Nafarroa, Gipuzkoa, and Bizkaia to the coast where they could be
picked up and returned to England. And her parents—I hope
they died peacefully at home in their beds. But all things being somehow equal, they too might have been in the underground and died resisting the fascists. They would have been
somewhere in their eighties and so their work would have
been based on stealth not physical strength. But that's the
hallmark of Basque resistance—stealth. Maybe when the war
ended and it became clear that peace would bring no freedom
to the Basque people, they died of broken hearts. It's romantic but unlikely in that if a broken heart could kill the Basques
they would never have survived past the Roman Empire much
less through the centuries of Spanish and French rule.

Think of Adam and Eve as the first astronauts. Held in
suspended animation, their ship dropped in a blaze of light
to earth and they awoke. Like that moment in *Galaxy Quest*
when the heroes come down in a landing module looking

for a new Beryllium Sphere to power their hyper drive outer space motors. They're all a little nervous being B grade TV actors who've been pressed into saving an alien species from the unspeakable cruelty of a monster whose name is the same as that of a famous film critic.

The Questerian wannabe who appeared in episode 81 of the series but was killed before the first commercial and has inserted himself into the show begins to weep and says, "I changed my mind. I wanta go back."

Alan Rickman who plays Alexander Dane, a former Shakespearean actor fallen on hard times so now playing Dr. Lazarus, a Mr. Spock knock-off in a pink and purple latex bathing cap reminiscent of a chambered nautilus, says, "After the fuss you made about getting left behind?"

And the wannabe whom we know only as Guy says, "Yeah, but that's when I thought I was the crewman that stays on the ship and there's something up there and it kills me but now I'm thinking I'm the guy that gets killed by some monster five minutes after we land on the planet."

Tim Allen as Jason Nesmith playing Commander Peter Quincy Taggert says, "You're not going to die on the planet, Guy."

"I'm not? What's my last name?"

Taggert looks around at his crew and, in a somber tone, admits he doesn't know.

"Nobody knows because my character isn't important enough for a last name, because I'm gonna die."

By now the module has settled down on the planet's surface. It's a world of sulphurous stone and dust and intense burning sunlight. Tony Shalhoub who plays Fred Kwan playing Tech Sargent Chen opens the hatch and Guy screams, "Hey, don't open that. It's an alien planet. Is there air? You don't know." Then he takes a big breath, closes his mouth, and ducks his head to the side as if he might avoid the poisonous atmosphere.

Shalhoub wrinkles his nose a little, puffs a breath or two in and out of his mouth, turns and says sweetly, "Seems okay."

The Torah says that on the sixth day of the universe's existence, God made man and woman in his image and told them to be fertile and increase and also everything on this planet belongs to you, you first man and woman and the day ended. But then on the seventh day, God forgot what he'd done the day before and made man again and again forgot to make a companion. For the second creation he explained that it was from the dust of the earth that man was made.

This part seems the most compelling to me—from dust we come and to dust we will go. And I'm telling you how sad I am that Zelestina has gone and here I am rambling on about the Bible and science fiction parodies when really I simply miss the old woman. Her stories helped me find a way to live in Wyoming, a state that along with Alaska is the only part of the United States that the census bureau still defines as a frontier. But they don't define a frontier; they just say Wyoming is one. It's an alien land to those of us dropped here by God from our mother's wombs and even more alien to those of us like Zelestina and me who found our way here by some twist of fate.

The second man in the creation was as unhappy in his solitude as the first—filled with a longing he couldn't name. It was also true that with so much work to do on the new planet he needed a helper, an apprentice, a gofer, someone to go to bed with. God put him into a deep sleep as if to send him again into outer space, where he would pass years, maybe eons, hurtling through the darkness, the stars whistling past.

As the man slept, God reached inside his body and removed a rib which he whittled into the shape of a woman. The spaceship, after an infinity of traveling in circles landed again on earth and both man and woman awoke. They were woozy and uncertain where they were, even who they were. God announced that the plants and animals, the fishes and birds, belonged to them and he told them to be fruitful and multiply. That part was the same as God's first try at making human beings. He just repeated the charge.

I can see the man there with his chalkboard under a baobab tree saying, "I get the addition and subtraction but multiply, it's hard."

Why did God pick multiplication? Some creatures on earth reproduce without sex. They simply divide.

I wonder if the man and woman who were created on the sixth day were sent on a separate interstellar probe that landed elsewhere and on that distant planet there is a mirror of our own experience. Maybe the second couple was sent away and we are that pair's descendants, children of exile—aliens in our own world. I know I'm repeating myself but it feels so strange to be here. I look up at the Wyoming night sky filled with stars and I wonder as we lurch on, bringing the planet again and again to the brink of ruin.

I'm guessing God was pretty uneasy about forgetting the first couple and doing the whole thing over. It's not a good start for an entity that bills itself as all knowing, all powerful, and all loving. The power might still be there but the story ends up short on both knowing and loving.

The reasonable solution would have been to leave all four of the new beings on earth. Better for the gene pool, too. It was a big planet, especially in those days when people walked almost everywhere. You could put one couple in the Great Rift Valley of East Africa and the other in the forests of Bali or in the Andes near the spot where one day we'd find the ruins of Macchu Picchu. The odds were good the two couples would never meet.

This leaves out curiosity, longing, greed, development, desire, and intelligence. In short, it leaves out being human. Everyone knows God told at least one of the couples they could eat anything they found on earth except the fruit of the tree of the knowledge of Good and Evil. If they ate that fruit they would die. And everyone knows too that the serpent told the woman God had lied to them. "You won't die," he said. "Just the opposite, eat that fruit and you'll awaken to your own existence and know the difference between good and bad. You'll finally be fully alive. And one day you will travel into space and find your lost twins."

The woman ate and told her husband to eat which he did. Confronted by God, the man blamed his helper and the two were ejected from Paradise because of God's concern that they might also eat of the tree of eternal life. It's strange God didn't mention the tree of eternal life at all as if you had to know good and evil before you could even be aware of eternity. God put locks on the gates of Paradise and assigned cherubim to keep humanity out forever.

The man and woman, by now named Adam and Eve, had two sons—Cain and Abel. Cain killed Abel, God cursed Cain, Cain moved to Nod, married, and had children. Where Cain's wife came from is never explained. Adam and Eve had another son named Seth. After that third child, Adam lived to be 930. Seth lived to 912. His descendants were equally long lived—Enosh, 905; Kenan, 910; Mahalalel, 895; and Jared, 962. All married and had more children. Again, no mention of the children's mothers. Later God remembered to tell us that Adam and Eve gave birth to both sons and daughters and while the daughters are never named and we know nothing of how old they were at death, these daughters are the only possible wives for the sons.

Did God create Adam with a penis and testicles? Or did he add that when he created woman? If, when he started, God had no intention to create woman then man wouldn't have needed sexual organs. What about the mixing of sexual and excretory functions? The two systems share some body organs and that implies that sexuality was an afterthought. Or else urinary excretion was the afterthought. If God had no plan to make male and female humans, why did he make male and female mammals—dogs and cats and deer and cows and horses? From the get go the animals had to copulate to reproduce. Primates too—monkeys, chimps, gorillas, and such. Everything was male and female with penises and vaginas and sexual reproduction except for man. It's very weird— man alone who would live forever in his loneliness. He would work as master gardener, plumber, carpenter, and electrician doing the maintenance on the entirety of creation. And all around him the animals would be having sex.

Maybe it was just the gardening work. There was no way a single man could keep up with the landscaping on Paradise not to mention naming everything. This is the twenty-first century and scientists are still finding new unnamed species. Even napping in his post creation exhaustion, God must have seen that. At that point, he could have created another man to give earth two hardworking genial companions busy from dawn to dusk keeping things shipshape. But no, God took that rib and whittled a woman with a slender waist and functional hips and breasts—there's God with a Swiss army knife stroking the bone and slowly carving out a spot for a vagina.

You get my meaning. If God first made just the man— imagining him not only to be skilled laborer but also first ranch manager, a bachelor committed to the ranch owner's wellbeing and to the perpetual viability of the hayfields and the cattle and there was no idea of the woman, then surely there would have been no genitalia in Genesis.

If I set that aside and assume God knew all along that he intended to create woman and that since he'd used animals to work out the concept of vaginal sex in which sperm are implanted in the uterine wall and a new being begins to grow there, if he'd worked that out, well, ok but then I wonder how old Adam and Eve were at the moment of creation. I picture a handsome upper middle class white couple in their early thirties. The man spends at least three mornings a week at the YMCA weight room. The woman is a long distance runner who looks like a late sixties playmate of the month. She is lovely but not so thin as models of our own latter days and not so large breasted as pornographic fetishists demand.

This is all wrong. If God intended them to be fertile and multiply, they would have come to earth at the moment of sexual awakening. They would have been neither thirty-year-old suburbanites nor five year olds standing at the school door on the first day of kindergarten, holding their mother's hand and trying to be brave. You don't tell a five year old to be fertile and multiply. Neither do you create the first incubator couple at an age that will mean they've lost fifteen to twenty of their prime childbearing years. And why should they have been white?

In science we learn that the simplest explanation is often the best one. But God's story is the reverse—filled with incongruities, complexities, contradictions, and an endless stream of moral questions with no clear answers. How can we expect a man and a woman who were never infants or children to care for their own infants and children and a God who has never been human to create human beings?

One evening God was walking in the cool of the Garden and called to Adam and Eve, "Where are you?"

Adam stepped out of the bushes sporting a fig leaf as underwear and said, "I heard the sound of you in the Garden, and I was afraid because I was naked, so I hid."

"Who told you that you were naked?"

Again, I repeat myself but the story expands in never ending concentric circles. Having explained to Adam and Eve that there was only one rule in all of Creation—don't eat the fruit of that one tree—then finding they'd broken the rule I might have thought God would have been angry. Lord knows he had a wicked temper, but he was quite gentle. Seeing how uneven the stitches were on the fig leaf, God sewed garments of animal skins for the unhappy couple.

In this way God was the first tailor. My friend Cookie Se-
gelstein's father was a tailor. He was also a Holocaust death
camp survivor. Cookie told me that she was surprised on en-
tering school to find that the other children hadn't learned to
count by using the numbers tattooed on their parents' fore-
arms.

All through college and long into her adult life, Cookie
sent her off-the-rack clothes to her father for alterations.
Finally, she decided it was silly to keep mailing dresses and
blouses from New York to Kansas City and she took some new
clothes to a local tailor. When she next went home for a visit,
her father noticed she was wearing a dress he'd never seen
before. He looked carefully at the seams, the darts, the collar,
and the way the shoulder had a slight pooch as it rolled over
onto the upper arm. He said, "So, you took this to someone
in the city?"

"Yes, Pop."

"And this man was a tailor?"

"Yes, Pop."

"He had a shop of his own?"

"Yeah, sure, of course he had a shop."

"Tell me, is this shop on a busy street?"

"Very busy."

"Busy enough to have a bus line?"

"Of course, I said it's a busy street.

"So there is a bus that passes the shop, yes?"

"Yes."

"Good. So you go back to that shop and you tell this tailor
that the next time a bus comes, he should step out in front of
it. God forgive me, that's how bad this workmanship is."

And that's about how I feel about God and the tailoring he
did on Zelestina's life. Exiled at sixteen, never married, never had children, her one great friend gone back to the world
from which she'd come, her parents and brothers never seen

again. Bad workmanship and when he finished he put a sign on his shop door that read, "Had an errand. Back at 2:30." He got in his spaceship and flew away and no one's seen him since.

18

Zelestina's Last Oldsmobile

So many years gone by and Aitzol Goikoetxea was still a blacksmith and metal worker. He'd never opened a body shop and Zelestina's were the only cars he'd ever painted. Still, she took her new Olds to him and waved her arms over the hood as if she were a magician with an upside down top hat out of which an endless stream of rabbits was about to emerge.

As usual, she asked for a color that no one used for cars. Aitzol had painted the Curved Dash a creamy ivory in a time of black only. He'd painted one car a blue that was as pale and sharp as the sky above the tree line in the mountains, and one a green as translucent as bull kelp.

"What are you smiling about?" Zelestina asked.

"Nothing. Am I smiling? I never smile." He was remembering the clown's nose red car and the inky purple one that shone like the skin of an eggplant.

"I would like this one the same color as the Curved Dash. You remember that color?"

"I'm not sure I do. It's been a long time. Is something

bothering you? You've never asked me to repeat a color."

"No, I never have. I'm fine."

"You're not worried about getting old, are you? We all get old. Nostalgia's a bad habit."

"I told you I'm fine. That first car was a beautiful color. They don't make those colors now. Are you smiling? It looks like you're smiling."

"I told you I never smile. Have you ever seen me smile?"

"You're right, I never have."

He smiled. "I guess it wouldn't be so hard. I might even have some notes on what I mixed, it being so strange in those days."

"Yes, so you can tell me how long it will take and how much I'm going to pay. How long is important as I have against all odds and as you have so rudely mentioned become an old woman and sometimes get tired walking. Not like when I was a young girl going all over the countryside. I remember being twelve or thirteen and walking up and down the hills around Arnegi surefooted as a mountain sheep. Now I have to step very carefully." She lifted one foot off the ground and set it back down. "Like that. If I go crooked on a rock I might twist my ankle and fall over—pow—onto the ground. Maybe I'd break my hip and then what? So I need the car before I'm too much older."

"I've already admitted we're getting older but neither of us is that old."

"Now you are flattering an old woman which brings me again to the price. I notice it goes up with each car."

"Of course it goes up, the price of everything goes up— paint, too. Then they keep making the cars bigger and you keep buying the biggest ones. This one's big enough for a herder to live in and you don't need a horse to pull it. Of course, you might not want your dog messing up the uphol-stery."

"I like a big car. It's safe. Maybe you can put some glue on the window rubber and an oxygen tank on the seat and I can drive to the moon. Like those Americans last summer."

"Well, they didn't go in an Oldsmobile. Plus the speed leaving the atmosphere would burn all the paint off so there'd be no point in wasting money on a new paint job."

Aitzol looked at the Oldsmobile. There wasn't a scratch on it and it shone so brightly that a person couldn't look at it in the sunlight bouncing off the snow. They'd done a good job with the finish. But Zelestina was right to want it repainted— the factory color was a hideous metallic tone reminiscent of the worst features of modern life. Then he said, "Maybe no one actually went to the moon. How are we to really know?"

"Some people say the whole thing was done in a Hollywood movie studio. They think it was a trick to keep the Russians from building a rocket like the Americans."

How many years she'd lived in Wolf and she still talked about the Americans. It was neither pride nor alienation. She just wasn't American. Who were the Americans anyway?

"The important thing is not the truth or lie of the moon voyage but the color of the car. *Dena den guk biok urte asko ondoren egunero ikusiko duguna dakigu.*"

"My Basque is not so good anymore," Aitzol admitted. "I been here too long." He walked twice around the gleaming car, crawled under it for a moment, opened and closed the doors, peered at the molding around the headlights, and went for a pen and paper. When he arrived at a bid that seemed to him fair, he deducted five percent and quoted this price to Zelestina.

"Are you trying to become a thief in your old age?" He took another five percent off. "Good, yes, call me when it's ready, please."

Most everyone in town breathed easier when Aitzol Goikoetxea was painting one of Zelestina's cars as it meant she wouldn't be on the road for a week or so. Her driving made fellow drivers leave their cars in the garage. Children, normally fearless as they played in the mostly empty streets, fled to their backyards. Even dogs recognized the sound of her wheels scraping curbs and the way she'd gun the engine then slam on the brakes. Or maybe they could just smell the burning rubber. They dove behind the hedges.

Sometimes Aitzol told Zelestina he couldn't get a certain compound for the paint mix or he claimed the heaters in his makeshift drying room were on the fritz or he had an emergency job he had to finish. Usually these stories were invented to keep the car a little longer. For this public service, Aitzol was highly esteemed in Wolf.

Every street Zelestina navigated became one way in the direction she was traveling. Other drivers pulled to the curb and waited when they saw her coming, as if she were driving an ambulance or a fire truck. Even the local sheriff's deputies turned discretely down a side street or alley to avoid her. It was as if she were a formula one racer heading for the stretch. Or a passenger riding in a coach seat on the train, turning her head to inspect the other passengers and staring out the window at the passing scenery, confident that the engineer was guiding the train safely down the track.

Zelestina was heading up the curving incline of Main Street. The large Oldsmobile, freshly painted the Curved Dash cream tone that in sunlight glowed like antique ivory, looked, in the lightly falling snow and early morning darkness, merely gray and dirty, as though streaked with alkali and sand. The falling snow muffled the rumble of the car's engine and so the Olds seemed to move silently in the manner of a ghost.

There was a stretch of ice and the rear wheel drive car fishtailed slightly. In the Wolf Den Café a line of ranchers debating whether they should go out in the cold and do the morning feeding heard the car's engine rpms go up suddenly when the rear wheels began to spin. That was sufficient to convince them it would be fine to have a third cup of coffee. Maybe it would warm up if they waited a little longer.

Or maybe it wouldn't. On any given winter day, Wolf, Wyoming can have the climate of Fairbanks, Alaska or Albuquerque, New Mexico.

At the counter, a Basque sheepman named Gorka Ahalaberria put his hand over his cup when the waitress came by to refill everyone's coffee. Gorka had known Zelestina Urza all his life and had worried about her driving most of that time. When he heard the engine's sudden high-pitched whine, he stood and went to the window but couldn't see through the fogged over surface. He began to rub the glass with his coat sleeve then thought better of it and went to the door. Outside, he pulled up his collar and looked left and right. At the lower end of the street he could see the greenish glow from the Production Credit Office's time and temperature sign—29 below zero. Too cold for snow but it was snowing—crystalline ice.

There was a look about the snow and a feel in the air that made Gorka nervous. He turned away from the Production Credit sign and squinted toward the high end of the street. The same greenish glow was visible, this time from the sign outside the Wolf Trust building—16 below. The two financial institutions were in competition and even the temperature could become a matter of who was right and who was wrong. The PCA always read the coldest, and the Trust the warmest. Out at the Ranchers and Farmers' Co-op, the new Savings and Loan, hoping to get along, put on its sign a temperature between those at the Trust and the PCA.

Gorka wiped the icy snow out of his eyes and saw the Olds sweep left and right up the street, narrowly missing parked cars on both sides. The swirling red glow from the taillights made Gorka dizzy and he couldn't tell if the Oldsmobile was continuing up the street or drifting backwards downhill.

The day before, the temperature got into the twenties, high enough for the surface of the snow, driven over, to melt. With the temperature well below zero that night, the surface refroze so that now the road had a silvery sheen.

Gorka began to walk toward the red glow. As he passed under the awning of the hunting and fishing store, he involuntarily hunched his shoulders and pulled his lips back as he gritted his teeth and whispered, "Look out." An arm shot out the window of the car. It was so sudden that it might have been ripped from the driver's shoulder and thrown away. "Look out," Gorka repeated.

Zelestina was waving her hand vigorously in the direction of a pickup parked in front of the Morning Star Diner, a breakfast and lunch place started by an ex lawyer from Philadelphia who'd dreamed of being a cowboy or at least a cowboy writer. He'd gotten to Wolf too late for either and so settled for short order cook. He was good, too. Made a mean meat loaf and a hot enough chili, but the Morning Star was, in the estimation of the old-timers, marred by a number of modern touches—lime juice drizzled over the breakfast steaks and scalloped garnishes of honeydew and cantaloupe next to the cheese omelets. There were also pictures of General George Armstrong Custer on the Morning Star's walls. It was better than calling the place Custer's but not by much.

Zelestina had noticed the pickup's headlights were on and rolled down her window. The glass dropped into the door channel with a slight grinding noise. Or maybe it was only the wind biting at the bare branches of the trees. Certainly the window went down smoothly enough. She steered to her left and crossed into the wrong lane. It was important to make sure the pickup's driver would be able to hear her when she shouted at him but as she slowed and started waving, she saw that no one was behind the wheel.

A white cloud rose from the pickup's exhaust pipe. That meant the engine was still running and the truck's owner had probably just run into the Morning Star for a cup of coffee and a cinnamon roll to go.

Zelestina was about to move back into her lane and roll up the window when she noticed two boys playing in the back seat of the truck. *Oh, bai, it's them Iberralde kids, good kids*, she thought.

It was awfully cold, though, and she wondered if they were all right. She also wondered if the boys' dad Iker was actually in the Morning Star. Iker was one of the locals who was deeply offended by the new diner so ate only at the Wolf Den. What was his truck doing here?

The two boys were wrestling and shouting. One of them—Txema, she thought, pushed the other—Peter—hard and the second boy disappeared from view. When his head popped back up, he bumped into the gun rack that was anchored to the roof above the seatback. He yelped and rubbed the back of his head with both hands.

Then Peter turned and looked at the metal with which he'd collided. The lower section of the rack held a fishing rod but Peter showed no interest in this. It was the rifle that drew his attention. He reached out but Txema did, too, and the boys began wrestling again, the gun bouncing around between them.

Zelestina leaned out the window and began shouting. "Txema, Peter, *ez. Ez!*" She took her right hand off the steering wheel and now had both arms out the window, waving wildly. "*Ez, geldi zaitezte! Entzun!*"

Gorka, who'd been walking carefully up the icy sidewalk, stopped.

In her concern for the boys, Zelestina had completely forgotten that they knew almost no Basque. She'd also forgotten she was driving. She switched to yelling in English. "Peter, Txema, you hear me? Put the gun . . ."

Before she finished the sentence, the rifle went off. The sound of the shot ricocheted off the bricks of the two-story buildings that lined the street. The bullet ripped through the sheet metal sidewall of the truck's cab. The snow stopped falling and the two boys tumbled together onto the floor-board of the truck.

Zelestina gasped. For a moment, she thought that the bullet must have hit her in the center of her chest. She felt a heavy weight, a sensation that her entire body was being crushed. The pain radiated out from the center of her chest and into her neck then down her left side and into her arm. She jerked and felt herself yanked back inside the Olds. She thought she should roll the window up then suddenly felt hot and noticed that she was covered with sweat. She was amazed thinking that she could be sweating in such cold. "*Hogei gradu zero azpitik gutxi gorabehera,*" she said out loud.

When he heard the shot, Gorka, too, jerked. He'd thought that whether it was forward or backward, Zelestina was go-ing slowly enough that she wouldn't be a danger to herself or anyone else. Now he leapt into the snow-packed street and began trotting toward her car as it drifted backward toward the creek.

Zelestina's arms were back inside the car but thrown away from her body to her sides. Her head was twisted so that she seemed to be looking backward over her right shoulder in preparation to change lanes. Despite her symptoms, no bullet had entered her chest. Having managed to claw its way through the two layers of steel in the truck's sidewall, the tiny plug of lead was spent. Like the last two-year-old in a long line of cows heading for water, the bullet wallowed slowly out from the truck. Halfway to Zelestina's open window, it dropped to the street where it would lie until midmorning when a deputy county sheriff, a half Chinese, half Northern Cheyenne named Will Song Fire who'd only that fall graduat-ed from the state police academy would pick it up and put it in a plastic bag to be filed as evidence.

Not that there was a crime. And the explosion Zelestina

felt had nothing to do with the bullet. It was just her heart giving way of its own accord. As the pain increased, she tried to wrap her arms around herself. When the convulsive electric shock hit her, her body flew apart. Her hand struck the back of the bench seat and bounced back, slapping her in the face. Knocked unconscious, she slumped forward and struck the top of her head on the steering wheel. Blood ran from her nose onto the Oldsmobile's floorboard. The snow began to fall harder.

Now Gorka was not trotting but running and I was running behind him. I'd been at the Wolf Den having breakfast while the local ranchers made fun of me for drinking mint tea and asking for my eggs and hash browns with no meat—no bacon, no sausage, no ham, no rib steak—no meat. No pork drippings in my coffee—assuming one day I'd tire of mint tea and order coffee. The Oldsmobile was picking up speed. I had just reached Gorka who'd stopped running and stood, his eyes narrowed against the snow. Not until Zelestina was almost upon him did he leap aside.

As the car passed, I saw the cloud of breath that hung in the air around Zelestina's head. I was relieved as it meant she was breathing. Gorka and I stood for a moment watching the car recede. Then unwilling to accept that there was nothing we could do, we started running again now with the headlights shining on us. It was like we were an incompetent stand-up duo at an amateur comedy contest on local TV. We'd finished our act and lost the contest only we wouldn't admit the loss. We tried to stay in the spotlight but the Oldsmobile's headlight beams, made erratic by the car's undirected motion, left us one moment in brilliant light and the next in darkness. When we took off running again, our feet slipped on the icy street. I fell, got back up, and limped on, my knee throbbing.

When the street curved slightly to Zelestina's left or, if the back of the car was the front, her right, the Oldsmobile decided to steady itself. Not curving with the street, it bounced up on the sidewalk, missed the light poles in front of the Mission Lounge and the Egindakoa Basque Club, knocked over Hartzall Drugstore's sale on aspirin sign, took out the town's new public trash can at the alley, caught the edge of the bridge railing along the creek, and went trunk first over the embankment. It hung weightless for a moment in space then fell toward the ice through which one could just make out the dark swirl of water.

There had been a strange mid-winter warm spell the week before and the usually sturdy ice had become fragile enough to open up for the Oldsmobile. The voluptuous car broke through and sank into the black water. Its momentum kept it somersaulting backward and it ended not quite upside down, halfway submerged, its headlights shining on a spot of cloud slightly above the heads of the early customers at the Wolf Den. These customers had nearly all risen from the counter and now stood at the window facing the creek.

Phil and Peanut Arno, the Wolf Den's owners, rushed from the grill and out the door, followed by the other customers. That left only the ghost Thomas Teague sitting at the counter. Yes, the same Thomas Teague we thought was gone so many times before.

It's hard to get rid of the dead. They die but refuse to leave the earth. Eduardo Galeano in the first volume of his trilogy *Memory of Fire* tells us that the one who made the sun and the moon warned the Tainos about this. The dead don't cause many problems in the daytime when they hide in the bush and stuff themselves on guava, but at night they go looking for trouble. They challenge the living to duels and when the duel is ready to start, they vanish. They offer themselves as sexual partners to both men and women but as the act is about to be consummated the lover is left lying with arms around empty air.

You must be careful to treat only with the living. Thankfully, it is easy to tell the living from the dead. You move your hands along your partner's body and if there's no belly button, your partner is dead.

When everyone rushed toward Zelestina, Teague walked along the counter and around the tables sniffing at coffee and cinnamon rolls, eggs and home fries, sausage. Not that he could eat for he had no digestive system. That's another way to know the dead—they never have to use the bathroom. Finding out this way though is less pleasant than running your hands along another person's body.

After inspecting the left over food, Teague made his way to the window where he stood amongst the living and tried to make out what was happening outside. With the snow coming down harder and the tipped-over car's headlights shining into the Wolf Den, it was hard to see anything. In the creek it was even harder. Up and down were confused. The sunless sky and the snow-covered ground were the same color so the buildings either had no shadows or were only shadows.

When Gorka stopped running, I nearly banged into him. "Oh, God," he said, and I, like an idiot, repeated, "Oh, God." Gorka slapped himself and turned in a jerky circle. People were shouting to call an ambulance and call the fire department and Search and Rescue and the EMTs and a doctor. This was before cell service so there was a lot of running from store to store to use the phones.

Gorka took the last steps toward the creek. When he reached the bridge, he pulled himself over the railing and slid down the slick embankment into several feet of icy water. I saw a shudder pass through him as he grabbed the door handle and pulled himself up to look in the window.

Zelestina's head, nearly upside down, seemed to be turned in a vague effort to get a better look at the water flowing under the car. He could see that she had been thrown against the seat then forward into the steering wheel. Her nose was swollen and twin lines of blood ran from her nostrils. Because the car balanced on its rear bumper and Zelestina's head was thrown back, the blood from her nose ran across her eyes and forehead into her hair.

In the cold, Gorka's hands were turning purple and he was shaking all over. Still, he pulled himself into the car through the window, falling across Zelestina and onto the floor beneath the dashboard. The Oldsmobile rolled another foot backward. Gorka slid up or back or something and ended on the roof in the back seat, his motion making the Olds again move backwards.

He pulled himself into the front seat and tried to open the passenger side door. He gave up and climbed over Zelestina to get out the driver's side window. Standing in the creek, he could reach her but couldn't pull her out through the window.

Seeing Phil and Peanut and the customers from the Wolf Den leaning over the bridge railing, staring at him, he said in a hoarse voice, "Help."

I jumped, as if awakening from a trance, and ran across the bridge to the other side of the creek where I worked my way down to the water, now flowing over the broken ice. I'd grabbed a broken off cottonwood branch and managed to prop the car door open. While I held the branch to make sure it didn't slip, Gorka pulled Zelestina out of the car. Once she was out I let the door fall shut and the two of us lifted her out of the creek and onto the edge of the street.

"Wait," Peanut said. "Let me get a blanket or something, you know, don't put her down there." She ran back to the Wolf Den.

Gorka and I lifted Zelestina again, this time with Phil's help, and we followed Peanut while someone yelled, "Hold the door open, will ya?"

As soon as we were inside, Peanut ran the length of the counter, sweeping plates, bowls, coffee cups, and silverware onto the floor. There was a great clattering of broken china and bouncing knives, forks, and spoons.

"What the hell?" Teague growled as Peanut knocked him off a stool and to the ground. She stepped on him twice as she ran down the counter. She stepped on him twice again as she ran back.

"Ok, lay her down right up here," Peanut said. She slapped the cleared counter and kept running, now to get a blanket. When she came back, Gorka held up his arm and shook his head no. Peanut dropped the blanket and looked down at the blood on Zelestina's face and head, and at the angry blue skin around her eyes.

Outside the Oldsmobile finally rolled over onto its roof. There was a heavy splash and breaking of more ice and a rough grinding noise as the car moved a few inches downstream before stopping completely. The walls of the Wolf Den shook.

One of the customers leaned forward to ask, "Is she alright?"

"Is she alright? That's a good one," Teague said, as he picked himself up from the broken glass and china that covered the floor. "For Chrissake, she's dead. I can't say I feel so bad about it. And you," he said, pointing at Peanut. "You could watch where you're going."

"Gorka?" Peanut asked, then looked at me.

"They're both soaked," Phil said, then he too began to shake.

"I'm sorry," Peanut said. "I don't know what I was thinking. You'll be frozen." She looked around the room and saw the blanket she'd dropped. "Here, take this. Take off your wet clothes. I'll run for more blankets. I'll...." She turned and disappeared.

Gorka and I stood there in shock, icy water falling from our clothes. Peanut returned not with blankets but with two large winter coats and a wool hat. She draped one of the coats around Gorka and one around me. Suddenly both anxious and angry, I let the coat fall from my shoulders and ran to the door. When I pulled it open, the snow swirled and blew in, stinging my face. Someone said, "Wait" and I answered, "What?" I grabbed for the door again, fearing I'd fall over.

They pulled me back and made me sit down. I don't know why I remembered a joke Zelestina had made about how if someone really did go to the moon maybe they could give it to the Basques and the Indians. "For the first time in hundreds of years, they will have their own countries again," she said. "As long as they can figure out how to breathe."

Standing there I felt a certain clarity, insight even, into the life Zelestina had led so far from home. How we are all far from home. It seemed important but now seems only banal. The men who went to the moon came home. Zelestina never would. A moment later I noticed that my head was pounding, my knee hurt like hell, and I was still shaking, shaking hard enough that I bit my tongue and for a moment could taste blood.

Afterword

Whales and the Graveyard

By the sixth century of the Christian era, the whales were moving farther out to sea. It wasn't like the days of the *aitatxi* and *amatxi* when one of the Basque villagers would go each morning to the beach and wait, watching the crests of the waves and the changing light until a whale came. Usually, it was one of the smaller *Bizkaikoak* but now and again it would be that whale's larger cousin *Erraldoia*—the giant.

Sometimes the whale was sick and landed sideways on the sand, belching and groaning. Sometimes it was marked by open wounds and empty eye sockets and a tail half eaten. Sometimes the whale was already dead and appeared as a bit of flotsam driven in with the tide.

Healthy whales that beached themselves were seen as offerings—the whales knew the Basques needed them and so they came. Maybe. But maybe the whales were only disoriented by the earth's changing magnetic poles and had no intention of giving themselves to anyone. No one knows what the sick and wounded might have thought and everyone knows the dead have no thoughts. That's another topic. A dead whale was worth more than ten thousand of the wild pigs that were hunted in the mountains.

The forces of nature do not explain everything. That's why we have history. Now and again, a whale rose up from the water of its own accord and walked on its tail onto the beach, coming to rest before whichever villager was there that day. After settling into the earth, such a whale would roll onto its side, one great eye pressed against the sand and the other staring unblinking into the sky. Then there would be the exhalation, a storm of spouting vapor, and silence. Such a whale could be seen as nothing other than a gift and after standing for several moments giving thanks, the villagers set to the work of turning the animal into oil, meat, tongue, and bone.

Although those days are gone, someone still waits on the beach. A whale might yet approach land, swimming toward the rushing clouds, or feeling electricity in the air after a storm. Mostly the lookout sits staring into the distance, hoping that a whale might breach and there will be a visible plume or the sound of the great swimmer breathing. The whale, lifting out of the water and settling back into it, will create the waves it then swims to shore on.

As the whales moved farther out to sea, the villagers built wooden platforms. The watchers stood on these and squinted into the distance. Later, they built boats and men began to follow the whales. At first, the boats were small, unable to stay out at sea more than ten or twelve days. The captain encouraged the four to six rowers while the harpooner stood ready. When they got within a few boat lengths of the whale, the harpooner would thrust the iron tipped blade hard into the animal's flesh. Stung, the wounded whale might turn and swim across the boat, dashing it to pieces. Or it might lash out with its tail. That too could bring the same end. If in its death struggle the animal dove, then the rope had to be quickly cut or the boat would be pulled under. If all went well, the whale swam, dragging the harpoon, the boat, and the men behind it. Several days might pass before the animal died of loss of blood and exhaustion. Then it might take days more to tow the animal to land.

Some said the disappearance of the whales was connected to the appearance of men who claimed to have been sent to earth by a God named Jesu Kristo. This God had nothing to do with the sun, moon, or stars. He was a human God who came to earth from the heavens. He had a human mother but no one knew how she came to be his mother. When the Basques asked they were told only that she was a virgin and that her impregnation was spiritual and magical, that it had never happened before and would never happen again. The story was unsettling and that was enough to link it to the disappearance of the whales.

A practical people, the Basques decided it would be better to follow the whales than to follow an invisible God born of a woman said to be a virgin. They built bigger boats and rowed up the coast of France to Brittany, England, and Ireland, then on to Greenland and Newfoundland.

Seven hundred years later, soldiers of the Christian monarchs Ferdinand and Isabella drove the last Moors from Andalusia, and the King and Queen, giddy in their success, ordered that all Muslims, Jews, Gypsies, and Basques were to convert to the faith of Jesu Kristo or be executed. That fall an Italian sailor was approached by a Basque whaler who had information about an unnamed land on the other side of the sea. The Basque suggested that the new King and Queen might be interested in this. If the Italian could convince them to fund a voyage, the Basque wanted no more than to go along. And he did.

Now Zelestina is dead and I go to her grave each winter on the anniversary of her death. Sometimes the snow is deep and I can't find the grave marker. They don't put up headstones much anymore. Just those flat concrete markers with a brass plaque or engraved letters. In summer the parks workers can finish mowing the lawns in half the time since they don't have to jockey their ungainly machines around the cumbersome headstones. When it rains heavily in June the markers and plaques are nearly covered by Walt Whitman's "...beautiful uncut hair of graves." Even so the mowing machines make an ungodly roar as if we hoped we might wake the dead and ask them to explain.

In winter it might be thirty below, or it might be thirty above but the middle ground is more common—zero, the wind blowing, the gray shadowless light nearly one with the snow. I take the pack off my back and pull out a *trikitixa* accordion. I play two songs, the same songs I played at the grave when Zelestina was put into the ground. The old Basque men came to me after the service to say how beautiful it was and would I be willing to play for them when they died. I'm older myself now and for the last few years my daughter has gone with me. We stand together in the snow and while I pull the *trikitixa* from my pack she pulls a violin from hers. We play like the Basques did in the old days—accordion and violin and I have no idea if we're doing this for Zelestina or just for ourselves. What about my daughter who never met Zelestina? I guess she's doing it for me.

The two songs are "Txoria txori"—The Bird is a Bird—and "Loreak"—The Flowers:

Hegoak ebaki banizkion,
nirea izango zen,
ez zuen alde egingo.

Baina honela,
ez zen gehiago
txoria izango

eta nik, txoria nuen maite
eta nik, txoria nuen maite.

If I had clipped its wings,
it would have been mine,
it would never have gone away.

But this way
it would have no longer
been a bird

and I, I loved the bird
and I, I loved the bird.

Loreak ihintza bezala,
loreak ihintza bezala,
maite dut dama gazte bat,
hari hainbat nahi diodanik.
Ez da munduan beste bat.
Loreak ihintza bezala,
maite dut dama gazte bat,

Zu bazinake arbola,
Zu bazinake arbola,
ni banintz txoria,
arbol maitagarri horretan
egingo nuke kabia.
Zu bazinake arbola,
ni banintz txoria,

Inoiz ikusi gaberik,
inoiz ikusi gaberik
pasatzen badut aste bat
bihotzean banatutzen zait
halako gauza triste bat.
Inoiz ikusi gaberik
pasatzen badut aste bat

Honekin agurtzen zaitut,
honekin agurtzen zaitut
baina denbora gutxiko.
Zurekin oroitu gabe
nola ez nuken etsiko.
Honekin agurtzen zaitut
baina denbora gutxiko.

This one's more complicated. The beauty of the young woman is like the dew on the flowers. There is no one else in the world the young man could have loved the way he loved this woman. If she had been a tree, and he a bird, he would have made his nest in that beloved tree. Even a week without seeing her would break his heart. In the end though there is only the end and with these words, he must say goodbye. Memory is all he has and while memory is something, it's not enough and he remains without consolation. But really, I don't know if it's so important what the words mean or about consolation or its absence or any of that. You can go on the internet and listen to the songs and decide. And if you haven't Googled Gernika yet, you can do that, too.

Acknowledgments

Thank you to my mother-in-law Dollie Iberlin and my late father-in-law Simon Iberlin for introducing me to Basque-American life and welcoming me into their family. Thanks also to the Basque people of Buffalo, Wyoming, the Zaharrer Segi Basque Dance Troupe and its directors Teresa Fieldgrove and Tina Rodriguez, Vikki Chenette of the Johnson County Arts and Humanities Council, and Ryan Fieldgrove of the Bighorn Basque Club. Cynthia Twing and the staff of the Johnson County Library gave me access to the library's Basque text and photo archives. Conversations with Jeanne Marie Etchemendy and Madeleine Iberlin Harriet got me started writing *Zelestina* and studying Euskara—the Basque language. Alyson Hagy, Bob Southard, and Mark Jenkins commented on early drafts of *Zelestina* and Victoria Banales and Kimberly Daggett proofread the manuscript. Thanks also to Amaia Iraizoz, Ziortza Gandarias, and Cameron Watson for proofing and correcting the Basque that I use in the book. The Caitlin Long Excellence Fund, the University of Wyoming English Department, and the Wyoming

Cultural Trust provided funding that assisted in the publication of this volume. My wife Margo Brown has supported me as a writer and person and I am deeply grateful to her.

Made in the USA
Middletown, DE
18 March 2020

86107307R00168